About th

James Ellis is the author of *The Wrong Story*. He has published a number of prize-winning short stories, a travelogue of his journey through Central America and a regular column for *The Gudgeon* magazine. He gained an MSt in Creative Writing from the University of Oxford and presented his paper, *Parallel Explorations of the Boundaries Between Fiction and Real Life*, to the International Flann O'Brien Society in Prague. He is a presenter on Frome FM's On-Air Book Group, a contributor to Carers UK's creative writing campaigns and was an ambassador and volunteer for Shooting Star, a children's hospice charity caring for babies, children and young people with life-limiting conditions. He currently lives near Bath. *Happy Family* is his second novel.

Happy Family

Happy Family

James Ellis

This edition first published in 2020

Unbound
6th Floor Mutual House, 70 Conduit Street, London W1S 2GF
www.unbound.com

© James Ellis, 2020

This book is a work of fiction and, except in the case of historical fact, any
resemblance to actual persons, living or dead, is purely coincidental.

ISBN (eBook): 978-1-78965-052-5
ISBN (Paperback): 978-1-78965-051-8

Cover design by Mecob

Printed and bound in Great Britain by Clays Ltd, Elcograf S.p.A.

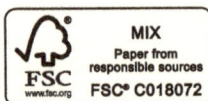

MIX
Paper from
responsible sources
FSC
www.fsc.org   FSC® C018072

To the ties that bind – Joe, Dan, Lauren and Camden

With special thanks to Sally McGuire

Super Patrons

Paige Balas
Hazel Barkworth
Angharad Brown
Susie Campbell
Paul Campy
Louise Casey
Sue Cass
Sue Clark
Geoffrey Clements
Benny Collins
Deborah Collins
Mungo Coyne
Gwen Cremin
Rachel Darling
Pearl Davis
Laura Deutsch
Yvonne Dewing
Lauren Ellis
Joe Ellis
Dan Ellis
Camden Ellis

Giana Elyea
Nicky Fagan
Brooke Fell
carla garner
Alan Garvey
Mark Goody
Manish Gupta
Richard Havard
Nicola Howle
Maggie Hunt
Alice Jolly
Simon Kelleway
Dan Kieran
Amanda Lloyd Jennings
Declan Logue
Simon Lovell-Smith
Scott Macpherson
Ruth Marks
Patricia McGuire
Sally McGuire
Barry McGuire
Charlie McIntosh
Dale Melita
John Mitchinson
Leonard Montgomery
Clare Morgan
Marian Nicholson
Laura O'Connor
Kizi Padden
Dominic Perry
Justin Pollard
Gordon Porter
David Preece

Pete Thomas & Sue Ransom
Becky Ravenscroft
Tom Ravenscroft
Hannah Robins-Frank
Amelia Rowe
Phillipa Ryan
Anna Sabine-Newlyn
Bobby Stevenson
Oliver Tuhey
Graham Tutt
Christian Uta
Kevin Venus
Chaz Warriner
Gemma Warriner
Darla Warriner
Lois Warriner
Natalie Watson
Pete Wood
Keith Woodgate

Prologue

Barbara Hannah moved to the Regency Palace Residential Retirement Village and was very happy there until a blood clot blocked an artery in her heart, and then travelled upwards and temporarily stopped the flow of oxygen in her brain. Although this small vascular tour took less than twenty seconds, it was a life-changing twenty seconds; a beginning-of-the-end twenty seconds. Hardly a day's illness in her life and then bang-bang: a heart attack and a stroke, double-whammy, bingo.

Eighty years old, she woke up in hospital to find she was now dependent on the kindness of strangers. She had lost all movement down her upper left side and all of her lower body. She couldn't swallow properly, and her left field of vision was gone which meant she could no longer read or write. Following words from the end of one line to the beginning of the next was impossible – there was no beginning of the next line; it started in the middle.

No more books, no more crosswords, no more turning over in bed, no more getting dressed on her own, no more pottering around, no more making a nice cup of tea.

'I am a head in a bed,' she said.

Her children, Tom and Caroline, began to use the word 'trajectory' a lot. *Her trajectory of recovery. Her trajectory of medication. Her trajectory of life quality.* It boiled down to this: her trajectory was not good.

'You don't think about this side of things, do you?' Tom said. 'You don't prepare for this. When you think about someone having a heart attack or a stroke, it's like you think about it as an event; a bad moment; a thing. But that's not the half of it. It's what comes afterwards, it's what that event takes away from your life – and everyone else's.'

And then, less than a fortnight into her trajectory of not-recovering-at-all, a nurse telephoned Tom at seven-thirty in the morning and told him that his mother's breathing had changed and now would be a good time to be by her side. He called Caroline and said, 'It's me, this is not "the call". But I think we're close. They want us to go in now.'

When Tom walked into his mother's room her head was turning from side to side as if she were watching a slow-motion tennis match and her chest was rattling loudly – terribly, painfully, heartbreakingly loudly.

He went to her side and kissed her forehead. She gave no sign she knew he was there. He watched her for a while, her head turning from side to side, and then he took a 3DHD MultiSenz SmartCam from his bag and placed it on the table at the foot of her bed.

'I hope you don't mind,' he said.

He kissed her again and sat by her side, holding her hand. Every few minutes a nurse looked in to check on her and after half an hour they injected her with morphine and Midazolam, which lessened the rattling, and they brought Tom a cup of tea. They were kind people, but they offered no hope. Tom had no doubt they had seen this scene many times before: the bed, the dying, the wretched relative.

They gave Tom a booklet called: *End of Life: Respect the Moment*. It told him that withdrawing from life was a natural phenomenon; that the rattling congestion in her chest signified her organs were closing down and that shortly she would stop being alive and would be dead. It made for brutal reading, but Tom found it kind and honest.

He continued to kiss his mother's forehead every few minutes. He probably kissed her more in the last hour he spent with her than he had during all the previous years of his life. He held her hand as tightly as he could without hurting her and when she suddenly sat forwards and took a deep breath, he held his breath, too. He watched her fall back into her pillows and not breathe for a long time, and then she took another deep breath followed by another long pause and then another big, deep breath. Tom waited. She did not breathe again. The room was very quiet and she was very still. After a few minutes he kissed her forehead and pressed the 'assistance' button. He switched off the camera and put it back in his bag. Then he phoned Caroline who was on her way to the hospital, and said, 'I'm sorry. This is the call.'

Later that day, in the afternoon, after Caroline had arrived and Barbara had been taken to the funeral director and her bed had been stripped, Tom and his sister sat opposite each other in their mother's room.

'How are you doing?' said Caroline. 'I'm sorry that I wasn't with you and you had to be here on your own. Was it awful?'

'Not awful, no. It was… I don't know. Strange? Odd? The transition from somethingness to nothingness. Odd watching the mechanics of dying, watching Mum's body shut down, or resisting shutting down. When she actually died, that actual moment, it looked normal – so easy and natural – I felt I could have gone with her; just held her hand and stepped through to wherever. Or nowhere. It didn't look so bad. It was anticlimactic but momentous at the same time. The implications... but for her it must be like going to sleep. Do you think? When you go to sleep you never actually know you've gone until you wake up. So for her... so for her, she doesn't know she's died.'

'It just stops.'

'I don't know if she could hear me, or knew what was happening. What's that phrase – in the midst of life we are in death? That's how I feel at the moment. Numb and kind of okay, but knowing that the emotion is piling up somewhere. A tsunami of grief that's just out of sight, waiting to fall on me.'

'I'm sure it will come.' Caroline squeezed his hand. 'We're orphans now.'

'I'm not ready for this. I don't have a philosophy.' Tom sighed deeply. 'I don't approve of this dying thing. What's the point of being alive if we're going to be dead? All our imaginings and dreams and hopes and knowledge. Our experiences. Love and hate. It's a flawed process. They should have made an exception for Mum. She wasn't doing anybody any harm. Just pottering about. No one would have minded if she lived forever.' Tom laughed and looked out the window. 'I never thought I'd watch my mother die.'

'There's a Mum-shaped hole in the world.'

'But why?'

'Who knows?' Caroline shook her head. 'But we should make the most of being alive. Give life some point and a meaning. You're a long time dead. Mum had a good life apart from the end bit. Everything else was good. And you, you're creative. You're leaving your mark. People will remember you. Your life isn't meaningless...'

'But what does it matter when you're dead? I struggle with this, Caroline, I really do. I struggle with this concept of nothingness – before I was born, after I have lived, the extinction of awareness, the absence of me. It's all unimaginable. What do you mean when you say it all just stops? What is nothing? In a hundred years I'll just be another name on our family tree. Think about all the people who have ever lived; and all the animals and the insects. Ants: how many...?'

'You're a lucky human being. Enjoy it.'

Tom gazed at the bed in which their mother had been alive. 'I don't know. Have you ever thought about that phrase: "a long time dead"? How long is long? How long is forever? Mum's barely begun being dead. Dad's been dead for years and he's barely begun. The first person who ever died, they've barely begun. They're going to be dead all the way until the world ends, and then until the universe ends, and then for all the ever and ever that comes after that.'

'It's not like it's a long time, though. It'll be like a dot.'

'Like a dot?'

'Yes.'

'How big a dot?'

'I'm being serious...'

'Will I fit in? I'll need a big dot. What do you mean a dot...?'

'Hear me out. When you're dead time stops. It must do, for you. Everything stops. So, it's not like the years are going by without you. You're not part of that... of that system, any more. So, for you, forever isn't a length of time; it's no time. Mum and Dad are at the beginning and at the end and all the way around the sides. They're in the dot. The dot has no dimensions, no time, no anything, no nothing.'

'Where did you get all this knowledge?'

'It's just how I see it: when you die you stop and stay in the dot of time.'

'The dot of time?'

'Yes. Stop laughing.'

'Do we each have our own dot? What happens if they join up? What's outside the dot?'

Caroline laughed too. 'It's not like a dot on a page – not something you'd draw. It's like a moment between two ticks. A moment dot…'

'Are you even my sister? I've never heard you talk like this.'

'I thought about these things after Dad died. I tried to imagine what was going on, and I imagined this big lake of black tar, and we rise out of it for a while and then we sink back into it. So, for all of time, forever, infinity, outside the system, almost all of our existence is like we're lying deep down in a lake of black tar. Which is actually a dot. That's normality. And then, for a cosmic moment or two, for some reason, we flare up like a match and we're not in the tar. That's how we are now, alive. But it's the exception. Normality is being in the tar. Normality is nothingness. We rise up for a moment, have some somethingness, and then we fall back in. Mum's gone back to that. She's gone back to where she came from.'

Tom leaned back in his chair and stared at the ceiling. 'She's gone back to the tar? But what's the point? What's the point of the tar?'

'I don't know. To keep us warm?'

AUTUMN 2021

1

History will view *Happy Family* as a cultural phenomenon: a game for everyone, a lifestyle, an essential accessory. A game that everybody played; that was played everywhere.

Remember the first version of *Happy Family* – a simple smart device app? No cartoon spin-off, no books, no TV or film. Just a game. Players could select a set of family members and friends from a configurable cast of characters – a husband or wife or partner, children, other relations, friends, colleagues, pets, neighbours, lovers, enemies – and the app would decide which character would appear where and when, send text messages, emails, even make phone calls.

It had two starting points: *Things Are Good* and *Things Are Bad*. But, however it began, the game was skewed to make things worse until everything was as bad as possible. All kinds of characters could show up and all kinds of bad things could happen. Arguments, fights, unwanted pregnancies, job losses, death, injury, explosions, car crashes – all part of an individually tailored soap opera with augmented characters overlaid on the gamer's real world.

The goal of the game has not changed since that first version: to reach the highest level and find sanctuary in the Garden. The Garden is a good place: sunny, peaceful, pleasant, trouble-free and safe. A gamer at that level owns the Garden and nobody and nothing can come in, other than their own personal happy family. There is still an online leader board of less than a thousand *Happy Family* players who have made it that far; most people fail and end up in the Bin. The Bin has spawned its own subculture. T-shirts printed with logos on them – a favourite is: 'Battered, Bruised & Binned'. These days there are Bin chatrooms, Bin forums, Bin clubs – even a Bin dog-walking group.

The second version of *Happy Family* was a step change in the game. Packaged with an AR play-record visor, it now included soundtracks, third-person narratives, whisper hints and character backstories. Another new feature was the option to play nested games, a 'mise en abyme' effect that layered one augmented reality onto another and allowed players to seek the Garden from different levels simultaneously.

Visor recordings of real events could also be imported into a game to create a composite augmented present. This was known as multilayering: a way of exploring different outcomes to a past real-world event. Combining this with nested game-playing usually resulted in a condition called a 'head-wreck', and a fast route to the Bin.

Then came Version 3.

Two years in development, Version 3 gamers could configure their fictional family to be any species they wanted, including creatures from other times, other planets or from worlds of their own devising. Version 3 also introduced artificial intelligence for speech recognition, and the real game changer – the iLets. Gone were the visors. Light and durable, iLets covered the wearer's eyes with a clear film, attached to the skin with a vacuum ring and a hair-thin wire stem that pressed against the face. When they were switched on the iLets synchronised with the wearer's pupils and then, although the real world was still visible, what the wearer saw, including lighting, shadows and colour filters, was under the control of the game.

Who can remember a world without iLets?

These days iLets come with volume control, retina logon, their own internet hub and TVA – Temperature Variation Alert. TVA uses the wire stem to change the iLets' temperature depending on what's happening in the game. And if you don't like the feel of these on your face you can now buy iLet-Inserts* – contact lenses with view and playback, invisible ear-buds and even, in some countries, nasal implants. Not just augmented reality, but augmented senses.

Always an artist with his eye on popular appeal, *Happy Family* defined its creator. All hail the master, Tash, and long may he serve the games industry.

*Editor's note: iLet-Inserts are not supported by Borkmann Augmented Realities Corporation and should not be worn for prolonged periods. It is strongly advised not to use iLet–Inserts in conjunction with standard iLets.

2

Night time. A back door opened and a shaft of harsh yellow light fell onto the patio along with a large man. He landed heavily on his knees and there he remained, head down, his long tangled greying hair and unkempt beard obscuring his face. He looked older than he was.

'Ouch,' he said.

It had been a peaceful scene until then; the quiet time that comes in the early hours before the birds wake and the dew settles. Now this man was here, breathing heavily and staring at the paving slabs.

'Hard,' he said.

He stood up, stiff-legged, almost losing his balance. He was wearing a dressing gown, open and untied with the cord hanging loose. He was naked underneath. He raised and lowered each leg and his knees crackled as cartilage moved where it hadn't moved before.

'Very hard.'

He took a half-bottle of whisky from his dressing gown pocket and drank from it extravagantly, tipping back his head and holding it above his mouth. He held it there for a long time, as if he'd become frozen or fallen asleep, and then carefully bent forwards to put the bottle on the ground, shuffling in his slippered feet to retain his balance, and placed it in the centre of a paving slab. He stood up, looked at it and bent down again, risking toppling onto his face, and moved the bottle a millimetre to the left.

'Better.'

He rubbed his hands but stayed where he was, his eyes closed now, swaying. Again, it seemed possible he had fallen asleep until he shouted, 'Come on. Do it.'

He took a deep breath and, nodding at nothing in particular, set off across the lawn towards a bank of shrubbery and a dark mass of woodland beyond. Along the way his slippers caught on the grass and became twisted on his feet until finally they fell off. He left the lawn and passed through tiers of landscaped bushes that had once been tended and nurtured, but now grew wild and uncared for, and entered the prickly, drier area of the trees.

Silence and stillness returned to the garden – and then two shapes detached themselves from the shadows on the lawn. One was a dog: big, heavy and threadbare; his fur flecked with grey and a broad white stripe running from neck to nose. The other was a teenager who had been sitting cross-legged on the grass away from the light. She might have been an elf or a sprite.

Her name was Alta.

The dog walked onto the patio and sniffed the whisky and knocked the bottle over trying to get his tongue into the neck. Alta watched him struggle and then made a clicking sound from her back teeth. The dog left the bottle and came back to her.

She was small and wiry and wore jeans and a baggy jumper and ruined flip-flops. She swung a knapsack from her back and rummaged through it until she pulled out an object wrapped in a faded blue towel. It was an old-fashioned Spanish dagger. She ran her finger along the blade.

'This is why you have to look after things,' she said. 'To keep them sharp.' She looked down at the dog. 'Come on.'

She left her knapsack on the patio next to the bottle and set off across the lawn, picking up the discarded slippers as she went.

In the northwest corner of Spain are the forests and mountains of the Galician Massif. Here, the great *Nuberu*, the Cloud Master, brings storms and rain to punish the Galicians while the *Santa Compaña*, the Holy Company, process through the isolated villages at night looking for new recruits. The procession of the dead in the world of the living.

In the lower reaches of the mountains facing west, much of the forest gives way to low, thorny plants and bare, dry land. Here the winters are long and cold and in the summer the sun is high and hot. Trees huddle together sucking what sustenance they can from the dry, rocky soil, growing bent and deformed, twisted and ugly. Life that survives in these parts is tough and resourceful.

The trees through which Alta and the dog walked were mostly oak. The pair were at the far western edge of the Galician region, the end of the known world as the Romans called it, walking through the thick outer ring of the man's property, high above the sea where the air was clean and carried the scent of berries and plants and leaves.

They made little noise as they walked, but ahead Alta could hear sounds: a creaking, a snap of wood, a huffing and puffing. She slowed down, touching each tree trunk as she crept past it as if making her way from one vertical stepping-stone to another.

'We have to be quiet now,' she whispered.

In her hand was the dagger. She moved forwards, lifting her feet slowly, creeping like a cartoon character, transferring her weight from one leg to the other in long exaggerated steps.

'This is fun,' she giggled.

And then, ahead, she saw him. The woodland thinned and gave way to a gentle leaf-strewn hollow. Trees grew in a circle around it and a toppled trunk lay amongst them as if they had slain it. The man had climbed onto the fallen tree. It was thick, about two metres in diameter, and although it was rotten and dead it was taking his weight. His dressing gown was on the ground and he was naked; his heavy, pale, bulky body looked vulnerable and out of place against the hard, dark roots and sharp branches that surrounded him.

He had lassoed one of the branches of a standing tree with his dressing gown cord, pulled it tight and was now looping the other end around his neck. He pulled it into a knot and then turned away from the tree, facing towards the hollow and Alta and the dog who were hidden in the night shadows on the far side. He took a deep breath and whispered, 'Back to the tar.'

He clenched and unclenched his fists and then lifted his hands and felt the cord around his neck. He touched it gently as if caressing it, feeling its contact against his skin. And then, making up his mind, he straightened his back and let his arms fall by his sides. He adjusted his balance and closed his eyes.

This was it.

Alta and the dog watched. The man stood naked in front of them, his big body sagging downwards, his bruised knees trembling, the noose around his neck, the knot under his left ear. He took another deep breath. And then another. And then another. And then he stepped off the tree trunk.

A lot happened and it happened all at once. The branch creaked, dipped under his sudden weight and then lifted again, taking him upwards. He broke wind loudly and leaves fell from above as he spun around on the cord, his flailing legs creating momentum and causing the cord to tighten into a smaller and smaller knot. His hands scrabbled at his neck and he began to choke, his tongue sticking out as he tried to breathe. His eyes rolled upwards, bulging towards the stars.

'Wow,' Alta said.

She ran round the hollow, climbed onto the tree trunk, waited for the man to spin past and grabbed the cord, holding it as still as she could while she attacked it with her dagger. It was hard going but halfway through it tore and the man fell onto the ground, his legs folded beneath him; a pile of wheezing hairy flesh.

She jumped down, knelt beside him, found the knot and tried to get her finger underneath it. It was cutting into his throat and there was no room even for her skinny fingers. She had no choice but to slip the blade in, twist the cutting edge away from his flesh and pull. There was a moment of tension and then the cord frayed and gave way, freeing his windpipe.

He sucked in air.

'Ouch. Ouch. Ouch.'

Alta grinned and said to the dog, 'He's a seal.'

She climbed back onto the tree trunk and sat watching him. Then she clicked her tongue and the dog wandered over and began to lick the man's face.

Earlier, when he had imagined how it would be to die and, more importantly, what awaited him afterwards, the man hadn't imagined a large, rough, evil-smelling tongue would play a part.

'What's happening?' he said.

Satisfied he would live, Alta threw his slippers at him. 'Stay there.'

She jogged back to the house, to the unlocked back door,

and poured cold water into the empty whisky bottle from the kitchen tap. She returned to the woods and found the man where she'd left him, lying on his back on the ground, still naked, staring up at the sky. The dog had finished his resuscitation duties and was now attending to his own rear end. Alta picked up the dressing gown and dropped it over the man's stomach.

'Cover up.'

She sat with him on the ground while he took sips of water, wincing as he did so.

'Painful,' he said. His voice was hoarse.

Alta nodded. 'What do you expect?' She spoke English but her Spanish accent was strong. 'A gun is better. Or a knife. You can use my dagger if you want. It's sharp. You can cut your throat or slice your wrists or stick it into your heart. Do you want me to stick it in your heart? I don't mind.'

She made a stabbing motion with her hand although her dagger was now safely restored to her knapsack. 'Or we can throw you off a cliff or set fire to you. I can make a list if you want.'

'List,' he repeated. He sipped more water and then he said, 'Who...?'

She ignored him. 'Your neck is hurt.'

He felt his throat and the tender, purplish, yellow-speckled bruise that was spreading where the cord had cut in. 'Ouch.' His head was filled with memories of spinning in the dark with trees revolving around him, his legs kicking out for purchase, the pain in his throat, the pressure pushing deep into the top of his head, forcing his eyes out of their sockets. He took another sip of water and then squinted at Alta.

'Do I know you?'

'Are you still drunk?' she said. 'You get drunk every night. We watch you through your window.'

'We?'

'Badger and me.'

'A badger?'

'Not *a* badger. Just Badger. Him.'

He looked at Badger who was still delving deep into his own interior. 'Dog.'

'Yes. But look at his stripe. See? He looks like a…'

The man rolled onto his stomach and threw up into the dirt. Ants and insects that had been asleep woke up to find they were covered in whisky-flavoured bile and scurried away. He moaned as the acidic contents of his stomach burned his damaged throat. Alta bent forwards and watched.

'It's coming out your nose,' she said.

When he finished, he heaved himself onto his back and lay motionless, staring at the sky again. His dressing gown was twisted around his body and there was sick and leaves and twigs in his beard and hair. He looked up at the stars and pronounced: 'I am a mess.'

Alta watched him and nodded. 'You should go home.'

'I am home.'

'I mean inside.'

'I am inside.' He was starting to fall asleep.

Alta shrugged. 'Stay here, then.'

'Did you tell me your name? I can't remember.'

'No.'

'Oh…' He closed his eyes.

'It is Altagracia Maria Rosario de Mendoza.'

She spoke her name as if it were the beginning of a poem or a lyric, rolling each syllable across her tongue and giving each word its own space. 'I let my good friends call me Alta.' She said that proudly, as if she had many friends and made special provision for those who were at the top of her list.

'Alta,' he murmured, his eyes closed. 'It must be nice to have good friends. My name is Tom. Thomas Arthur Stevenson Hannah. But you can call me Tom.'

He passed out.

3

In Tom's garage there was a power-assisted flatbed trolley which he used for moving crates, furniture and any other kind of cumbersome, unwieldy object. Alta used it to move him. It took longer than it should to bring him home because she had to stop frequently to chase Badger away who kept sitting on his chest so he could be pulled home too.

She bounced Tom over the doorstep and dumped him on his stomach on the living room floor along with all the leaves and twigs he had collected during the journey. She sat on a large sofa and fanned her face with her hands.

'You eat too much,' she said to Tom's unconscious body.

She looked around. Although she had explored the grounds many times this was the first occasion she had been inside the house. 'What do you think?' she said to Badger. 'Welcome to the inside!'

Badger ignored her and lay on the floor. It was late and he was tired, and he hadn't been fed for a long time.

'Are you sulky?'

Alta went into the kitchen and locked the back door. She checked all the doors and windows and made sure that they were all closed and locked too. Then she lowered the blinds, switched on all the lights and went exploring.

In the basement she found a utility room, a games room and a door with upwards access to the gardens. She locked and bolted that too. Badger padded along beside her while they explored, checking corners, sniffing under cabinets and cupboards, and jumping up and peering into shelves. At one point, as he eyed a rug speculatively, Alta knelt down and held his face to hers and said, 'No going to the toilet inside the house.'

On the ground floor the rooms had cherry wood floorboards and thick rugs, with wall-sized windows and high ceilings. There was a kitchen, a living room, a study and a library, and two guest bedrooms with their own bathrooms. A spiral staircase led up to a mezzanine level where there was a dining table and chairs, and a separate staircase led from the ground floor to the first floor where thick carpeting muffled their footsteps and they found more bedrooms and bathrooms.

On the roof terrace was a hut, like a boat's deckhouse, with a locked door. Alta threw her shoulder at it a few times until the lock broke and the door opened. It was a studio. There were drawings and giveaway merchandising and plastic models of the *Happy Family* characters. She jammed the door shut again, using a piece of the splintered door frame.

'I'm hungry,' she said.

She went back to the kitchen and found some bread, cheese and ham which she cut up and put on two plates and took into the living room. It was just before five o'clock in the morning.

While she and Badger ate, Tom opened his eyes. There was grass and earth in his nose, his bruised and damaged knees hurt, his swollen throat felt as if someone had filled it with broken glass and there was a cold patty of sick under his tongue.

'Floorboards,' he said. 'Dust.' He tried to swallow and couldn't. 'Ouch.'

'You're alive,' Alta said.

Tom looked up at her without lifting his head. 'Who's that?'

'It's Badger and me.'

'Badger and me?'

'Badger and *me*.'

'Badger…'

'You have drunk six cans of beer, two bottles of wine and a half-bottle of whisky,' Alta said, bored with the Badger and me conversation. 'You tied your neck to a tree, you were sick on the ground and you have a very ugly body. Sometimes you drink more. We bring you back most nights. Did you know that? But you don't normally try to kill yourself. So, this time we've stayed with you.'

'I…'

'Can we live in your house?'

Tom remained on the floor until the sun rose and filled the room with light. Then, with Alta's help, he got to his hands and knees and heaved himself to his feet. He bent over in a swaying bow-legged position with his head hanging down and his hands brushing the floor, and then, with one mighty effort, he stood upright. His dressing gown fell to the ground.

'You are a human again,' said Alta clapping. 'Cover yourself up.'

She led him upstairs to one of the many bathrooms and ran a hot bath for him. She left him to his toilet and then returned and sat with him while he lay beneath a mountain of soapy bubbles.

'Do you want me to hold your head under the water?' she said.

Tom carefully cleared his throat. 'Why?'

'I thought you might still want to kill yourself.'

He stared at the bubbles and said nothing. She brought him warm water with salt to sip, and a towel, and when he had dried himself she led him to his bedroom where she left him. He slept the entire day and most of the night, awakening early the following morning before dawn. When he opened his eyes, Alta was sitting on a chair, watching him. Badger was guarding the door and he smelled of musk and woodland and hill breezes. It was a strong smell but not unpleasant. Alta was wearing jeans and one of Tom's t-shirts, which hung from her meagre shoulders like a poncho. It had a picture of four cartoon animals on it, standing like superheroes with an angry-looking woman running towards them in the background.

'You snore a lot,' she said.

There was water on the table by his bed and he leaned on his elbow and took a small sip. 'Thanks.' He looked at Alta and Badger and nodded thoughtfully. 'You're still here.'

'We're your guests.'

Tom stared at the glass of water in his hand. 'My guests.' He spoke slowly as if listening to himself explaining what was going on. 'Do I have any other guests?'

'No.'

'More on the way?'

'No.'

'Just you and…'

'Badger. This is fun. Ask me another question.'

Tom sat up in bed. 'You're Spanish?'

'*Sí.*'

'Your English is very good.'

'*Gracias.*'

'Much better than my Spanish.'

'*Mucho.*'

'You must have good teachers. Your parents…'

'Next.'

Tom drank some more water, wincing as the cold liquid ran through his swollen throat. 'How old are you?'

'How old are you?'

'Forty-six.'

'Really, you look older. I'm eighteen. So, you don't have to worry.'

'About what?'

'About being naked.'

Tom pulled the covers higher. 'What?'

Alta grinned. 'Don't look shocked. If you don't want people seeing your naked body you shouldn't leave it hanging around in the woods. Don't worry, I'm not going to be your girlfriend. Do you have a girlfriend?'

Tom closed his eyes. She looked younger than eighteen, he thought; a skinny stick of a creature with angry eyes and jutting chin. 'It must have been an upsetting thing to see…'

'Not really.'

'What I did; what I tried to do…'

'No.'

'Well, I'm sorry that you had to see it anyway. Thank you for helping me.'

'And Badger for licking you back to life.'

Tom opened his eyes. 'Yes. I remember that. Horrible. So, look, I'm okay now. Thank you for trespassing and sorting me out. I want to give you something. A reward. Something. Some money…'

'I don't want money.'

'A gift then. To take home with you.'

'I want to stay here.'

Tom winced. He was more tired than he realised. 'Obviously, you can't stay here. Do your parents know where you are? Someone will want to know where you are, that you're safe.'

Alta came over to his bed and looked down at him. 'I know what you see when you sit in your chair every night and wear your iLets. What you see when you get drunk. I looked while you were asleep. I watched what you watch every night. That old lady.'

Tom was a big man with a bruised neck and a hairy head and face. He wasn't strong enough for this though. 'That's private. Precious.' He stared at her. 'You can't stay; you have to go.'

Alta stood up and clicked her tongue. Badger clambered to his feet and waited for her. 'We're going out,' she said. 'For an hour or so. We'll be back. Don't kill yourself while we're gone.' They left and the bedroom door clicked shut. Tom was alone. He fell back into his pillows.

That old lady.

'That was no lady; that was my mother.'

4

When Alta and Badger returned, Tom was up and dressed and waiting for them in his living room. He said, 'You're not really eighteen, are you?'

Alta grinned. 'Is that what's worrying you? Not quite. But soon.'

'How soon?'

'This much.' She held up her thumb and forefinger with a tiny gap between them. She squinted through it. 'A few days.'

'Can I see your passport or something? Your identity card?'

'No. Those things were at my house. But now my house has gone, and I am gone. I am like a spirit, a puff of gas. Forgotten.'

Tom noticed that her Spanish accent was becoming thicker, dominating her English words.

'You're a runaway?'

'Of course. And Badger, too.'

'What about your parents? Are they alive?'

'They're fine.'

Tom sighed. 'Should they at least know you're all right?'

'They know.'

'And?'

'And what? I'm happy, they're happy. Everyone is happy.'

'Are you in trouble?'

'Pregnant? Do you think all women should be pregnant?'

'Of course not. I meant in trouble with your parents – hey, what do you mean your house is gone?'

'In my mind. It's gone in my mind.'

'Not in real life? You didn't...'

'Burn it down?'

'Yes.'

Alta sat on the sofa. She put on her stern, patient expression, the same one she used when she had told Badger not to use the house as a toilet. 'I am not in any trouble. And I won't be any trouble. There are no police. And no little Alta waiting inside me.' She smiled. 'Please may Badger and I stay here for a little while? Just a little while? It will be all right.'

Tom ran his hands through his hair and stared at the floor. What was he to make of all this? A young woman, a teenager, technically a child, and a dog in his house, runaways, how could that possibly be all right? How would the days unfold without further drama; where had normal gone?

'What about clothes and things?'

'I have everything I need and what I don't, I can get. I like your t-shirts, though. And in a few weeks I'll be eighteen.'

'Days.'

She smiled again. 'Yes. Days.'

Tom shook his head. What to do?

'I need to think about all this. But you can stay. For the moment. But no looking at my things, you know... especially... the old lady thing.'

Alta smiled. 'I like those words. For the moment. I want everything to be for the moment.'

'But we must have rules.'

'No, we mustn't.'

Alta continued to sleep in the garden until Tom insisted that she move into one of the guest bedrooms and, yes, Badger could have his own room too – if he must. Tom's necklace bruise from his dressing gown cord turned a multicoloured rainbow of greens and yellows, purples, blues and red, and he spent the early days trying to recreate those hues in his studio.

'Why?' Alta said.

'They are wonderful colours and soon they'll be gone.'

Alta nodded. 'I like that. Are you an artist?'

'Of sorts.'

'What sort of sorts?'

'Cartoons – and games. I'm a cartoonist and I'm a games creator.'

After two weeks they ran out of food and drink and toilet paper. Tom said he would go to the village and order more provisions. Alta shook her head and folded her arms.

'Why not?' said Tom. 'What are we going to eat – and don't say things that grow in the woods. I am not eating leaves and berries.'

'I can get everything we need. We'll look after you until you are better.'

'I am better.'

'No, you're not.'

Tom laughed. 'Okay, you get all the things we need. But legally. Buy them. I pay, you buy. Deal?'

'Deal. And we'll help you.'

'Help me do what?'

'Get better. I'll tell you what to do.'

Tom laughed again. 'Ah-ha, that old trick. What will I have to do? Sign over my things to you?'

Alta clicked her tongue and Badger jumped up next to her. She put her arm around him and kissed his head. 'That wasn't a nice thing to say. I didn't say you have to do what I say. And I don't want any of your things or any of your money or anything you have at all. If you don't want me to help you, I won't. I don't care. Get drunk every night, fall over, hang yourself, cut your wrists, howl at the moon. Put on your iLets and drive yourself mad.'

She got up and she and Badger left him alone.

In the evening Tom found them sitting outside on the grass. He sat with them and said, 'I'm sorry. I shouldn't have laughed.'

'No. You shouldn't.'

They said nothing more until Alta turned to him. 'I like the outside more than the inside.'

'Yes,' said Tom, looking up. 'I think I do too.' He sat cross-legged, his hair long and unkempt, his beard big and his moustache wide.

'You're famous, aren't you?'

'Not really.'

'Where are your hangers-on?'

'I don't have any. I have business people, art people, an agent, publicists, family – well, a sister at least. So, not too many friends.'

'We're not hangers-on.'

'No.'

'Do you still want to kill yourself?'

'I don't know. But if I did I wouldn't inconvenience you. I'm not saying I do. I'm just saying you wouldn't have to worry about... about seeing anything.'

'I'm not worried about seeing things. Not dead things. I've seen lots of dead things. You'd just be a bigger dead thing. I've seen a dead horse. You're not as big as a horse.'

Tom drank his whisky. 'Not yet, anyway. Your English,

I know you don't want to talk about it, but where did you learn…'

'We travelled.'

'You and your parents?'

'Why did you want to kill yourself?'

Tom looked at his empty glass and then rolled it across the grass to Badger who licked it clean.

'It's complicated. I suppose everyone says that. But it is. Part of it is this: my mother died and I can't get that moment out of my head. I was there. I saw it. I saw her senses diminish, her movements slow, her breathing stop. I saw her change state, the mechanics, that moment of being and then not being, the transition from somethingness to nothingness. Her last breath. I filmed it. I don't know why but that scene, with me in the room with her, I have to keep playing it. It's important.' He looked at her.

Alta chewed on a stem of grass. 'I think the world should not be how it is. And how it should be, is not anywhere. It doesn't exist.'

'When you said you'd make me better, what does that mean?'

'It means not being an artist or a famous person or anything. Be like when you were born. Like an animal. Or a tree.'

'A tree?'

'You have to stop controlling things; making things how you want. You have to stop wanting things. You have to be apart from those things. If it rains, a tree gets wet. If a wind blows, a tree gets cold. For a tree, life happens. That's it. All it does is grow towards the sun. One moment at a time.'

'But I'm not a tree…'

'Imagine there was no one else in the world. What would you be then? Would you still give yourself a label? Say you were a person who draws? A cartoonist and a games creator? Or would you just be Thomas Arthur Stevenson Hannah?'

Tom stared at the grass and thought about being a plant. 'There are a lot of trees in the world,' he said. 'Do you think there might, amongst all the trillions of trees that ever existed, be one that chose to turn towards the shade, one rogue tree that chose death in the dark over life in the light?'

'No.'

'Oh. You know that, do you?'

'Stop being a famous person, an artist, a cartoonist, and become a thing that occupies space. Eat and drink and breathe and move. Don't control. Just be.'

'Like a tree?'

'Yes.'

'Can I wear clothes?'

'Of course you can wear clothes. I don't want to see your disgusting body.'

'I mean I don't have to wear bark or leaves or robes or colourful trousers or anything like that?'

'Wear what you want.'

'Can I drink alcohol?'

'If that's what you want.'

'iLets?'

'No iLets. And no people. We'll put up signs to keep people out. And a fence or a wall. And we'll need alarms and cameras and dogs.' Badger looked up. 'Proper dogs,' she said rubbing his ears. 'That look like they can bite.'

'Is this about keeping people away from me, or from you?'

'You don't have to do anything I say. We won't rob you or hold you prisoner or do anything to harm you, like you keep thinking we will.'

Tom lay on his back and looked up at the darkening sky. Badger rolled over and fell asleep, and Alta lay on her back too.

All three of them remained there until they were merely three shapes in the night, three bumps on the lawn.

'No past and no future,' Tom said. 'Just the moment. The now. And, no me?'

'There is always you.'

More silence and then Tom said, 'My mother's death was only part of it. The other part is this: I stare through my windows and watch the trees change with the seasons and I drink whatever I can and I sleep wherever I fall. I do that because I can. There are no consequences other than death and that happens whatever I do. I've seen it. It's easy. We just stop. Life is pointless, Alta, and therefore I am pointless too. And I'm tired. My bones are tired. My mind is tired. I'm tired of waking up every morning and I'm tired of going to sleep every night. Time is heavy. I've had enough. I want to stop.'

'Want or wanted?' said Alta.

'Want.'

'Go ahead, then. I don't care.'

'I'm not talking about what you're thinking.'

'What am I thinking?'

'I'm not going to hang myself from a tree or anything.'

'Good.'

'You've given me another way.'

WINTER 2022

1

Restart.

Germaine Kiecke waited outside a restaurant and studied her reflection in its window. It was raining and she was smoking. She looked at herself and at the other people as they passed behind her and imagined her reflection turning to join them, leaving her alone to look at nothing.

Germaine was thirty-six years old. She was slim, slight and boyish looking with her blonde hair cut short. She wrote columns for art magazines and journals and presented an occasional late-night arts series on television called, *Kiecke in Conversation*. She lectured at the Université de Liège and went to galleries and attended openings and exhibitions. Her life was infused with art, but she did not create any herself.

She finished her cigarette and dropped it on the ground. Die, sucker, she thought and then smiled. '*Die zucker*,' she said aloud with a German intonation. 'Tobacco: *der zucker des lebens*.' The sugar of life.

Germaine was once interviewed by a student reporter for the university newsletter and when she was asked about her cigarette habit she said: 'I smoke because smoking connects me to death, and therefore to life.' That was how Germaine talked. It wasn't true, though. She smoked because she liked the barrier it created between her and other people.

When the student reporter asked if her break-up with the French abstract painter Valerie Morin, who called herself *La Jaune*, had affected her views on abstract art, Germaine said, 'No. For me art is more important than the artist. It is the end, not the means, that matters. I'm not saying that an artist's life isn't interesting. It is. But…' She shrugged.

The student reporter then asked if the break-up had affected her views on relationships. She laughed and said, 'Is this what students want to know? The messiness of life; the ins and outs of my life? I don't know – what is a relationship? Perhaps, if we had tried harder, if *I* had tried harder, the *relationship* might have lasted longer. But we didn't try harder, or I didn't, and, in the end, we are what we do. Or don't do. And I suppose I don't do relationships.'

The student reporter asked if they could talk about her time at Chateau Giselle, but she just smiled and said, 'No'.

Germaine knew she could be a prickly customer but why not? She was a *vondeling*, a foundling, raised in Chateau Giselle, a Liège orphanage, run by a lay religious order dubbed by the press as the *Motherhood*. She told people that she had not been born; she had been discovered, and she laughed when she said that. But other people were unsure about laughing because they knew being discovered and raised by the Motherhood wasn't a good thing.

The Motherhood was a semi-monastic, quasi-religious community made up mostly, but not entirely, of women. They did not take formal religious vows and their doctrines and ceremonies were a canon of pain and humiliation. Within the buildings and grounds of their commune, Chateau Giselle – a drab and dreary manor house to the east of Liège – abandoned, lost and runaway children were imprisoned, abused and trafficked.

The Motherhood existed for over twenty years under the noses of the Belgium courts, the Office for Protection of Children and the National Children's Agency. It was a national scandal; a litany of atrocity. The moment of reckoning came in 2000 when the police arrived with social services and a team of clinical psychologists. Thirty or more children, ranging in age from two to sixteen, were found and taken to safety. Germaine was fourteen. For most, the wounds they suffered in Chateau Giselle were too deep to ever fully heal. Scars remained that could bleed no matter how much time passed by.

Occasionally, Germaine wondered who her parents were and why they had abandoned her and whether or not they were still alive. Did they think about her? Had they sought her out in the past, watched her from a distance, followed her career? Were they watching her now from a street corner, a shop window or a passing car? Did they care?

The student reporter had also asked Germaine why she was so preoccupied with the artist Thomas Arthur Stevenson Hannah, also known as *Tash*, the creator of the *Scraps* cartoon strip and the *Happy Family* augmented reality game.

'Am I preoccupied with him?'

He pointed out that Germaine's PhD thesis had been titled, *The Vixen God: A Study of Female Violence in the Tash Oeuvre*, that Germaine had written over thirty articles on Tom Hannah's art, that Germaine had interviewed him numerous times, had interviewed his mother and was generally accepted to be the foremost authority on the *Scraps* strip cartoons, with the exception of Tom Hannah himself.

Germaine had become cross and found herself answering a question she hadn't been asked. 'Again. It is the art, not the man. I am not *preoccupied* with Tom Hannah. Yes, he is an artist who has defined a generation. And it's true, *Scraps* has informed my thinking as much as any other life experience, as much as any other teaching or research or reading. And, of course, I was sad when he stopped drawing. I felt bereft. Many people did. He drew in the *ligne claire* style, you know – uncluttered, unadorned, minimalist. That's why I like it, because even in an empty outline there is something. And *Happy Family*? Yes, I play it. Who doesn't? Tell me that. Who doesn't?'

The rain was becoming heavy. Germaine checked her phone. It was time. She nodded to her reflection, pulled her raincoat tighter and went inside.

Waiting at a corner table, motionless and expressionless, was Gerard Borkmann. He had two whiskies in front of him. Had the student reporter been there he would have rolled his eyes with an *I-told-you-so* look. Gerard Borkmann was Tom Hannah's agent. He stood up when Germaine walked in and they looked at each other and he said, 'Hello, Germaine'.

Sometimes when she flew to Brussels from outside of Belgium the people in the customs booth would say to her, 'Welcome home'. She liked that. They'd call her *Mejuffrouw* or *Mademoiselle* depending on which part of Belgium they were from. She liked that less. *Mejuffrouw*: Miss. A label. But now, whenever people visited her, she always liked to say, 'Welcome'.

'Hello, Gerard, welcome to Belgium.' She looked at the whiskies. 'If you want a double they can put it in one glass.'

'Funny. One's for you.'

She sat down. *Always be on your guard with Gerard Borkmann. Nothing was nothing with him. Nothing was always something.* 'It's eleven o'clock in the morning. I'll have a coffee with mine.'

He caught the eye of a waiter in the far corner of the room and mimed drinking a cup of coffee. 'Coffee,' he called and held up two fingers. '*Deux, s'il vous plait.* With milk. *Au lait.* Please.'

'They'll come to the table if you're nice to them,' she said. 'You don't have to glare like that.'

'Like what?'

'Like that. Like you're outraged. Why are we drinking whisky?'

'I'm on holiday.'

'Oh really?'

It was more bar than restaurant, dimly lit, and at that time of the morning still quiet. The lunchtime rush was an hour away and there was only the two of them and a table of tourists sitting by the window who were poring over their maps. The sounds outside of rain, buses, cars, taxis and mopeds were kept out by heavy double doors and the thick opaque windows with the name of the restaurant, *Le Chat Noir*, etched in the glass.

'Thank you for coming over,' she said. 'I didn't expect you to swap London for Liège so easily.'

'I liked your email,' he said. 'I thought it was interesting.'

'Is that sarcasm?'

'Not at all. I am interested. Really.'

Germaine sat back and studied him. 'Please don't let this be one of those meetings where you say one thing and mean another, and I don't know what's going on, and then at some point you get what you want.'

'Aren't all meetings like that?'

'Only yours, Gerard. In my world it's more straightforward.

And I think, as we're in Belgium, which is technically more my world than yours, we should try it my way. A social experiment. I'll ask you a question and you answer, "yes" or "no". What do you say?'

'Yes.'

'Good. Are you going to set up an interview with Tom Hannah for my new book?'

'Ah yes. Your book about new art. What is new art exactly? When did it stop being old art?'

Germaine sighed. 'Gerard. Tell me you haven't come all this way just to say no.'

'I haven't said anything yet.'

'You have that look on your face. The one you always have whenever the subject of Tom Hannah comes up. I should have gone straight to him.'

But she knew that would never work. When Tom Hannah was starting out no one was interested in animal-based cartoon strips. They had had their day. Only Borkmann was willing to take on the unknown artist who wanted to create a world in which an eco-friendly fox called *Scraps* conducted a war on waste. Borkmann signed him up, incubated his talent and turned Tom's aversion to meeting people to his advantage, making it hard for the critics to get close to the artist while exploiting the Borkmann network to market the work.

The *Tash* brand became ubiquitous but the man himself was in short supply. *Scraps* was syndicated around the world and the spin-offs and merchandising made him, and Borkmann, very wealthy. And obtaining any kind of interview became virtually impossible.

And then life with all its unruliness caught up with the neat and ordered world of Tom Hannah. Lauded and applauded, his fall was all the heavier for it. Divorce, alcoholism, drug dependency and a traumatic accident took him out of the art world. The Tash era began to be spoken of in the past tense.

But Tom Hannah moved to Spain, set up a small studio in his house, locked the doors and reinvented himself as the creative force behind an augmented reality game. Borkmann set up a games company as a vehicle for the new style of Tash artistic output and put his protégé in the centre of a lucrative Borkmann-built cocoon. The result was *Happy Family* – a games success that picked up the Tash brand where *Scraps* had dropped it.

The waiter brought the coffees. Borkmann and Germaine sat back and looked at each other and, without dropping her gaze, she poured her whisky into her coffee.

'Oh, surely not,' he said.

Germaine smiled. 'We can all be annoying.' She took a sip. It was stronger than she'd expected. 'Anyway, don't focus on "new" being an adjective for "art". Turn it round…'

'I would if I had your brain.'

'Thank you. Let me interview him. You know how significant Tom's move into the games market was. He's one of the great graphic artists. You're his agent not his mother. It will be pure publicity for you. And perhaps he needs it – I haven't heard anything of him for well over a year now, maybe even two.'

Borkmann shook his head. 'His mother is dead. You should bear that in mind when you meet him.'

'I know she's… *when* I meet him?' Germaine put down her coffee.

Borkmann nodded.

'I like that.' She looked at Borkmann and he looked at her. 'So, I can interview him?'

Borkmann leaned forwards. 'You can interview him with my blessing. Interview away. Have multiple interviews.'

'But will you set it up? Have you talked to him?'

'I would but I no longer represent him.'

Germaine looked at him. 'Really?'

'Really.'

'I don't believe you.'

'I can't help that. It is what it is.'

'I'm shocked. This is big news. Massive news.' She tried to read his face, but it was like deciphering a wooden mask. 'How long?'

'A few months.'

'Really?'

'Yes. Again. Really.'

Germaine ran her hand through her hair and sighed. 'Gerard, in real life, why are you here? It's not about my book, is it? What do you want?'

'I want you to interview Tom. In Spain. Soon. If you can.'

'And? Don't pull that face. There is always an "and".'

'And perhaps you might bring him back.'

'To Belgium?'

'Metaphorically back. From the brink. Yes, that's what I want. I want you to bring Tom Hannah back from the brink.'

'The brink of what?'

Borkmann smiled and his face looked like a pupal case splitting open. 'Treat it as an exercise in existentialism. Another coffee?' He started gesturing and miming at the waiter again. 'Two coffees; two whiskies.'

2

The waiter was quick with the drinks, perhaps mistaking Borkmann for a man who tips big. Germaine asked, 'What does "no longer represent" actually mean? You still own the games company, don't you? And Tom Hannah is still the creative director?'

'Yes,' Borkmann said, 'but as an agent and as a business manager, I'm out of a job.'

'So, what happened?'

Borkmann took a moment as if seeking a way into his tale, and then said, 'A while ago, last summer, I realised I hadn't spoken to Tom for almost three months. There had been some emails, a few bland words, but we hadn't actually talked. That's fine, things crop up, time gets away from us. So, I called him – and there was no answer. I emailed him and there was no reply, and then I called the office and no one had heard from him. Finally, I called my contact in the village near his house – and he said that I should go to Spain.'

'Why?'

'They had seen some things.'

'Things?'

Borkmann looked at Germaine's half-empty glass. 'Another?'

'Are we getting drunk? I warn you; I have a naturally strong resistance to alcohol.'

'I'm pleased to hear it. I don't.' He signalled to the waiter and held up his glass and two fingers. 'So, I flew to Spain. I hired a car and drove to the village. This is not an easy place to get to. It's on the far side of the mountains on the extreme west of Spain. It's bleak. Tom lives way out, overlooking a village called Las Sombras. I call it La Zombies.'

'That's very cosmopolitan of you.'

'It's typical Tom. He's found a home no one can get to easily, and no one would want to even if they could. Which is fair enough. He's a private man and I respect that, I always have, but even so I like to have someone in the village keep an eye on him – just in case.'

'In case he comes tumbling down the hill.'

'Precisely.'

The whiskies came.

'We should eat,' Germaine said. She was beginning to feel relaxed and that would never do with a Borkmann circling in the water. Food was required.

'This is on me.'

'But you're a guest in my country.'

'I insist.'

'Now I am worried.'

Germaine focused on the menu and ordered pasta. She didn't normally like its stodgy, doughy blandness but she wanted to soak up the alcohol. Borkmann ordered a plain salad, no dressing. The lunchtime rush was beginning, and the tables were filling up around them.

'What is his house like?'

'He's called it *El Callejón – House of the Alley*. A throwback to *Scraps*. It used to be stunning. Views of the sea on one side and mountains on the other. His own wood, shrubberies, a rose garden. Floor to ceiling windows, big balconies, verandas, terraces, patios – all that sort of thing. Wide and spacious and, as I'm sure you can imagine, minimalist. No clutter.'

'But not stunning any more?'

'I didn't get to see much of it on this trip. I went to the village first, for an update. A husband and wife team: Rodolfo and Teresa. You'll meet them if you go there. You'll like her. Very sociable. Rodolfo said he was under the influence of a demon. Also there had been some character with an expensive car wandering around the place – always on his phone. A technical type. Not one of ours. Rodolfo said they were there a month. He said that Tom had stopped coming to the village and no one had seen him since the wall had gone up.'

'The wall?'

'Around his house.'

'Oh.' Germaine thought about that. 'Is he drinking again?'

Borkmann raised his eyebrows. 'I haven't said anything about that.'

'Come on, Gerard. It's a valid question. We both know Tom's vulnerabilities. I'm not going to gossip, you know that.'

Borkmann nodded. 'I do, which is why I'm telling you this. I don't know if he is drinking or not. I don't know what he's doing. Anyway, after the village I drove up to the house to see what was going on. The main road zigzags and about a mile up from the village there's a dirt track that leads to Tom's property. It's now blocked by several tons of earth. I had to get out of the car and scramble over it to get to Tom's place. And when I did, I saw what Rodolfo had been talking about: a huge stone wall around his property. Stone walls and a massive gate – big vertical iron bars that were very definitely locked. Even his woods are now hidden from view. It's all cut off and contained. Cauterised. No bell, no intercom, just a camera pointing down at me. I looked through the gate, but I couldn't see anyone. So, I waved at the camera and I tried to call him again on my phone, but I couldn't get a signal – obviously. It's Tom Hannah's house. Why would I expect to get a signal?'

The food came and Germaine reminded herself that it was not what Borkmann said that required her attention, it was why he was saying it.

'Did you manage to get in?'

'No, but I met the so-called demon. She was sitting on top of the wall: a tough-looking teenager, unkempt, throwing stones at me. Actually, not throwing, flicking. She was flicking stones off the top of the wall and she had a good aim, I'll give her that.

'I said, "cut it out", and she said, "I'll cut you out." They were her exact words. Charming. Fortunately, Tom finally came to the gate. He had three big dogs with him that were not pets. I didn't like the look of them nor the female on the wall. She was grinning the whole time, as if she were watching a play and knew how it would end. I said to Tom, "what the hell is going on?"'

'And?'

'I couldn't understand him at first, he said things that I couldn't catch. He looked a mess. But I got the message in the end. He said I had to go. He said I wasn't to come back. He said I wasn't representing him any more.'

'Just like that?'

'Just like that.'

'After all those years you've been together?'

'After all those years.'

'But why?'

'He's changed, Germaine. He needs bringing home.'

44

Borkmann continued with his salad while Germaine finished her third large whisky. His story felt unreal, distant and strange compared to the rainy world of Liège with its wet pavements, parks and boulevards.

Borkmann put down his fork and spoon and looked at her. 'You know, I came here because you emailed me and asked to talk about an interview with Tom Hannah. Well, as it turns out, I want you to have that interview. I want you to go to Spain and visit him, to talk to him about new art and old art, and any kind of art that takes your fancy; and about his life and his work; and to remind him of that world, the world he belongs in and should be living in – not locked up behind prison walls with a stone-throwing hooligan for company.'

'But you could do all that. You've known him longer than I have.'

'I can't. Not in the same way you can. You are his context, his audience, you appreciate what he does. You give him credibility and value and respect. You authenticate him. I care about him, but I can't reach him in that way. He knows you; you can connect with him in ways I can't. You asked me what bringing him back means – it means reconnecting him to his world.'

'And if I do reconnect him, then what?'

'Then – I hope – his lights will switch on, and he'll get rid of that girl and the dogs and the walls. You get your interview; I get my client back. And my friend.'

'I do want to go,' Germaine said. 'But I'm not an artist. I'm an observer. I have no influence on his behaviour or his art. I'm not trying to be a blocker because I do want to go, but you're more integral to his world because you helped him to create it. And if he's rejected you why would he see me? I could go all that way only to have stones flicked at my head.'

'He respects you.'

Germaine laughed. 'That's nice. Some people do.'

'I'm serious. Do you know why?'

'Why?'

'Because you're simple.'

Germaine raised an eyebrow. 'Careful, Gerard.'

'In a good way.'

'Explain?'

'You're orderly – in your thoughts and your looks and in your academic ways. I can see it. You think and express yourself in straight lines and sharp corners and clear colours. There is no ambiguity in you. No clutter. That's why Tom Hannah respects you. You are unadorned and uncomplicated. Untextured. And that's what he wants in himself. That's why we've always given you interviews: you're like one of his cartoons – no shading. He will see you, I'm certain of that, and he'll see how far he's drifted from his ideal. You'll be the shock of realisation that he needs.'

'I'll be a shock of realisation?'

'Yes.'

'Lack of shading?'

'No grey areas.'

Germaine sat back in her chair. 'Well. That was illuminating.' She put down her cutlery and laid them in parallel columns beside her plate. 'I don't know what to... did you say, unadorned?'

'I did. And uncomplicated.'

'I heard the word untextured.'

'That too.'

'Well, well, well.'

Borkmann crunched on some cucumber and looked at her. 'Everything all right?'

Whisky fumes were rising behind Germaine's eyes, which were already starting to ache. 'Not everything.'

'What is it?'

'It's not polite to describe a person in front of that person's face.'

'Whose face?'

'My face. You can't call someone unadorned just because they're not... don't appear to be adorned. You don't know what's underneath. I could be particularly well adorned underneath. The only person who has any right to describe a person in front of that person's face... is that person whose face it is.'

'I apologise.'

'I am not antiseptic.'

'I didn't say you were.'

For some reason, and Germaine suspected it might relate to the three large whiskies, she no longer liked being in the restaurant. And so what if she was neat and orderly and clean and tidy with her black jacket and white shirt, black trousers, short functional hair, no make-up, a book for the train, nails done, cigarettes, lighter, change for a coffee, tissues in a packet (best to be safe), keys on a fob, phone in an art-house cover (Hockney: *A Bigger Splash*), fish for supper, a book at bedtime, clean teeth, moisturiser, bed, sleep.

She wanted a cigarette. 'I'm sorry but I have to go.'

Borkmann stopped eating. 'Dear Germaine,' he began as if writing a letter. 'I didn't mean to offend you. It was meant to be a compliment. You haven't finished your meal.'

She stood up. She felt hot. 'I think I've eaten something. I don't feel well.' She swayed. The room swayed. There was too much swaying going on.

'Let me get you some water.'

'I don't want any water; I want to go. And it's not the whisky. I'm a good drinker. Ask anyone.' She looked around for someone to ask. 'It's caught up with me a bit, that's all.'

Borkmann was on his feet now, looking as concerned as his

predatory face would allow. 'How about some fresh air – find somewhere else to sit down? I'd still like to talk about the interview. Do you want dessert? A coffee?'

'No. Thank you. Thank you for the lunch and the coffees and everything. Thank you for telling me all about Tom too. It sounds awful. Really awful.' Germaine started to put on her coat. She was in a hurry to go but she didn't know why. 'Let's talk about the interview later. Not this day. Another day.' She wondered what she was talking about.

'Are you going to be all right?'

'I don't know, Gerard.' She stepped to one side and then back again. 'I'm usually so resilient. I mean, realistic. What is that R-word? Resistant. That's it. Let me pay for the meal.'

'It's on me. Take your time and I'll order you a cab.'

And now Borkmann looked quite kindly as he tried to mime ordering a taxi at the waiter. Germaine's heart sank. She had been rude and ungracious.

'I am sorry,' she said. 'You've come all this way. I do want to interview Tom. From the brink.'

'That's fine. I understand.'

And she thought he did because he then said, 'Sometimes in trying to get my thoughts across I don't always choose the right words. These days there are very few people for whom I would leave London. Very few. And you are one of them. It's been a pleasure, Germaine. Let's talk again soon. I mean it. I really do want you to interview Tom. I think your book will be a great success. I hope I haven't upset you.'

Poor Borkmann, she thought, all he wanted was his friend back and now she was abandoning him. But she still wanted to leave and so she did.

3

Germaine walked to the train station. The cold air, the rain and two cigarettes partly cleared the alcohol fumes from her mind. The whisky had left a sour taste in her mouth and was now sloshing around with the pasta and bread, building a small furnace in her stomach. When her train arrived, she found a corner seat and slumped against the window.

'Stupid,' she said and closed her eyes. They were watering. 'Stupid, stupid, stupid.'

Had she really stood up and walked out on Borkmann? What was she thinking? A wiser head would now be discussing the logistics of an interview with Tom Hannah. She could be planning her travel. Instead, she would have to call Borkmann and apologise and try to meet him again, and he would undoubtedly be awkward – and who could blame him? Why didn't she have a wiser head?

She replayed their conversation in her mind. Whatever Borkmann had told her, it probably wasn't the whole story. The teenager on the wall, the village, the dogs, the gate – some or all of that might be exaggeration or deliberately misleading. And why had he made that point about Tom Hannah's mother being dead? Why mention her at all?

Germaine peeled her thoughts away from the meal and turned them towards her book – *New Art*. She could imagine it clearly: a philosophical deconstruction of the word 'new' and a reconstruction through the prism of art. It would be a heavy hardback crammed with exposition, illustrations, photographs, maps, timelines and biographies; an academic book of importance. It would be on the bookshelves of every art department in every university in Belgium, perhaps even Europe. It would be her showcase; her certificate of eligibility; the step onto the next rung of her ladder to:

Associate Professor.

A permanent academic position; a position of high academic attainment.

She had heard there would be a vacancy for such a position the following year and she wanted it. She was young, she knew, very young for such a position, but she wanted it so much that the desire was a lump in her throat, a stone in her shoe, an ache in her belly, a constant itch. It was an immovable, implacable yearning. She wanted to squeeze time and jump to the moment when it was hers.

Her book would be crucial to her success. It would be the key differentiator between her and the other candidates. And yet she had walked out on Borkmann.

'Idiot,' she said as her train pulled out.

Her phone rang. Germaine looked at it and debated whether or not to take the call. She wanted to ignore it, but the display told her it was her agent, Catharina Caboulet. She looked around the carriage. She disliked talking on the phone in public but there were few people on the train, and no one in her vicinity at all. She took the call.

'Hello, Catharina,' she said. 'How are you? How were the calls with the publishers?'

'Fine.' Catharina's accent always made Germaine think of

50

heavy velvet, red velvet – but that day her tone was light. Deceptively light. 'The interest is there.'

Germaine may have drunk three large whiskies, but she knew a euphemism when she heard one.

'How much interest?'

'Enough. I'll explain but tell me about Borkmann first.'

'It went well,' Germaine said slowly. 'Up to a point.' She decided not to mention the getting drunk and walking out part. 'The big news is: he's not representing Tom Hannah any more.'

'You're joking.'

'That's what he said.'

Germaine could imagine Catharina sitting in her office tapping her pen against her perfect teeth. She huddled closer to the window. Her unwise head was throbbing. She was dehydrated. 'Tell me about the publishers.'

'Well, I spoke to the big three; the multimedia ones. I went through your outline and the synopsis, and our proposal for a documentary spin-off. We talked about the BBC and Netflix. They were interested. They liked the concept.'

'Great, so what's the "but"?'

'They think it's dry.'

'Dry.'

'And wide.'

'Wide.'

'Covering too much ground.'

'Ground.'

'They liked the focus on the artists – their personalities, their lives, that part. They liked the angle that new art comes from old art – a new generation of artists breaking the mould. Old art dead; new art born. That sort of thing.'

'But new art isn't the opposite of old art. And old art isn't dead. There is no *old* art. There's just art. My book is something different. It's about what "new" is, it's…'

'That's what I said.'

'Did you? Anyway, this is a scholarly book. It won't be too dry or too wide or cover too much ground for scholars.'

'They were less keen on the scholarly side of things.'

'Oh.' Germaine tried to laugh but it came out as a squeak. 'That's the whole concept. Do they want the book to be just about the artists? Should I call it *New Artists* and…'

'That's good.'

Germaine looked around the carriage and tried to keep her voice to a whisper. 'Catharina, this book is meant to be underpinned by sound, rigorous, *detailed* academic research. It is meant to be about what "new" is through the prism of art, and the ways in which artists interpret it. Gifted interpreters, yes, creators too, wonderful creators – but it's not meant to be a populist book about a dozen or so contemporary artists. I need this book to be accepted as a scholarly…'

'They also suggested you cut back on the number of artists.'

'Oh, they did, did they? They said that?'

'To six.'

'That's a third of my proposal.'

'It would fit with a television series. Six artists, six episodes.'

'But what do you think…?'

'I think we'll get a deal if we go for six artists. And Tom Hannah is mandatory. If you get Tom Hannah in the book, we'll get a deal and an advance. And we'll go for a two-book contract. Book One can be about the artists; Book Two can be your bestselling academic reference book. And there's nothing to stop you writing them as one book. Structure it so you can lift one from the other. Then, when the second book comes out, we can pitch it as a companion piece.'

'But…'

'It will be the best of both worlds: Germaine Kiecke the arts communicator; Germaine Kiecke the arts academic. You'll own new art by the time you apply for your professorship.'

'Associate…'

'If I could sell it another way, I would. You know that. This makes it all real. If I go elsewhere, we could lose what we have. But you need Tom Hannah in the book.'

'I know. I want him in the book…'

'So, is Borkmann a dud or what?'

'I suppose he's still an influencer…'

'Let's get him round the table. Do you want me there?'

'The thing is, I had a bit too much…'

'Everything is going to be all right.'

Germaine stared at her reflection in the window. 'Okay,' she said.

Germaine lived on the fifth floor of an art deco block of flats overlooking the river. The foyer was the best feature of the building with original geometrical designs on the walls, chequered flooring, tall mirrors and a small gated lift that was slower and took more effort to use than walking up the wide stone staircases.

Germaine let herself into her flat and made a cup of coffee and then stood on her balcony, smoking and looking across the river at the city, wondering if Borkmann was already on his way back to London, cursing his wasted trip and vowing never to talk to her again.

It was only four o'clock. She should call him straight away, but she didn't. Instead she went into the living room, lay on the sofa and put on her iLets. It was time for some augmented reality therapy.

Putting on the iLets was to enter a bubble; a bubble in

which it was hard to detect where the game ended and reality began. The game made all the decisions about lighting, atmosphere and points of view. Characters and props could appear all around, above or below. A light fitting on a ceiling through which water dripped might be part of the game or not.

Germaine believed that the best of fiction could be a genuine life experience; a visceral, tangible experience – frightening, exciting, joy-making and often exhausting. And for her, *Happy Family* was exactly that.

In the past, game-players had mistaken real people for characters; had tried to follow game characters through non-existent openings in the real world; had fallen asleep with their iLets on and awoken in somebody else's game. For many people *Happy Family* augmented not just their reality but the quality of their lives. For many of those people, inside the bubble was better than outside.

Germaine launched *Happy Family* and there was a moment when indistinct shapes and colours flashed in front of her eyes as the lenses synchronised with her pupils, and the app on her phone paired with the other devices in her apartment – and then her living room came back into view. It looked the same as before except a human-sized, semi-aquatic amphibian was sitting on the sofa, reading a book. His name was Mr Venus and he was a salamander, and, in this game of *Happy Family*, he was her father and she was a salamander nymph.

Defining and naming characters was one of the delights for Germaine and she liked to mix the frivolous with the bookish. She had named her game father Kevin, after the Dutch impressionist, Kevin De Gunn, and she had given them the family name 'Venus' in tribute to the Roman goddess: a force of womanhood, a power in a male-orientated pantheon of immortal gods. As for deciding they should all be salamanders, come on, who wouldn't want a salamander as a parent; a symbol of power and protection, rebirth and passion.

The rendering of Mr Kevin Venus was not of some goofy-looking cartoon creature. He didn't wear clothes or twirl a cane or put on a collar and tie in the morning. Germaine had not wanted to immerse herself in a comic; she had wanted to enter a parallel real world, warts and all.

Mr Venus was an athlete – powerful, versatile, equally at home on land as in water. His tongue could explode outwards with devastating and instantaneous power. He was khaki coloured, his skin dry and rough and generating enough toxins to kill an adult human. His body was long, slender and strong – merging into his head without any appreciable join or neck. He had a huge thick tail. His arms and legs were overly muscular and there was something thrilling about the speed with which he could move across a carpeted floor.

Germaine left Mr Venus on the sofa and went into the kitchen and blended some fruit and yoghurt. She logged it on her phone as *Happy Family* lifestyle bonus points, banked half and kept the rest in her game purse, just in case. Back in the living room she jumped onto the sofa.

'What are you reading?' she said.

She had heard the *Happy Family* creative team had fun with product placement, but she couldn't see the title because his large webby hands were obscuring the cover. Mr Venus looked at her, registering her voice and running speech recognition algorithms over her words.

'*Le Petit Chien,*' he said.

She sighed. Perfect. She sat back with her chin on her chest and stared at her feet. Through the iLets she too was physically a salamander. She wiggled one fleshy webbed foot, then the other, then both together. Then she crossed her legs one way, then another, and then back again.

She watched and enjoyed the visual motion. Such clever technology. And what might be possible in ten years' time? Or a hundred or a thousand, or in ten thousand years' time? One day people would visit museums and look at the technology she was using and marvel that anything so crude could ever have been used – just as she marvelled at exhibits of early dentistry and wire-framed spectacles and pedal-driven machines for polishing lenses. Probably the sort of equipment that Borkmann still used.

Mrs Venus, or Rachel as Germaine had named her salamander mother, came into the room. She was small and slim; she liked to paint; she was cosmopolitan and cultured; she adored children. And, as usually happened whenever she saw Mrs Venus, Germaine was reminded of a short exchange with La Jaune shortly before they broke up.

'I do get it. You don't have to look at me that way. I play the game to engage with a childhood I never had. You don't have to run the psychology test.'

'You play it too much.'

But what was too much? Where was the rule book? Where did one game end and another begin, or were they all just one long continuous cycle?

Mrs Venus sat next to Mr Venus and they looked into each other's eyes as if sharing some deeper electronic bond. 'How was your day?' she said.

'Fine,' he said. 'Just fine.' His voice was gentle and reasonable. He had a job in the city.

Germaine looked around her living room. Nothing else was happening and the iLets were neither hot nor cold. She got up and checked all her rooms and looked out into the communal hallway. Nothing lurking, no bags of good luck, no shadows, no feet behind curtains, nothing. The version of the world within her iLets was the same as her real-life world. She went back into the living room.

This was how she liked to play it: a game where *nothing ever happened*. Whenever she started a new game, she always switched off the plug-ins, reduced the levels to one, minimised the danger settings, turned off the game trainers, muted the whisperers and set the age range as four to seven. In doing so, she turned it into a static scenario in which her happy family sat at home, watched television and read books together. As much as any game could be, it was a still-life into which she could insert herself.

'I need the bathroom,' Mr Venus said.

He stood up and scampered into the hallway. In earlier versions of the game the iLets had registered any large rectangle as a door and it was quite usual for a *Happy Family* character to exit through a chimney breast or a grandfather clock – or go to sleep in a bidet or a coffin.

She watched him leave the room and felt a faint sense of apprehension. The problem with being a lizard-like amphibian was when bad things happened they were usually very bad indeed. The story of a children's game in which a frog had his legs chopped off by a sous chef, who then tossed the still-moving head and torso into the shrubbery outside the toddler's virtual front door, had gone viral.

Germaine sat on the sofa with Mrs Venus and wondered about her behaviour with Borkmann. Had he inadvertently touched a nerve? Had she behaved in such an infantile way because deep down she knew he was right; that she appeared uncluttered because in truth she had nothing with which to be cluttered; she was unadorned because she had no… adornings; that she was, in essence, an empty canvas, an outline, a space defined by the shapes of other people?

Even in an empty outline there is something.

When it came right down to it, all she could say for sure about her own being was that she had been born and that she existed. Everything else was pure speculation. She turned to Mrs Venus and said, 'I have to make a call.'

4

Germaine turned off the app and removed her iLets. She stood up, ignoring the vertigo that always came when she finished a game, and took her phone onto her balcony where she lit a cigarette, took a deep breath and dialled Borkmann's number.

He answered immediately; too immediately because she hadn't prepared her opening line. She had wanted to sound cool and calm; measured and authoritative; an academic version of Catharina. Instead she gabbled as if she didn't know how a telephone worked.

'Oh. Hello? Gerard? It's Germaine. Yes. Much. I know. I feel so guilty. Thanks. Are you – oh good. Yes. No. I was wondering. How about – yes. This evening. No, you'd be very… not at all. I could order something. I'll text you my address. Okay, that's perfect. Just after seven. I'll see you then. Thank you, Gerard. Yes. Goodbye. Bye. Bye. Bye.'

She hung up. God that was a fast call. But it was done. Situation retrieved. He was coming to her flat. Was that good? She didn't know.

'Take a breath, Germaine,' she said. 'Slow down.'

She stood on the balcony and finished her cigarette, imagining Borkmann in her home, his long legs stretched out across the carpet, his glittering eyes taking in everything she owned – assessing, quantifying and cataloguing. She imagined him in his shiny black business suit, dusty from the day, pressed against her furniture. She imagined the two of them sitting at her glass dinner table sharing a *rijsttafel*.

She checked her phone and texted him her address, and wondered if she should invite Catharina as well. It was now five o'clock. She went back into her flat, moving slowly through the rooms, not doing anything, just thinking. She paused in front of the hall mirror.

'What's bothering you?' she said to her reflection.

I don't know.

'Is it Borkmann coming to your home?'

Maybe.

'Or do you just want to call Catharina?'

What do you mean?

'You know what I mean.'

I genuinely do not know what you mean.

She ran a bath and stretched out beneath the bubbles with the back of her head and her ears in the water. Sounds of the city that came through her window were now muffled and remote. She lay there until the water became too cool for comfort and then washed quickly, showered her hair, climbed out, wrapped herself in a towel and went into her bedroom. She sat on her bed, staring into space, and then picked up her phone and called Catharina.

'Hello? Catharina? It's Germaine – I know, twice in one day. Crazy. I'm glad I caught you, I – no, no I haven't changed my mind. Can I ask you a favour? Are you busy – no, this evening? Borkmann's coming over – yes, it would be nice to have some support – it won't be late. A discussion, something to eat – a takeaway – I know. Would you mind? Are you sure? Wonderful. Thank you, Catharina. No, whenever you can. Seven-thirty? Perfect. See you then.'

She put her phone on her bed and looked at it. She was getting better at these sorts of call.

At seven o'clock her doorbell rang. Borkmann was waiting with a bottle of champagne.

'Hair of the dog,' he said.

Germaine laughed. 'Was I that bad? Thank you. Come in. Look around. Make yourself at home.'

Her flat was large and open plan. The living room and dining room were all one room, with a kitchen area behind a bar. Wide windows led onto the shallow balcony, and along the hallway were the bathroom and her bedroom. The furnishings were a mixture of artwork and functional necessities. A single Inuit painting dominated the hallway. An antique chair was draped with an ancient African leaf – dried and painted with vegetable dye. The bathroom door was made from rows of opaque bottle bottoms. A large South American fertility sculpture marked the border between the dining area and the living room. Borkmann hung his jacket on it. Other paintings, large and small, had been carefully placed throughout the rest of the flat. Suspended light fittings which looked like insects' legs protruded from the ceiling.

Her furniture was either ornate, asymmetrical and handmade, or harshly bland and utilitarian. A hand-thrown pot of red clay stood in stark relief against a slim silver vertical sound bar on an otherwise empty shelf.

'Still moving in?' Borkmann said.

Germaine gave him a look. 'I have a rule not to throw out my guests as soon as they arrive. But I can make exceptions.

By the way, I've asked Catharina to come over too. Catharina Caboulet, my agent. I hope you don't mind.'

'Not at all. I know Catharina.'

Germaine offered Borkmann a drink. He chose a glass of tap water. She chose a lime and soda and felt virtuous. He sat on the sofa and stretched out and she sat on a chair facing him.

'What time is Catharina coming?' he said.

'Soon, I think.'

'Good. And then we'll talk about your trip to Spain.'

'And the salvation of Tom Hannah.'

Borkmann raised his glass. '*Proost*.'

'*Santé*.'

'I get confused, Germaine, Dutch or French?'

'I don't mind. But I live my life here, in Liège, a Walloon city, so mostly French.'

'And how's your Spanish?'

'Basic.'

'Which is better than mine.' He looked around and saw her iLets. 'Well. What do we have here – Standards? Good. I don't trust the Inserts. You don't use them, do you?'

The doorbell rang before she could answer.

Catharina blew in full of breathless conversation, bringing with her a swirling cloud of perfume and rustling clothes, carrying bags of food and drink, her face bright and cold from the night air. She was tall and wide shouldered, and her face was angular with strong, dark eyes that seemed to see everything. Germaine always felt she could just sit and watch her, and envy her sense of place, her sureness of being, the ownership of her identity.

'Thanks for coming,' she said.

Catharina gave Germaine a hug. 'Straight from work. You smell nice. I picked up some Thai food. I hope that's okay. I

4

thought it would save time.' She threw her coat onto a chair and Borkmann stood up, his hand outstretched.

'Hello, Catharina.'

'And hello to you, too.' They cheek-kissed and she stepped back and looked him up and down. 'Looking good, Gerard. Games suit you.'

This was not true. Borkmann didn't look good at all. He was gaunt and bony and breathless. His limbs seemed too long, too frail, needing too much power to keep them operating. They sat on the sofa while Germaine unpacked the food and laid it out in dishes on her glass dining table.

'I'm starving,' Catharina said.

'Drinks?' said Germaine.

Catharina had a whisky and ginger and Borkmann had a glass of red wine. Germaine chose a glass of white wine. *Just the one*, she thought. *Lunch and learn.* They sat at the table and ate.

'Nice,' Borkmann said. 'Very nice.'

Catharina pointed her chopsticks at him. 'So, what is all this about Tom Hannah? Germaine tells me he's cut loose.'

Borkmann took his time answering, chewing slowly. 'Temporarily, I hope,' he said.

'But who is the new girl? Are they together? What's the situation?' She smiled. 'It's not like you to be outmanoeuvred.'

Borkmann sat back and grinned or, to be precise, he exposed his teeth. 'Shall we talk about Germaine's trip?'

'Let's.'

Germaine poured more wine for Borkmann and added more whisky to Catharina's glass. She looked at her own glass and topped it up too.

'Before we get down to business,' Catharina said. 'I want to make sure we're all talking about the same thing. Germaine's writing a book about six artists. Six contemporary artists. It's going to be big, Gerard, and we're pitching for a network follow-up. I've got three publishers interested, the big three, and I might take it to auction. Tom Hannah is a desirable inclusion. Desirable for the project. So, it's important that, if he's on board, he's on board for the whole thing, television too.'

'Well, that's interesting.' Borkmann looked at Germaine. 'It's not quite how you described it. I thought it was going to be more of a scholarly work. This sounds different. I like it better.'

'It's part of a suite,' Catharina said. 'The book; the TV series; and then the scholarly, academic book.' She helped herself to more food.

'I'm going to write it as a single...' Germaine began.

'But,' Catharina said to Borkmann, 'should we be talking to you or his new girlfriend?'

Borkmann shrugged. 'I can only tell you how it is. Tom Hannah has implied that he would, for the moment at least, like to conduct his business through a person who sits on walls and throws stones at people. She is not an agent of any sort – I've checked. The locals say she's been living rough. If that sounds like someone you'd rather deal with than me, someone who's not even in the business, then fine. I wish you all the joy in the world and do let me know how it goes.'

Catharina looked at Germaine, and Germaine looked at Catharina. She might have looked too long because Catharina raised her eyebrows and then turned back to Borkmann.

'But technically, in reality, Tom Hannah is no longer your client. Right?'

Borkmann laid his cutlery against his plate. 'Look, I've known Tom for over twenty years. I'm his friend as much as his agent and business manager. We all know every now and then that things get on top of him. It's a pattern. Yes, I'm worried about him, of course. That's why I wanted to see Germaine. I like the sound of her book – even more now – and I think it would be good for him to participate in it. But he will come back to me. He always does.'

Germaine helped herself to some more rice and topped up everyone's glass again. Catharina looked thoughtful.

'Okay,' she said. 'So – where do we go now?'

Germaine was feeling tired. Her ears and nose were aching as if she had a cold. She felt grateful that Catharina was doing all the work. Through her half-closed eyes she thought her agent looked great. 'Let's sit on the comfortable chairs,' she said.

They left the food and dishes on the table and Germaine fetched more whisky and wine, and en route she had a quick puff of a cigarette on her balcony.

'It's quite bright in here,' she said coming back in. She turned down the lamps and flopped onto a chair.

Borkmann and Catharina were sitting on the sofa.

'Gerard has proposed something interesting,' Catharina said.

'Marriage?' Germaine said, and as she did so she realised with an awful clarity that she was drunk again. What was wrong with her?

'I was suggesting,' Borkmann said, 'that I might fund your trip to Spain. That I might, in fact, publish your book.'

Germaine nodded and frowned, wanting to convey both enthusiasm and gravitas. 'That is good,' she said. She chose each word carefully. They seemed appropriate but she suspected she now sounded like a robot.

Borkmann said, 'I'll publish your book. You said it yourself – a book about Tom Hannah is bound to do *Happy Family* some good. So why not? We already publish the *Scraps* books. We'll distribute through the same channels, or I'll set up an arts imprint. It makes sense. I don't know why I haven't done it before. And I'll publish both books. The follow-up thing too.'

'It's going to be an academic reference...'

Catharina waved her glass. 'It's a fantastic offer. Thank you, Gerard. And just to clarify – it will be a proper publishing contract? Copyright sits with Germaine. Industry standard. And it will have the Borkmann marketing machine behind it? You'll promote and distribute?'

Borkmann smiled. 'Yes, yes and yes. It's an honest offer. No auction, though. Commit to me. No advance either, but I'll cover Germaine's expenses for interviews with all six artists and any reasonable research and writing costs – although my stipulation is that she interviews Tom Hannah first.'

Catharina looked at Germaine. 'What do you think?'

Germaine frowned. 'I think it's great,' she said. 'Is it hot in here? I might open a window. I'm hot. It's very hot.' Germaine levered herself out of the chair and opened the balcony door as wide as it would go and almost fell through it. She made her way back to her chair and tried to look serious and sensible. 'There.'

Catharina turned back to Borkmann. 'We're talking book rights only?'

Borkmann drummed his long fingers on the arm of the sofa and Germaine watched them go up and down, up and down, like big spider legs. A spider dancing a jig. She noticed that everything now seemed to be either very close or very far away. She must have had at least a bottle of wine to herself and now there was whisky in her glass. She was a terrible person. 'Does anyone want any dessert?' she said.

'I want first refusal on the television rights,' Borkmann said.

'I've only got sorbet.'

'I think,' said Catharina slowly, 'that we should shake on the principle tonight and talk contracts and detail tomorrow. Let's bank the moment and come back to it with a clear head in the morning.'

Germaine watched Catharina with admiration. She wished that she were that sensible and wonderful.

Borkmann stood up and raised his glass. 'Fine. To the principle.'

'To the deal.'

'To the toast.'

They drank and shook hands and Borkmann sat down and Catharina prised her hand from Germaine's. Then they had more food and wine and whisky and talked about the trip to Spain, and, at some point, Germaine put on music. Later they went onto the balcony and Germaine shouted at passers-by. Catharina and Borkmann had a row about e-books and then they made up, and then they had another row about self-publishing while Germaine lay on the floor.

Much later, Germaine was sick in the sink in the bathroom and poked the bits down the plughole with her chopsticks, and much, much later, at some point in the early hours, her guests made sure Germaine was lying on her side on the sofa and covered her with a blanket before leaving.

5

When she woke up her neck was stiff and she was cold. It was dawn. She got up and went to bed and lay there reviewing what little of the previous evening she could bear to remember. It wasn't good for her to drink, she decided. It was the opposite of good. It was very, very, very bad.

She supposed Borkmann had gained what he wanted: control of her and control of the situation, whereas she had achieved a hangover and a mosaic of memories, which included insulting her neighbours as they walked beneath her balcony. She would buy them flowers and leave them on their doorstep along with a note of apology, and then she would emigrate to Planet Venus. It would be best if she were never seen in public again.

It was difficult to separate the feeling of anxiety, caused by the certain knowledge she had made an embarrassing spectacle of herself, from a deeper, more intellectual unease that things were – were what? Incomplete? Misaligned? Wrong?

'Enough thinking,' she said. 'Get up.'

Despite a thudding headache she got up. Her flat was untidy: cold and congealing food, empty and almost empty bottles, sticky glasses. She walked amongst the day-after-party clutter but couldn't summon any energy to clear up.

She stepped onto her balcony. It was one of those days when the air was still and close and the clouds were low and grey and oppressive. It put her on edge, and she felt that nothing good would happen to her on a day like this, and that she should return inside and curl up in her bed and lie there for a long time. So she did, and fell asleep. It was late in the day and the sky was growing dark and her phone was ringing.

Still half-asleep, her head deep in the pillow, she put the phone on her cheek and said, 'Hello?'

'It's me.'

'Hello, Catharina.'

'Who spiked the drinks?'

'I did. I feel awful. I'm an idiot.'

'Nonsense. Anyway, what do you think about Borkmann?'

Germaine passed a hand over her forehead. Borkmann, what did she think about Borkmann? That was a good question. What was the meaning of Borkmann? Why Borkmann? Whither Borkmann?

'In what sense?'

'In the sense he's offering to publish your book?'

Talking and listening and being awake was making Germaine feel nauseous. 'I don't know. What do you think?'

'Better a peck than a promise, that's what I think. Although I can't help wondering what he really wants.'

'He wants his client back.'

'I'm going to talk to him today and get the ball rolling. I'll try for a letter of intent and ring-fence the expenses for you. Can you start thinking about the trip? Flights, hotels, questions, that sort of thing.' Catharina fell silent and Germaine waited, her eyes closed.

'You know, if we do get a Tom Hannah interview, we'll

be in a good position however things go. Borkmann wants his client back, I agree, but perhaps there's a specific reason. An urgency he's not talked about. What if Tom Hannah is drawing again, a new *Scraps*, perhaps? Going back to cartoons. That would be interesting, wouldn't it? Especially if he's un-agented. Are you still there, Germaine?'

'Just.'

'Are you feeling poorly?'

'Alcohol is bad.'

'I know. I knew a woman who used to check herself into a hospital and put herself onto a saline drip to rehydrate. You know you're properly hungover when your blood turns to powder. What you need is some fast food. Instant gratification. A burger with cheese and fries. A double. Bacon too and lots of salt. You'll be fine. Although now I think about it, that woman is dead.'

The line went quiet and Germaine couldn't raise the energy to do anything other than listen to her blood pulsing in her ear. She remembered Tom Hannah's mother whom she had interviewed just before her death: one small blood clot travelling up through her body while, unsuspecting, she went about her daily business.

His mother is dead. You should bear that in mind when you meet him.

'I was thinking,' said Catharina after a while. 'It can be difficult for an agent when they lose a client, you know, *lose* a client, especially when someone else has control of the back catalogue. All that copyright sitting with someone else who's not under contract. Maybe that's what Borkmann is worried about. This new person – girlfriend, woman, devil, whatever she is – getting her hands on Tom Hannah's estate.'

Germaine let the words float on the surface of her mind. 'Do you think Tom is ill?'

'I haven't heard anything. But he can hit the hard stuff. Hey, maybe this girl's his drug dealer.'

'I don't think so.'

'Maybe. Anyway, let's divide and conquer. I'll deal with Borkmann and you get some details on the place where Tom Hannah lives. And look on the bright side, if all this doesn't work out you still get a holiday in Spain.'

Germaine lay in her bed in the dark. She would cancel the entire day and wake up tomorrow when she felt human. She was too lightweight for this lifestyle. But she was hungry. Catharina was right; she should eat and then sleep. Eat and sleep. That was all that really mattered. In the Motherhood, Germaine had seen much of the worst in people; a society in which love and family bonds, kindness and generosity were luxuries. The true goals in life, humanity's highest values, were the needs to eat and sleep undisturbed. Interfere with those and wars could start.

Growing up in Chateau Giselle the children had often been fed the animals that lived in, or wandered into, the orphanage's grounds. Rats, cats, mice and squirrels; pigeons, magpies, blackbirds, crows. The choicest meat would go into the pot for Sunday dinner, the rest would be served up throughout the coming week – stew and soups of offal and marrow; jellies and rinds; scrapings. Germaine had been a vegetarian since leaving the Motherhood but occasionally, in her sleepier moments, she caught herself salivating over the thought of a freshly plucked magpie.

Certainly, now, she wanted more than salad and leftover rice. What was required was a slab of fried cheese under a massive mushroom, dripping with olive oil, topped with a layer of ketchup and wrapped in a starchy white bread bap. And fries. And cheesecake. And full-fat coke.

Germaine rolled out of the bed, got to her feet and went into the bathroom. She cleaned her teeth, washed in the sink she had been sick in, pulled on jeans and a jumper, put on a coat, squashed a baseball cap over her unbrushed hair and went out.

Take a look at this, Borkmann, and tell me I'm clean and neat.

Outside, she smoked as she walked, holding her cigarette outwards between two fingers as if she had a dog on a lead. After she had been freed from the Motherhood, she had decided that never again would she drop her eyes before the look of another. Never again would she keep her head down and hope not to be noticed, not to be there, not to exist, not to occupy a space in the world. She blew smoke before her like a steam train and held the centre line along the pavement with her head up and back straight. She might not be tall, but she was there. It was a small rebalancing of a much larger wrong.

There was a burger restaurant near the river that had both a vegan and a vegetarian menu. Germaine sat inside on a plastic chair at a vinyl table and ate out of a box alongside students and families, tourists and teenagers. It was bright and garish and exactly what she wanted. Tomorrow she would be good. Tomorrow she would be Germaine Kiecke again. Today she would survive.

On her way home she passed a café in whose window there was a stand of cakes and pastries. She hesitated. There was surviving and there was gratuitous feasting. She looked at her reflection in the window.

'What do you think?'

Do it.

She went in and ordered a rich and creamy coffee and sat at

a table near the back by the kitchen, with a slice of chocolate cake and cream. She was beyond redemption.

A radio was playing nearby, low enough to be inaudible at the front of the café where most of the customers were sitting. It was two minutes past seven o'clock and as the news finished the familiar signature tune of *Tuscan Fields* came on.

Even Belgians who didn't follow the series knew this signature tune. Should any Belgian ever be abducted and dissected by aliens, and their thoughts and memories recorded and played back, the theme tune to *Tuscan Fields* would fill the spacecraft with its frenetic accordion sounds. It was a simple tale of simple people who lived and worked in a simple Tuscan village.

A large woman in a stained white apron came out from the kitchen where she'd been working and sat at an empty table across from Germaine. She looked at her and smiled.

'I never miss it,' she said.

Germaine smiled too and nodded. She ought to go home but she was comfortable where she was and the voices on the radio were soothing. No matter how many episodes of *Tuscan Fields* were missed, it was always possible to rejoin the story within moments of tuning in.

That night there were four story strands to follow: a missing tractor, bats in a barn, a car set alight and, towards the end of the episode, what appeared to be a lovers' tryst in a country lane. The characters were whispering to each other when there was a sudden sneeze in the background. It was a fantastic sneeze – a nasal explosion followed by rustling leaves. Clearly someone was lurking in the hedge and eavesdropping on the lovers' secrets. Who was it? The signature music came on; Germaine would have to wait until the following day to find out. The chef looked at her and shook her head.

'That's torn it,' she said.

Germaine nodded. 'Busted.'

'That was Bill Flapp listening to what they were saying. One of the bottlers up at the winery.'

'The sneezer?' said Germaine. She leaned with her elbows on the table, her chin resting on one hand. She felt liberated and anonymous in her cap and jumper and jeans. She could be anyone she chose to be.

'That's the one. Can't keep his mouth shut. It will be all over the village.'

'Are they having an affair?'

'That was last year. This year they're planning a surprise Spring Gala. No one is meant to know who the guest celebrity is going to be.'

'Exciting.' Germaine toyed with her fork and plate, redirecting the flow of cream around the chocolate crumbs. It reminded her of being sick in her sink. She smiled. 'He certainly knows how to sneeze,' she said. 'I thought the radio was going to fall off the shelf.'

'Sneeze double.'

'Pardon?'

'Sneeze double. A specialist actor who comes in and does all those noises. Hiccups, snoring, belches. It's radio. That sneezer has to conjure up a lot of images in a listener's head – why he sneezed, what made him sneeze, whether he'd been trying to stifle it, did he have a handkerchief. It's a craft.'

'I didn't realise.'

'The British do it best. They learn it at their theatre schools. Bodily functions voice acting. They get a lot of work in Europe. That one was Robin Rix. Replaced Charles Cubberley.'

'I've never heard of either of them.'

The chef looked around the café. 'I was in an episode of *Tuscan Fields* once. They had a scene where somebody asks somebody else to make a cup of coffee in a café. They wanted to record some background hubbub. The sound crew came here and recorded me.'

'Exciting.'

'It was. And the crew were all talking about Rix having a fling with Mrs Cubberley. There was a dust-up on the set. Punched him on the nose. Live on air. Apparently he's got a temper – Cubberley. He can't control the red mist. Cost him his place on *Tuscan Fields*. I don't know what he's up to now. But you can't go around punching people.'

'I suppose not.'

Germaine paid her bill, left the café and walked home thinking about many things: Borkmann's offer of publication, the possibility of meeting Tom Hannah at his retreat in Spain, Catharina's face, the calories inside her stomach, actors having flings.

When she got back to her flat, she stood in the bathroom and looked in the mirror. Her hair was flat where she had worn the baseball cap and her face was pale and washed out. She thought her nose was too small, her shoulders too narrow, her t-shirt too big. What did she see when she looked into her eyes? Who was in there looking out? Or was there no one – just two empty circles staring back?

She shrugged. She was too tired to think any more about these things. She checked her phone, turned out the lights and went to bed.

6

The following day, Germaine's hangover was gone and she decided to go for an early morning walk – to get some fresh air and restore her sense of self-worth.

In Belgium it was legal to wear iLets outside in certain designated open areas. The park near her home was one such area. She wasn't the only gamer out and about that morning. There was a man jogging with his iLets and talking to a non-existent running mate; and near the fence a woman was berating some unseen child or pet or wild animal or unnameable creature.

Germaine felt a keen anticipation, a familiar urgency to not just begin playing the game but to be in it, to be past the starting point and to be deep within, to fast-forward to a point of absorption. She wanted to reach the view without the climb. She put on her iLets, changed the narrative setting to 'exterior', synchronised her world with the app and set off across the grass. Now, either side of her, Mr and Mrs Venus appeared, human-sized, their heads looking this way and that, sticky tongues flicking in and out. A walk in the park with her parents, hand in webby hand.

Around her the drab, overcast day was enlivened by a beeping, buzzing soundtrack and the park was augmented with a colourful carnival scene of primary colours. Crazy creatures jumped up and down and squealed and giggled and threw water bombs at each other, while a kindly magician with a moustache that Tom Hannah might have coveted threw Good Luck tokens into the air for Germaine to catch.

A snail appeared in her path, carrying a heavy load on her back. A banner hovered above her head proclaiming that this was Sally the Snail. Only the bottom part of Sally was connected to the ground. The rest of her was vertical and, in the game, she was as big as Germaine.

'Good morning,' Sally called. 'You're in a rush. Do you want a lift?'

A *Yes/No* option flashed in Germaine's iLets. Yes was always the default option. She shook her head, the iLets registered the movement and the option disappeared. She had once asked a *Happy Family* developer why they had made it easier to say Yes rather than No. He told her that saying Yes always led to trouble and that was where the fun lay. This disturbed Germaine in ways she couldn't describe.

They passed a rockery and came upon a second character, an ant called Anuj, who was dragging a piece of burned meat behind him. Anuj was also as big as Germaine and his appearance would have fitted well into a 1950s creature feature.

'What's that?' Germaine said.

'It's from yesterday's barbecue. If I get it back to my anthill in one piece, I might win the 'ant of the day' prize and receive a granule of sugar from the queen's larder.'

'I'll give you a lift,' said Sally. 'Can you help us, Germaine?'

'Yes, you must go and help them,' said Mr and Mrs Venus in unison, which Germaine found to be a bit creepy. That was salamanders for you. 'Go and play.'

And so the simple, linear, pre-school adventure was set up. Germaine walked alone in one world and bounced along with her garden friends and freshwater parents in another; a world where colours were brighter, birds were louder and flowers larger.

What would her art colleagues make of this? What would anyone make of it? A grown woman in a child's game. But why not? There were enough adult games in the real world. She imagined herself to be at the centre of concentric circles in which, like millions of rocks circling the sun, there were people – the great and the good, the wicked and bad, the happy and sad, the lost and found – all absorbed in intricate and emotional adventures of their own devising; spinning faster and faster until they shot off into space.

'And good riddance to you all,' she muttered.

Perhaps the breeze took her words before the iLets could register them because neither Mr nor Mrs Venus answered. But a passing cyclist in the real world gave her a sharp look before noticing that she was gaming and smiled.

'Got rid of the bad guys?' he said.

Germaine stopped and took off her iLets. She had learned that mixing games with reality was too disorientating.

'Just thinking aloud,' she said.

'What are you playing?'

'Amphibians.'

The cyclist beamed. 'Not the one with the frogs? My children play that. It's great. Have you been in the one with the sous chef?'

'No,' Germaine said, walking on. 'Salamanders.'

The encounter disturbed her. Why did so many people seek the unpleasant things in life? People who had no idea of how unpleasant 'unpleasant' could be. She lit a cigarette and blew a large cloud of blue smoke into the air. '*Der zucker des lebens*,' she said quietly.

It was irrational, she knew, but it annoyed her that other

people played *Happy Family*. She wanted it all for herself. She didn't like to hear of other people's game experiences because, in some inexplicable way, doing so sullied hers. She had thought she would be immune to emotional distress after escaping the Motherhood; just to be alive and to sleep peacefully would be enough.

But when the *Happy Family* games suite had been infected by the *Bird of Prey* virus she had felt real angst. It had shown her how much the game meant to her. It was during that time that La Jaune had left her. Cause and effect? She didn't know.

Bird of Prey was developed by a hacking team led by the twin brothers Richter and Holst Bird. Their software worm added a 'cuckoo' to the base list of character attributes. When a gamer selected any of these attributes, the cuckoo appropriated their social media profiles, financial data, password key fobs, and family and friends contact lists – and then deleted them. The cuckoo installed itself onto every instance of *Happy Family* on every device on the wifi connection, and then rippled out across the internet. An added twist was that it profiled the gamer – changing the game to mirror key recorded events in the gamer's life, taking the gamer to dark parts of their psyche. Global penetration of the worm in the *Happy Family* game was believed to be over 35 per cent within a month, and rising.

Losing customers, Borkmann Augmented Realities Corporation released the *Deraptor* patch which was meant to delete the cuckoo before the game began. But the cuckoo adapted and slayed everyone in the game, virtually speaking – and still stole all their details. The explicit carnage created by this caused players to experience genuine, real-world traumas. Mental health professionals began lobbying governments to ban the game. In response, Borkmann released a full antivirus fix called

Coyote. This ring-fenced the game, killed all the characters at birth, including the cuckoo, and reinstalled a clean version. It seemed to work.

The Bird brothers, of course, were still out there somewhere. There were rumours of a split – an acrimonious fall out between the twins. Wealthy and sought after by governments and private concerns who wanted unauthorised back doors into social media and games platforms, Richter took the darker path, establishing a network of cyber-criminals – hackers for hire as they styled themselves. Holst, meanwhile, took a two-month tech-detox on an island off Norway in the South Utsire seas and watched puffins pick fish from the waves. When he came back, he reinvented himself as an ethical hacker.

Both brothers vanished from the grid, cropping up unexpectedly in various guises online, as avatars – threatening and cajoling; warning and protecting. It was as if they were carrying out a proxy sibling spat using the landscape of the internet as their battleground. Where one appeared the other soon followed, each trying to undo the other's handiwork. The flurry of hacks and fixes that would suddenly beset an online entity became known in the industry as the *Goth-Ungoth Syndrome* – due to Richter Bird's penchant for black clothing, pale face make-up and all things Bauhaus.

Germaine walked home, her iLets tucked away in her bag. She was an outsider now, separate from the clusters of gamers who haunted the park battling with their electronic destinies. When she arrived at her flat she made a cup of coffee and settled down at her desk, arranging her notes into neat piles along with her thoughts, ready to research the trip to Spain and begin the preparations she would need to complete before she travelled. The prospect of a few hours spent in quiet, methodical study smoothed whatever jagged edges remained after her recent encounters with booze and reality.

She began by looking into the area in which Tom Hannah had made a home. As Borkmann had suggested, Las Sombras was a village a long way off any beaten track. There was one road in, no train station nearby and according to an online itinerary only one bus a day. The route followed a wide clockwise circle that took in other coastal villages, hamlets and communities that were scattered across the foothills on the seaward-side of the mountains. An entire round-trip would take five hours.

There was also scant information on Las Sombras itself. It was a town that seemed to have appeared only to fill a space on a map. No armies had ever marched upon it, no battles had been fought over it, no kings or queens had fled there. The *Iberian List of Trade & Commerce* could only manage a lacklustre 'Fishing, Tourism and Other' in its listing of Las Sombras activities. Germaine did find one travelogue, however, written by the Victorian adventurer Joshua Waite who visited the area in 1842. He wrote:

> There is a village on the far side of the mountains, on a rocky peninsula of damp stones and slippery surfaces, where the days are brittle and bright and the nights roll in like a creeping gas. They call it the place in the shade: Las Sombras. In this place the houses crouch low against the ground and the villagers light their candles early, and the flames flicker in the draughts, and the wind whispers beneath their beds. A single cobbled street leads from the village down to the harbour. Either side of this street there are heavy stone houses. On one side the land behind the houses falls away into the sea and the crashing waves send thick, salty spray high above the occupants' gardens. On the other side the houses reach a corner, turn, and become a line of wind and sea-scarred buildings that run parallel to the harbour wall: a tavern, a fishing store, a chandlery and a shoemaker. Beyond this there is noth-

ing and the land returns to the rocks which climb back up to the mountains.

'Sea-scarred buildings?'

What romantic nonsense. Germaine tutted, happy to be back in her scholastic comfort zone. She found an online version of the local newspaper, *El Eco Diario*, which had an article in its Archives section on Tom Hannah, '*the famous cartoonist and games entrepreneur*' who was moving into the area. They'd conflated his name and pen name and called him Tash Hannah which amused Germaine. It made him sound as if he were one of his own characters.

Tash Hannah and the Shades of Las Sombras.

There was a grainy picture of his house taken from a distance and it appeared, as Borkmann had said, to be an impressive building with views out to sea and the mountains as a backdrop. She also found pictures of Rodolfo and Teresa in an old advertisements section. Teresa seemed to be a jolly woman in the photograph, standing outside a small hotel called *El Tesoro Escondido*, but Rodolfo came across as a dour character – a tall, bony man with loose folds of skin hanging from his neck and big, fleshy ears. He was turned to one side, as if wanting to be photographed looking over the top of Teresa's head, and the back of his skull seemed to lack substance as if someone had deflated it.

Rodolfo's name appeared in more than one advertisement. Apart from the hotel he also operated a local delivery service and a glass bottom boat business. In a photograph too blurred to expand, there was an empty plastic chair leaning against the harbour wall and a child's chalkboard on which was scrawled the words: *Glass Bottom Boat Trips – Every Hour On The Hour. €6.* Germaine could make out an old motor launch tethered to a lumpy iron bollard.

Bleak, Borkmann had called Las Sombras, and bleak it looked. Whatever had possessed Tom Hannah to move there? But Germaine knew the answer to that question before it had finished forming in her mind – solitude. Solitude and isolation.

She imagined Las Sombras to be a place where people were born and died without ever crossing the mountain barrier. But then, who was she to criticise? Abandoned as a baby in Liège, she was still there thirty-six years later. She had read that all of life can be observed from the vantage point of one's garden gate. God help us all, she thought, if it were the garden at Chateau Giselle with its wide urine-yellowed lawn; the high brick walls, cracked and flaking; the litter and scattered broken toys – a doll's head, a chicken bone, a three-legged chair. What could anyone learn of life from that, other than it was a messy, sordid affair? But perhaps that was all it really was.

SPRING 2023

1

It took Catharina three months to get written agreement from Borkmann that he would cover Germaine's travel expenses for the Tom Hannah interview. He had been indisposed all that time and contract negotiations were still at the 'speculative' stage.

'I don't understand,' Catharina said. 'I thought he was keen to get you out there.' And now, before Germaine could travel, Borkmann wanted a conference call.

When Germaine dialled in, Borkmann and Catharina were already on the line.

'Hello,' Germaine said.

'Germaine,' Borkmann said. 'Apologies for the long delay in proceedings. And I never thanked you for that takeaway evening. Most enjoyable.'

Germaine smiled, tightly. 'That's all right.'

'You were so happy. Singing, dancing, shouting…'

'Yes, thank you.'

'And your neighbours…'

'Yes, all good.'

'Hard of hearing, perhaps…'

'Shall we talk about Spain?'

'Of course. Dates all sorted out?'

'I'm going in two weeks' time. Staying for five days.'

'You've spoken to Rodolfo?'

'His son. Claudio. I'm booked into the hotel, *El Tesoro Escondido*. Thanks for arranging the flights.'

'My pleasure. And don't worry about a car. You'll be picked up at the airport.'

'Thank you.'

'It's the least I can do. I'll arrange for you to be met.'

'Not minders?' Germaine had seen this technique of constraining interviews before.

Borkmann sounded tired. 'No, not minders. Just two people who will do me a favour in exchange for some help. A couple. They'll work to your direction and they'll be useful.'

'Are you all right with that, Germaine?' said Catharina.

'I'm fine with it – but, if Tom Hannah is not welcoming visitors, they might be a hindrance.'

'Play it by ear,' Borkmann said.

Catharina said, 'Gerard, have you spoken to him yet? Tom Hannah?'

'I've tried. But he's not responding. I left a message and sent an email. It's been read so he knows you're coming – I've sent you his contact details. I assume I am still persona non grata.'

'So how is this going to work?' said Catharina. 'Let's imagine he won't answer the door. What happens then? Play that by ear too?'

'You have five days. Worst case it's a holiday on me. But I know your tenacity, Germaine. I have faith. So, are we all set?'

'I think so,' said Catharina. 'Germaine?'

'Yes,' Germaine said. 'All set.'

Borkmann wrapped it up. 'Good. You'll be met at the airport. He's British, she's Belgian. So, you should get along. Husband and wife: Charles and Margot.'

Had she been in a play Germaine would have looked at the audience and raised her eyebrows.

'What?' she said.

Germaine flew from Brussels to Madrid. She had discovered it was the cheapest flight to Spain from Belgium that Borkmann could have bought. It meant the remaining 370 miles to Las Sombras would have to be completed by car – with people she didn't know.

'Thank you, Gerard.'

But much as she disliked the idea of sharing the trip with two strangers, she was curious to meet them. Could it possibly be *the* Charles Cubberley and his wife, of fling and dust-up fame?

She came through to the arrivals hall trying not to wear that bewildered look most people adopt when they arrive at an airport – as if emerging into an airport was wholly unexpected after flying in an aeroplane. She spotted Charles Cubberley straight away, an older – and she was loath to judge so quickly – but seedier version of his IMDB photograph. He was standing by a waste basket, holding up a sign that read, *German Kake*.

She waited with her trolley a few feet from him while he scanned the arriving passengers, presumably searching for someone or something with the look of a Teutonic pastry. Had he not questioned that name, she wondered, not asked for the words to be repeated? Or perhaps in the entertainment business a person called German Kake was quite normal.

For some reason, perhaps it was the prospect of the long car journey ahead, she was unwilling to break the spell and was content for the moment to stand in the crowd and watch the ex-*Tuscan Fields* bodily functions voice actor. She decided that seedy was uncharitable. On closer inspection 'ramshackle' was a better description. His grey hair was uncombed, his tanned face was lined and unshaven, his blue eyes were bloodshot. He wore a white polo shirt with a stain on it, a blue jumper tied around his neck with frayed cuffs and shiny corduroy trousers. She knew he was in his late fifties, but he looked older.

She waited until most of the passengers had gone and then stepped in front of him and held out her hand. 'Charles Cupboard?' she said.

'Hyanh?' he said.

She pointed at his sign. 'I'm Germaine Kiecke.'

'Kake?'

'Kiecke.'

'Ah.'

He looked at her, looked at the sign and then folded it in two and dropped it into the bin. Germaine liked that. Decisive adaptation to changing circumstances. He made the noise that sounded like 'Hyanh' again. It was some form of breathy punctuation delivered through clenched teeth. His head twitched from side to side when he did it, like a trapped beast.

They shook hands.

'Have you been waiting long?' she said.

'Just arrived.'

She had expected a rich and sonorous actor's voice, but Charles's was hoarse and ragged. Throaty. It was a smoker's voice. She liked that too.

'From Las Sombras?' she said. 'You've driven three hundred and seventy miles and now you're going to drive all the way back…'

'Stopped for a tea, of course.'

'Of course. But…'

'Expensive place, Madrid.'

'Wouldn't Borkmann pay for an overnight stay?'

Apparently, Borkmann wouldn't. Charles ground his teeth.

Germaine had never seen anyone do that in real life and she found herself silently mimicking the action. They left the trolley at the airport's exit and carried Germaine's bags, but instead of walking towards the car parks Charles walked around the side of the building and set off along the perimeter road.

'How far is the car?'

'About twenty minutes.'

Germaine wondered if his clipped, staccato delivery was an affectation, an actor's habit, or genuine. She said, 'I'm having a cigarette. Do you mind?'

'Not at all.'

'Do you smoke?'

'Gave up.'

'Oh. I…'

'No, no. Go ahead.'

They stopped and she lit up and blew smoke into the air while they watched aircraft take off.

'When did you stop?' she said.

'Two weeks ago.'

'Two weeks? You should have said. This must be a torment. I'll put it out.'

'Wait, could I…?'

'You've given up. You can't.'

'Just a puff.'

'You'll break the seal.'

'I won't.'

Germaine laughed. 'You will. Okay. But I feel I've corrupted you.'

Charles took her cigarette and filled up his lungs. 'Thanks,' he said breathing out long tendrils of smoke. 'Good. Probably best not to mention this to Margot. Promised her. You know… I wouldn't. Spineless. But I'm an actor. We're all spineless.'

'I'm sorry to hear that.' She looked at him. 'How do you know Gerard Borkmann?'

'I don't. Wrote him a letter. Margot's idea. Good one too. Hard life being an actor's wife. Hard life being an actor. Lousy pay. Always resting. Then, when they want you, it's an early call in some godforsaken hellhole. Three years studying at Bristol – Shakespeare. Pinter. Molière. They called me "On-Cue Cubberley"; always on my mark. Blow raspberries for a living now. Ever heard of a man called Rix? Robin Rix? Shit bag. If you come across him, kick him hard in the face. I mean, hard. Really hard.'

Charles was livening up. Perhaps it was being beneath a hot Spanish sun; perhaps it was walking along a busy airport road; but his face had turned red. He took a final puff of the cigarette and stubbed it out on the ground, grinding it into the concrete until it ceased to exist. Germaine watched it go.

They picked up her bags and carried on.

'So,' she said. 'Why did you write a letter to Borkmann?'

'Voice audition. For that game thing.'

'You're in Spain for an audition? With Tom Hannah?' Germaine frowned. That was news. Borkmann had not mentioned an audition. Would that make it easier or harder to get an interview?

'Said he'd pay a bit extra if I did some running around for him. Borkmann, that is. Paid for Margot too. Very decent I thought at the time. The extra wasn't much, though. That was two weeks ago. And I needed the work. Rubbish, isn't it? Anyway, you're here now so that's all right.'

'What do you mean, I'm here now?'

'Well, you are, aren't you?'

'Well, yes. I am.'

'So that's all right.' Charles was now looking at a distant car parked in a lay-by. 'Have you got a mint?'

'A mint?'

'Breath. Giveaway.'

'Is Margot a non-smoker?'

'Yes.'

'Then forget it. You're busted. Non-smokers can always smell a smoker. It's all pervasive. It's not just on your breath. It's on your clothes, your hair, your fingers, your skin – trust me, a mint's not going to do it.'

'But have you got one?'

'No.'

The closer they got to the car, the smaller it became. Germaine should have known that if Borkmann was providing transport then it wouldn't be a limousine. And it wasn't. It was a small and ancient SEAT 600. He'd said it was the least he could do and so it was.

The passenger door opened and Margot squeezed out, stood up and smiled in greeting. She was not what Germaine had been expecting. She had imagined Margot to be a tall, willowy woman with mousy-brown hair who wore flowery dresses and flat shoes and ran jumble sales. A watery watercolours sort of woman.

Not so.

Margot Cubberley was small and compact, built like a bulldog. She wore a jumper that sported a visually disturbing geometric pattern in yellow and black. She wore white trousers. She wore black calf-length boots.

'Remember,' Charles said from the side of his mouth. 'Not a word about the… you know.'

'You're still busted.'

Margot came over and shook Germaine's hand. It was a bone-crusher. Had she been in a cartoon Germaine was sure she would have been slammed up and down on the ground.

Margot had small eyes, a plump face and thin hairs on her

upper lip and chin. She was round shouldered and pot-bellied. Her dyed-brown hair was cut in the shape of an old German helmet and some form of static imbalance lifted wisps of it into the air, which twined and combined like strands of candyfloss.

'You must be Margot,' Germaine said.

'And you must be German…'

'Germaine. Call me Germaine.'

'Somebody got her bloody name wrong,' Charles muttered.

'Somebody smells of smoke,' said Margot.

'That's probably me,' said Germaine. 'Sorry.' And changing the subject quickly she said, '*Vous êtes Belge?*'

Margot nodded. 'But I speak English all the time. Charles is very monolingual.'

The subject of the *Tuscan Fields* rumours rose unbidden in Germaine's mind but again she kept it there. 'Thank you for collecting me. Don't you want to have a rest before we set off?'

Margot opened the car door and started throwing Germaine's bags onto the back seat. 'It's an awful drive. I just want to get it over with.'

2

The tiny Spanish car must have been the cheapest Borkmann could find, possibly the cheapest car in Spain. Margot drove while Charles sat next to her and maintained a running narrative on the shortcomings of other drivers, Spanish roads, distant fields, lorries, the sun, animals, traffic signals and cyclists. It was tiring and Germaine wished that Margot would let him have a cigarette. Also, Margot was a poor driver. She would speed up and slow down and change gear for no reason. She fiddled with the heating controls and tried to tune the radio and adjusted the mirror all the time. This, too, Germaine found tiring. Too much unnecessary movement. Too much clutter in their mannerisms.

The noise of the engine ebbing and flowing and Charles's shouting made conversation almost impossible, and the smell of petrol and the throb of the rear wheels bouncing along the road began to make her feel sick. She passed the time trying to keep a splattered insect on the windscreen above the horizon, and, when this palled, she closed her eyes and rehearsed her interview with Tom Hannah.

Germaine, so good to see you again.
Thank you, Tom. It's good to see you, too.

93

I built a wall to keep Borkmann out. We flick stones at him.

That's nice. Have you met Mr Venus? My father. He's a sala-mander, you know.

Really? I'm a Pisces…

Germaine awoke with a snort and a gasp. She wondered if she'd been snoring. But the car was rattling noisily, and Germaine was still squashed into the back seat amongst piles of her luggage, so it was unlikely anyone had heard, even if she had. She looked out of the window.

The mountain range that had been a distant grey-blue smudge when they had begun the journey had solidified and taken on a more definite shape with more developed detail. The road was climbing, the traffic had thinned out and Germaine saw they had entered the foothills of the mountains beyond which Las Sombras awaited.

'Need a nature break?' Charles called over his shoulder.

'Perhaps something to eat, too,' Germaine said.

They stopped at a roadside restaurant. The light was fading and Germaine could feel the change in the temperature as the night gathered around them. She shivered. It reminded her of the iLets' danger signal.

'How much further?' she said as she crawled out of the car.

'Three hours, maybe four,' said Charles.

'What are the mountain roads like?'

'Windy, steep, big drops, poor lighting. Terrible to drive through at night.'

Germaine looked at Margot. 'And we'll be driving through at night?'

'Charles and I take turns,' she said. 'He's the one with a head for heights when it comes to driving in the mountains.'

In the restaurant they sat at a table by the window and ordered coffee and spiced meat and vegetables and tortillas, and while they waited for it to arrive Germaine went outside and checked her phone for emails and messages, smoked a cigarette and watched Charles watching her through the window.

When the food came Margot began searching through her bag looking for her purse, but Germaine said, 'I'll get this. I insist. You've come all this way to collect me.'

Charles seemed to cheer up after that and became almost talkative. 'You're a journalist?' he said. He had chilli sauce on his chin.

'Not really. I'm an art historian. I lecture and give talks. I had a late-night show on Belgian television once. Very niche. But not really journalism. Just interviewing people. I've interviewed Tom Hannah a few times.'

'And he's an artist as well as a games person?'

'Yes. In fact, an artist is all he really is. He's very good. I mean, brilliant, in his way. I like him a lot and, of course, *Happy Family* is massive. A phenomenon. But he's not technical. He's the creative force behind the concept. What part are you auditioning for?'

'Anything really.'

'Oh. Have they sent you a brief?'

'Borkmann said you'd arrange all that.'

Germaine sat back and let that one percolate. Finally, she said, 'Beg pardon?'

'Borkmann said you'd arrange all that.'

'The audition?'

'Yes.' Charles looked at her like a dog watching a bone that might be taken away.

'He hasn't plugged you into an existing round of auditions?' Germaine paused and shook her head. No, of course he hadn't – there were no auditions. 'What exactly did Borkmann say?'

'He said that when you got here you'd meet this Tom Hannah and explain to him what I do, and he would… you know… because it's all about contacts, isn't it? Hyanh.'

Germaine could feel her heart beating faster. What could she say to this poor, desperate man who had travelled 700 miles in one day on a promise that could not be kept?

'I suppose it is. Well, let's see what happens. You know, I'm not sure how much input Tom Hannah has to the acting side of the business. I'm not even sure I'll get to see him. Borkmann told me that he's resistant to visitors at the moment. He's done this before,' she continued brightly. 'When there's something bad in his life, he drops out of sight for a while.'

'And is there something bad now?' Margot asked.

'I don't know.'

His mother's dead. You should bear that in mind when you meet him.

'If I can get on the roster that would be enough,' Charles said. He looked at Margot and she smiled.

'Charles is the best in the business,' she said. 'When a scene calls for a character with hiccups there is no one better than Charles.'

'I bet there isn't,' Germaine said. 'Have you played it – the game? *Happy Family*.'

'Oh no. We don't play games. Do we, Charles?'

'A bit of Jenga here and there. Got to thirty-two levels once.'

Germaine felt homesick. Who were these people? 'I think you should learn something about the game before you audition.'

But as she spoke, she wondered if they were right and she was wrong. Perhaps it didn't matter if Charles knew about the game or not. He was offering a service. Pay him to hiccup and no one would hiccup better. You'd be getting the best in the business. A simple transaction; a straightforward contract.

She caught sight of her reflection in the window and smiled ruefully. It was going to be a long trip.

When darkness came, it came fast. They crossed the mountains with their headlights undipped and Charles no longer shouted. Instead, he hunched forwards in his seat, gripping the steering wheel and muttering 'Hyanh' at irregular intervals. Germaine hoped that when they tumbled over the edge, as surely they would do, the fact that she was wedged in tight amongst so many bags and cases and coats would save her life.

The upward part of the journey seemed to take days. Germaine lost all sense of time and direction. Were they going up or down? Fast or slow? She couldn't tell. She was aware of passing through small, weather-eroded communities that clung to the mountainside in the shadow of rocky overhangs. Occasionally bright lights squeezed past them from the opposite direction. Once, she opened her window and felt the chill of the night as they continued on the single-track roads, snaking from one hairpin bend to another, and saw that they were on the ridge of the mountain where the sky above was barely lighter than the ground below.

Here, the land fell away on all sides. It was where one municipality met another and where, due to an administrative error, there existed a narrow tract of no man's land that belonged to neither. For a few minutes they would be driving in an area without local jurisdiction, subject only to the broad brush of the province and of Galicia itself. A lawless, unconstrained area.

They passed a low-slung, sprawling wooden cabin where many years before people from both sides of the mountain had come to drink and gamble. It was as the Victorian adventurer Joshua Waite had noted:

… As good a place as the best man there, and as bad as the worst. Open from dusk until dawn, a brooding place amongst the howling winds and icy fogs, visible only by a single outside lamp that swung backwards and forwards, and a faint orange glow that shone through its mean and narrow windows. A place for the Santa Compaña and the harsh Nuberu to rest their feet and await the passage of unsuspecting mortals …

After that, they descended seawards and no doubt towards the end of their journey. In the dark they passed the track that led to Tom Hannah's walled fortress. At just after ten o'clock at night they left the mountain road and turned onto the cobbled street that led to the harbour, the sea and their hotel.

'We're here,' Charles said, and after the rattle and drone of the car's tiny engine his voice sounded strangely flat.

From amongst the coats and luggage, Germaine peered through the window. So, this was it.

The Shades.

The Shadows.

Las Sombras.

In the small hotel lobby into which the three of them could barely fit, they were met by a pale youth with soft, wispy blonde hair and an earnest expression. He spoke in English.

'Welcome, *Señorita* Kiecke. I am Claudio. How was your trip? Would you like something to eat – to drink? I will take your bags. Your room is on the first floor.'

Charles and Margot offered to meet her in the bar once she'd been to her room, but Germaine was too tired. She thanked them for their heroism and promised to meet them for breakfast when she hoped to be better company. Claudio took her luggage and led the way upstairs, opened her door and dropped her bags in the corner of her room.

'Thank you, Claudio. Here, this is for you.'

But Claudio wouldn't take her tip. He backed away with smiles and nods and vanished like mist through the door. Germaine locked it and fell on the bed and stared at the ceiling.

'Sleep,' she said.

But first she had to check her phone. She found the wifi password on a printed slip of paper and connected her phone, tablet and iLets to the internet.

'Civilisation.'

She showered and then, finally, warm, clean and weary, she climbed between the sheets and turned out the lamp. She was asleep moments after her head touched the pillow. She dreamed of lights and heights and tortillas. At some point during the night she heard footsteps on the cobbled street; footsteps that stopped outside her window. Later, she lay awake, turning over and over, unable to sleep, but when she finally woke up, and the room was light, she realised that too had been part of her dream.

3

Las Sombras. A visitor might think they had stumbled upon a ghost town or an abandoned medieval hamlet. Few of the houses were home to permanent residents. Few of the local people came onto the streets or gathered at the bar or met at the bus stop or leaned on the harbour wall to contemplate the sea. Who were these local people anyway? There are four of interest: Rodolfo, married to Teresa; their son, Claudio; his aunt Luisa – Teresa's sister.

Rodolfo, Teresa, Claudio and Luisa.

But Teresa had left just days before Germaine's arrival; gone to find her father who had already been missing for fifteen years. Or so Rodolfo said. He said she had received a letter with news of her father. He said she left in the night taking the letter with her, in such a state of anticipation she had no time to mention it to her sister.

Why would she do that, Luisa wanted to know? He was her father too. Why would her sister leave so suddenly without showing her the letter; without even telling her? And why, she asked, would her sister leave an idiot like Rodolfo in charge of the hotel and the glass bottom boat business? Or was it all a pack of lies?

Rodolfo, Claudio and Luisa.

Luisa lived in the house at the end of the road that led to the harbour, on the corner opposite the hotel *El Tesoro Escondido* where now only Rodolfo and Claudio and their guests were staying. Poor, depleted Claudio. Left with a warring father and aunt. No mother, no grandfather – and no grandmother either. She died when Aunt Luisa clawed and elbowed and tore her way feet-first into the world. That was how children were born in Las Sombras.

Now Teresa had gone, Rodolfo spent his nights sitting alone in his bar, gazing at the sea-splattered window in front of him, soaking up the sour local alcohol, *razik*. By day he ran errands in his truck or sat on the plastic chair next to the chalkboard advertising *Glass Bottom Boat Trips – Every Hour On The Hour. €6*, while Luisa watched him from her window and twisted her curtain into an unbending cord.

She blamed her family's ills on Rodolfo's drinking and gambling. His debts, she said, were a stain on their name. What mental aberration had led her kind, patient and sensible sister to give herself to a witless absurdity like Rodolfo? Her family's glass bottom boat had been a thriving business, she said, filling up six times a day and going out at night with flares and torches. People travelled for miles to sail on the glass bottom boat but that was when her father had been in charge, before he went missing – before he became absent; whereabouts unknown; an empty chair; a place at the table set but unused; a side of the bed left cold. And the family business that Rodolfo had married into, and which he now managed, sunk.

So that was how they were arranged: Rodolfo and Claudio on one corner; Luisa on the other; and between them, like chalked outlines on the cobbled street, the absent Teresa and her father.

Germaine leaned against the harbour wall and looked out to sea. It was her first morning in Las Sombras. Close to the rocks that supported the wall, the water was thick and sluggish, but beyond the shelter of the rocky barricades the sea skipped in from the horizon in choppy waves, as if affected by a lightness of spirit. In front of her, about a mile out to sea, was an island, an upswing of rock linked to the land by a submerged causeway. Behind her, the mountains gathered around the village and cast morning shadows over the coastline.

Germaine put on her iLets. There was a moment of nothingness and then they cleared, and she looked onto the bare, smooth, salt-eroded boulders below. Mr and Mrs Venus were sitting on a rock, watching her.

How did it work, she wondered? Mentally. How could her brain make sense of two overlaid worlds? What synaptic fireworks were exploding in her brain? She had played computer games since leaving the Motherhood and she was, she knew, an obvious cliché – a social maladroit who found contact with real life difficult and game characters easier to deal with. But then again, she had grown up in a house where children awoke with rat bites, so who needed real life?

In truth she had no real friends – nobody who would meet that definition; no person with whom she shared a bond of mutual affection, no confidante, no buddy. No soulmate. La Jaune had come close to filling that role but, in the end, Germaine had let that relationship wither – unfed, unwatered, unworked-at.

In the end, we are what we do. Or don't do. And I suppose I don't do relationships.

In her more self-analytic moods she worried about her growing dependency on the game and her normalisation of that fact. She could argue she was no more addicted to *Happy*

Family than she was to reading books or watching films or listening to music, or to any pleasurable pastime, but she knew that was playing with words. Look at her now: she had only been up for an hour, she hadn't even had breakfast, and already she was outside playing the game – and not in a safe, designated area.

Mr Venus stood up and called across to her. 'What are you doing here?' He didn't seem pleased to see her.

'What am I doing?' she said. 'I'm in the game.'

'Which one?'

'This one, of course.'

'You should be at home in bed,' Mr Venus said.

'In bed? It's the morning? And if I were, you should be there too, looking after me.'

Periodically, a wave splashed onto the rocks coating her with a thin layer of cold sea spray and appearing to overwhelm Mr and Mrs Venus. But they were immune to the real world. One day, she thought, there will be more mobile devices than there are stars and the universe will be filled with solitary people like me leaning over harbour walls and shouting at creatures nobody else can see.

'Go and play,' he said, pointing. There was movement on the periphery of her vision and she saw that Sally and Anuj were with her again. Only now Sally was not a fluffy-toy rendering. She was a proper snail, albeit as big as a human, secreting mucus and dripping slime. She had beady eyes on the end of her tentacles and she had teeth – a lot of teeth, rows and rows of them, thousands of tiny knives in her mouth. Conversely, Anuj was so poorly rendered that he was visibly shimmering in and out of focus.

'What's going on?' said Germaine.

'Go home,' Mrs Venus said. Her voice was quiet and calm in Germaine's ears. She looked around. Where were the crazy jumping creatures and all the squealing and giggling? Where was the moustachioed magician throwing Good Luck tokens into the air? Where were all the primary colours and the sing-songs and the bells and buzzers and the learning games?

Germaine's iLets were starting to grow cold although it was hard to be certain because she was already damp and chilly. She wasn't dressed for a huddling in front of an early morning sea-drenched harbour wall.

She wondered if the game was malfunctioning but then a face filled her iLets making her jump. It was Mrs Venus. She was no longer on the other side of the harbour wall but right in front of her – an enormous salamander staring into her face. Germaine stepped back onto the road – and had a car been coming she would have been knocked down.

'What's going on…?'

'You ran away from home,' Mrs Venus said. 'I will be guilty of neglect and you will lose two hundred Game Privileges unless you return to the house immediately. This is a Dilemma Point. Your choice. Press *Stay* or *Go* on your device.'

Her face vanished. Sally and Anuj stood on the pavement, waiting, while behind them, on the rock, Mr Venus stared at her.

'I don't get it,' Germaine said.

Somehow, she had been seduced by the narrative. Instead of keeping an eye on all her options she had allowed herself to follow one thread and now the game was going to punish her. When had that happened? And how? Her iLets were definitely cold but where was the danger – was it to do with the Dilemma Point or the current situation? She didn't know. Should she restart the game – come right out and start the whole thing again after all these months?

A countdown timer was running. Less than a minute to

resolve the dilemma or the game would do it for her. Mr Venus waved at her. 'Go home, Germaine.'

Twenty seconds remained.

Stay and *Go* were both flashing. The iLets were cold. Where was the approaching danger? The harbour road and the cobbled street leading through the village were empty. Were there sharks in the sea? A giant squid?

'Uh-oh,' said Sally.

'What?' said Germaine.

'Look up,' said Anuj.

Ten seconds.

Germaine looked up and saw, at last, the incoming danger. Sweeping down from a distant virtual nest, making her final hunting trip for the night, was a barn owl. According to a label floating above her head, she was called Harriet.

'I don't understand.' She had turned all the danger settings off. Why was this happening?

Germaine pulled off her iLets before Harriet could strike and the game stopped as soon as she did so, sensing the decoupling from her pupils.

'Stupid,' she said. It was unhealthy to leave a game this way. The climb down was too abrupt and she felt an odd sense of lightness as if her feet were about to leave the ground. She waited for the buzzing inside her head to subside, and then began to walk, concentrating on the touch of solid objects – the pavement, the harbour wall, a lamp post – while her senses slowly reasserted themselves. After fifty metres or so the land ran out and descended into rocky steps to the sea where waves curled towards her like chained snakes.

She stopped and lit a cigarette and watched the waves, and then walked back to her hotel on the other side of the road. It both distracted and amused her to see that the old houses facing the sea really were sea-scarred – cut for centuries by salt-filled winds. Joshua Waite had been right, and she had been wrong. She ran her hands along the walls, and felt comforted by both the roughness of the bricks and her error. There was a real world beyond the mind of Germaine Kiecke and she liked that. She needed that.

4

Her hotel room was also reassuringly normal. Small and clean, it had exposed wooden floorboards covered by a large, thin red mat and yellow walls, which reminded her of La Jaune. There was a bedside table, a lamp, a standalone wardrobe, a painting of the harbour above her bed, a louvered door to an en suite bathroom and a window that looked onto the cobbled street. A heavy cotton blind could be raised and lowered with a tasselled cord. If she pressed her face to the window and looked to the left she could see the sea. As a hotel room, it was adequate. As a hotel room paid for by Gerard Borkmann, it was a palace.

She checked her phone. Both Borkmann and Catharina had sent her a message, both asking the same question.

Have you arrived?

To Catharina, Germaine wrote:

Arrived safe but travel sore. Long journey in a tiny car. Is there a cap on my expenses? Met Charles & Margot. Nice but odd. He hopes for audition with TH. Bizarre. Borkmann said I would fix it. Seriously. WTF? All v curious. Las Sombras is well-named. Lots of dark areas. Visiting Casa Hannah today. Fingers x'd.

To Borkmann, she wrote:

Arrived. Great transport. Going to visit Tom Hannah today. PS, can you ask your techies if any cheats to reset a Dilemma countdown in HF V3?

It was now eight-thirty in the morning, and she was hungry having not eaten since the roadside meal with Margot and Charles the previous evening. She left her room and went downstairs again, in search of breakfast, enjoying the feeling of being in a new and unfamiliar place, the thick, bouncy stair carpet deadening her footsteps.

The hotel reception led to both the cobbled street and to a bar-dining area which had its own front door leading onto the harbour road. Charles and Margot were already sitting at a table in a nook by a large hearth. Germaine joined them. The place smelled of dust and polish, alcohol and fried food.

'Good morning. May I?'

'Of course,' said Charles gesturing at the two empty places. 'Strength in numbers.' His voice this morning sounded like dry gravel in a cement mixer.

'Are we the only guests?' said Germaine.

'We haven't seen anyone else since we've been here,' said Margot. 'It's very quiet.'

Germaine looked at the creased, stained and well-used paper menu. Hot coffee, sweet rolls and churros were the only items available for breakfast.

'Sleep well?' said Margot.

'I think so. I was tired.'

'The body knows,' said Charles, nodding wisely. 'Always listen to your body. It's not natural to travel hundreds of miles in a day.'

'No, I suppose not.'

'A few miles, that's all we're built for – a short walk from one village to the next. That's why you were tired. Body thinks you've walked hundreds of miles so you must be exhausted, therefore you are exhausted. See? That's how it works.'

'I see.'

'Natural satellite navigation system. Geo-something or other. Knows where you are on the planet. Spatial, that's the word. Geo-spatial whatsit.'

'That's a Charles-fact,' said Margot, booming across the table. 'Spoken like a fact; sounds like a fact; might even be a fact. But it's probably not.' She laughed like a donkey braying, which made Germaine laugh too.

'It does make sense, though,' she said. 'And I was very tired.' The ghost-like Claudio came to take their order and Germaine wondered if he were cook and cleaner too as there didn't seem to be anyone else working. 'Do you serve anything other than pastries?' she asked.

Claudio frowned and gazed at the menu she was holding and then said, 'Coffee'.

Germaine nodded. 'Of course. Coffee it is, then, please, and churros. Thank you.'

'Times *numero trois*,' said Charles.

'For each of us,' Margot explained.

Claudio left them and a tall, dejected man came in through the front door and sat at a table away from them, across the room. Germaine recognised him from his photograph: the bacon-rind ears, the deflated head. This was Rodolfo – proprietor of the hotel, Claudio's father and Borkmann's man on the ground.

Charles hissed, 'Odd fellow'.

Rodolfo looked across. He regarded them for a few moments and then stood up and came over to their table.

'*Buenos días*,' he said.

Germaine stood up and shook his hand. '*Buenos días*,' she said. 'Germaine Kiecke. You're Rodolfo?'

'*Sí.*'

Germaine could now see that what appeared to be skinniness from afar was better described as sinewy close up. The comical, oversized hands were actually strong and rough. His forlorn face was sharper and his watery eyes more penetrating than she had imagined. He pulled up a chair.

She recalled an article she had read about an imagined meeting between Homo sapiens and Homo erectus. They would have looked similar, behaved similarly but it would have been impossible for one to comprehend the thoughts of the other – just as she might look into the eyes of a cat or an insect or a fish. Or a salamander. She felt she and Rodolfo existed in very different worlds.

'You are going to the house today?' he said. 'Tom Hannah's?'

'Yes. Is it far?'

'It's not so far but there is a girl. A bad girl. You must not trust her.' He tapped his head. 'Not right. You understand? Dangerous.' He beckoned to Claudio who was waiting to bring their pastries and coffee. 'Come.'

Claudio put down a huge bowl of freshly fried churros, the smell of cinnamon rising with the heat. It made Germaine feel giddy.

'Thank you,' she said but Claudio was already being waved away by Rodolfo.

'He's a good boy but he has work to do.'

Germaine was sure he did.

Rodolfo leaned forwards. 'I'll tell you how it is. The artist, he moved here and all things were good. He brings money to the village. He drinks in our bars, he buys food from our shops, he eats in here, we look after his gardens, clean his house. I take things to him in my truck, collect orders, make deliveries. Sometimes other artists come here too and *Señor* Borkmann says to me, "Keep an eye on my friend. He is important to me."

110

So, I do. And then the girl arrives. We see her at night. She looks through our windows and steals from our gardens. We chase her but we cannot catch her. She is like an animal. She lives like an animal.'

Germaine nodded. Borkmann's stone-throwing hooligan.

'And this is when things change. The girl is living in the artist's garden. Perhaps in his house too. His bed. Who knows? She is cunning, clever, she plays with his mind. She becomes his guardian, his *guardaespaldas*. He stops coming to the village.' Rodolfo wagged his long finger at them. 'And now he doesn't order his food from us. He has it brought in, once a month, over the mountains. It is the girl. The devil.'

'Borkmann said a wall has been built and there are dogs?'

'Yes. The dogs came first. The girl controls them like she is a mother bitch. And then one day some people come and now house is in the middle of his new walls.'

A frame, Germaine thought. Tom Hannah has put himself inside a cartoon panel. Aloud she said, 'A boundary'.

'Exactly. These people who build the walls, they are from outside the village, but they do not stay with us and they sleep in the artist's garden in caravans. We get no money from them. No one wants any deliveries in my truck. It sits on the road and its tyres go flat. And there is this other man who comes to stay: never smiling. He sits in here, dressed in black like a raven, talking on his fancy phone and asks about my wifi and my broadband and my connections. He has a drink, eats lots of food, watches football on the television.'

'Did he say who he was?' said Germaine.

'No. But at least he spends some money here, not like the others.'

Rodolfo went quiet for a moment. Germaine noticed that Margot was staring at him, hanging on his every word and she wondered if this was the first time they'd spoken to him. How strangely insular these people are, she thought.

'When I see this happening and these people in his house,' Rodolfo said, sitting back and pouring a coffee for himself. 'I think, well, *Señor* Borkmann wants me to look after his artist, so I go up to the house. They are putting on the gate and I say, "Hey, I have come to see *Señor* Hannah. I have a message from his English friend." They say, "Sure", because they don't know any different, and I walk in and these big dogs are looking at me and there is the girl. She says, "Hey, Rudy, what's the message you're bringing?" How does she know my name? I say, "That's none of your business. *Señor* Borkmann sent me." I want to knock her down and she knows it, and the dogs know it too, which is not so good.'

'Devil dogs,' breathed Charles.

'I say to her, "This is not your home. You are *intruso*, you are a thief, a pusher-in. You are a nothing." And she laughs and says, "So you are mad at nothing. And nothing will set the dogs on you and nothing will come into your house and cut your throat while you dream about being something. Don't catch my eye at night, Rudy. Even while you're asleep."'

'That's a threat,' said Charles looking at them in turn. 'Clear as daylight.'

'Yes. Yes. She threatens me. And those dogs. Don't ever let those dogs come near you. *¿Entender?* Not without a gun and poisoned meat.'

'So, what did you do?' Germaine said.

'I left.'

'You left? You didn't see Tom Hannah?'

'No. He is a prisoner of this girl. That is what I think. A prisoner. She is a witch. A creature of the *Santa Compaña*. Cursed. She will cook him and put him in her pot and, when there's nothing left, she will take all his things and nobody will see her again.' Rodolfo stood up. 'So, now you know. Do you want a trip in my glass bottom boat? I'll give you a group deal. Five euro.'

They all shook their heads and he nodded as if this was the expected answer. He was about to walk away when he stopped and said, 'I'll tell you this too. When *Señor* Borkmann comes to visit there is a big argument between him and his artist. A big argument at the gate. I don't know what the artist says because I cannot hear him. I know that *Señor* Borkmann is upset. He shouts long after the girl and the artist have gone.'

Rodolfo left the hotel and from where she sat Germaine could see him take up position on the chair by the harbour wall, next to the glass bottom boat sign.

'Dramatic,' Charles said. 'But I've seen his type before. Likes an audience. Tells his story and adds a bit more each time to make it sound better. Before you know it, you've got a full-scale work of fiction on your hands.'

Germaine nodded. Possibly. But there were things to think about. The other man who was dressed in black, for example, with his fancy phone. Borkmann had mentioned him, a technical type, singled him out as someone who wasn't from the *Happy Family*. That had clearly annoyed him. And why had Borkmann, the Gerard Borkmann whom Germaine had known for years, the veteran campaigner, master of the long game, been driven to shout through a locked gate? That would show his hand too much. The Borkmann she knew always kept his powder dry. Borkmann never declared he was competing until he'd won. Now, looking around the empty hotel bar and restaurant, that thought made Germaine feel uncomfortable. Was she part of his powder?

5

It was time. After weeks of planning and preparing, Germaine was just over a mile from where Tom Hannah lived. She was breathing the same air he was, seeing the same sky and, with luck, preparing for the same meeting. She should have been happy, but she wasn't. Now she was here it all seemed wrong.

Tom Hannah had been generous to her in the past, granting her interviews where others were turned down. She knew about his issues, his fragility, his yearning for privacy and she did not like the way she was about to behave. She was going to doorstep him which felt like a betrayal.

After breakfast she went back to her room and sent Tom another email and tried his mobile again. She left a voice message and sent a text message, and then sat on her bed and tried to imagine how this was going to work. They would drive to his house, knock on the gate, receive no answer and come back to the hotel having wasted everybody's time.

She lay down.

Was it the effects of dropping out of the game so abruptly earlier, or was she still tired from her travels? She felt she was losing sight of herself. Since leaving the Motherhood she had created walls to keep the world at bay, barriers of academia between herself and humanity. She liked the world to be caged on canvas or frozen in sculpture or trapped on film – a one-way window.

Now she felt as if her walls were crumbling and she did not know why or how, or what would remain if they did fall away. Perhaps there would be nothing. The world in which she existed had no connection to her, did not know her, did not care about her, did not want her; and the only people with whom she had any connection were the utterly unreal Mr and Mrs Venus.

She went into the bathroom and looked at the mirror and stared deep into her eyes. 'Where are you?' she said to her reflection. 'Who are you?'

It was ten o'clock. She had an hour before she was due to meet Charles and Margot. Because they were so eager to come along, and as they had been good enough to drive hundreds of miles to pick her up, Germaine felt she could hardly refuse. Besides, she wasn't expecting to conduct any interviews that day; they would come later. She would be happy just to meet Tom Hannah and set some loose parameters for the project. She wanted him to be an enthused and willing participant.

She checked her phone again. No replies so she decided to call Catharina. But not indoors. Looking through her window she could see the clouds were clearing and the sun was out; she should be outside – after all, she was in Spain. She went down-stairs and found a bench by the hotel entrance where she could sit.

Catharina answered on the second ring.

'Hello, Germaine.'

She sounded cool and cosmopolitan and far away, and Germaine wished she too was far away, back in Belgium, in Liège, in her flat or in a restaurant or bar, at a gallery or at the theatre or cinema, or enjoying any of the distractions that were missing in Las Sombras.

'Hi, Catharina. I thought I'd call. We're going to see Tom Hannah this morning and I'm having a crisis of confidence. I wish we'd had some response from him. Have you heard from Borkmann?' Germaine could hear Catharina's breathing in her ear. It was like a gentle tickle. She closed her eyes and let the sun warm her face.

'No, I haven't. He's being his usual elusive self. Who is the "we" that's going with you?'

'Borkmann's bodily functions man and his wife. The cuddly Cubberleys. He told them I would arrange an audition with Tom for voice work on *Happy Family*. Don't ask me why.'

'I bet it's a side deal. Borkmann has more sides than a... what's that shape? The one with all the sides?'

'Polygon?'

'No. The one that sounds like a dinosaur.'

'I don't know, Catharina. Is it important...?'

'Like that bird. The one the sailors ate.'

'The Dodo?'

'That's it.'

Germaine waited. She was in the sun, she was going to see Tom Hannah, everything was going to be all right.

'Dodecahedron,' Catharina shouted. 'He has more sides than a dodecahedron.'

'Yes.'

'Anyway, keep the Cubberies in the background. What's the plan to get in?'

'Cubberleys. We'll knock on the gate. Borkmann said there was a camera, so I hope he'll see it's me and let us in.' It had seemed feasible at home but now, as she said it, it seemed ludicrous.

'And you've tried to contact him?'

'All the time.'

There was more silence; more breathing.

'There is something you could try,' Catharina said at last. She was back in the moment, back being an agent. 'Why don't you try *not* to see Tom Hannah when you go to the house? I'm thinking about his new little friend. As we know nothing about her you could pretend that the purpose of your visit is to interview her and not him. It's perfectly reasonable that you've not been able to set up the interview beforehand because she's not contactable. And you can honestly say that you've heard she's the new influence in our artist's life. According to Borkmann she's likely to pop up if you make a nuisance of yourself at the gate. When she does, focus on her. Don't mention Tom Hannah at all, get in with her and get to Hannah that way.'

'She wouldn't believe I've come all the way to Spain to interview her.'

'Why not? It's for your book. Your book on the role of muses and models in an artist's life.'

Germaine opened her eyes. 'Is that what my book's about now? It changes so much I can't keep up.'

'It could be. And if she is important to Tom Hannah's art then she'll be in your book anyway. I'm not suggesting you lie – just be fluid and see where it takes you. Use your allure.'

Germaine hung up and stayed where she was on the bench, thinking. Be fluid? Use her allure? Catharina with her white teeth, close to the phone and saying the word 'allure' like it was a breath at the end of a sentence.

Doesn't Assistant Professor Kiecke look alluring today?

Germaine Kiecke? She has natural allure.

Do you know what first attracted me to you, Germaine? It was your allure. Your alluring allure.

She laughed out loud. She felt foolishly happy.

The front door opened in the house on the opposite corner and a woman stepped onto the pavement. She was tall and hatchet-faced, and appeared to be wrapped entirely in black muslin. She crossed the road and walked up to Germaine, stopping in front of her and frowning as if Germaine were sitting on her bench and she was waiting for her to get up.

'Do you want to sit here?' Germaine said. '*Yo voy…*'

'*¿Hablas español?*'

'*Un poco. ¿Habla usted francés?*'

'*Habla Inglés.* So, sit. There's room for two. French?'

'Belgian.'

She nodded as if this were an acceptable answer.

'*¿Turista?*'

'No. Work. I'm going to visit Tom Hannah, the artist who lives in the house up the hill.'

'Ah. Journalist?'

'In a way. I'm writing a book. An academic reference book… new art… groundbreaking…' She trailed off. It seemed, somehow, an insignificant thing to say in this place, to this person in this over-bright morning light.

'I am Luisa.' She turned towards the harbour wall where Germaine could see Rodolfo was still sitting, waiting for customers that never seemed to come. 'And that is my brother-in-law. This is our family hotel.'

'It's very nice. I'm Germaine. Germaine Kiecke.'

'Kiecke – like a magpie's call. Khak-khak.'

Luisa sat down and they remained for a moment in silence; Germaine was never comfortable with small talk. But not saying anything seemed even more awkward so she said, 'Excuse me but may I ask, the young woman who's living with Tom Hannah, with the artist, do you know anything about her?

118

Have you seen her? Spoken to her? Rodolfo, your brother-in-law, he had very strong views on her.'

'Speak slowly. Don't gabble.'

Germaine laughed, both surprised and pleased to find that she didn't mind being ticked off by this haughty woman.

'Sorry, I…'

'Yes, I have spoken to her.'

'You have? Your brother-in-law said she is dangerous. A bit wild. Do you think she's dangerous?'

'Pah. That man. What is dangerous? You give a child a knife and it is dangerous. If the wind blows hard it is dangerous. She is just different. Why not? Don't look for what is not there.'

'She threw stones at someone I know.'

'Did she throw them hard or soft? You throw stones hard then it is dangerous. You throw them soft… you are just making that person go away. Not everything is about something.'

'Rodolfo thinks she controls him.'

'Hah. The only control that girl has is the control he gives. She is not a witch come to take his gold. She is a medicine, not a poison.'

'Do you know if they're… you know, involved?'

'Who cares? It's their business.'

They lapsed back into silence.

'It's going to be a hot day,' Germaine said after a while.

Luisa looked at her and then gestured widely with her hands, taking in the hotel, the street, the harbour wall and Rodolfo's pitch by the glass bottom boat. 'All this,' she said, 'belonged to my parents. Everything. My father was a strong and good man and then one day he disappears. Gone. And now…' She paused and took a deep breath as if whatever she was about to say required physical self-control. 'Fifteen years. Gone. And my brother-in-law… he runs things now.'

'I see.'

'Do you? I'll tell you a story. My father is just missing. I watch for him every day and I see two people, *turista*, walk down the street. They wriggle together like they have an itch, giggling and squeezing each other. "Is your boat for hire?" the man says to Rodolfo. "We are newly-weds," the woman tells him. So, Rodolfo charges them double for a honeymoon trip – twice around the harbour and then over to the island where he will moor up and lower the tarpaulin for their privacy.' Luisa rolled her eyes. 'I watch him take these people out to the island and then I hear shouting and the boat turns back. "There was something watching us on the seabed," the man says. My brother-in-law says, "There was nothing there. It was seaweed or a shadow or something. Unless… unless it was the Las Sombras mermaid." The next day, I look out of my window, I see a queue of customers all the way along the harbour wall – people want to see the mermaid. He takes out ten boats a day. The next week the queues are still there but he can only fill eight boats. Then four, and after that nobody comes. Since then he sits on his plastic chair and looks up and down the harbour road and he is alone. He sits there all day, but nobody comes. That was fifteen years ago. And now, Teresa has gone too. My sister. His wife.'

'Gone?'

'Gone to find our father. Or so he says. He says he saw her boarding the bus. Two weeks ago. No one else saw her boarding a bus. Now I think maybe another mermaid is coming.' Luisa laughed suddenly. 'Hah. Did you like that story?'

Germaine looked across at Rodolfo who sat alone on his chair ignoring their glances, his eyes fixed sightlessly on the empty street, his cloth cap stiffened with sweat, his sockless feet in his boots stretched out before him. She wondered what it would be like to be the target of a warrior woman such as Luisa, a woman who looked to be cut by nature into hard edges and sharp angles. A woman who waited like a cat for a mouse, hissing and twitching with her claws ready to strike. It would not be good, Germaine thought. It would not be good at all.

6

Germaine was relieved when Margot walked out of the hotel. Margot was wearing an orange cagoule, orange walking trousers and stout walking boots. She had a heavy-looking rucksack too. What could be in that, Germaine wondered. She had no coat and wore sandals. Normally so sure of herself and her decision-making, Germaine wondered now if she should change into something more rugged. But she didn't have anything rugged; she was not a rugged person.

She stood up. 'We're going now. Thank you, Luisa,' she said, although she wasn't quite clear why she was saying thank you.

Luisa waved her away as if she were suddenly fatigued. 'Enjoy your visit.'

Germaine and Margot walked up to the car. 'That was Rodolfo's sister-in-law,' Germaine said. 'Tough woman.'

'I've not met her.'

'Have you met anyone?'

'Not really. Charles is more meet-and-retreat than meet-and-greet.'

Germaine smiled. 'That's funny. I like that. Where is he?'

'He's going to meet us there.'

'How?'

'He'll walk.'

Germaine's smile faded. She felt a stirring of irritation. She didn't want any looseness in her plans. 'Does he know the way?'

'It's about a mile up the road and left at the track. We looked at it when we first came here. I suppose we could wait?'

'No. We'll go on.'

The hire car was parked up the cobbled street and as they walked towards it Germaine turned suddenly and saw Luisa watching them. Germaine waved and then wished she hadn't. It was like looking down on a painted canvas. Luisa didn't move or acknowledge her wave at all.

They got into the car and Margot pulled away. She fought with the gear stick, graunching the gears, the engine note rising and falling like a failing aircraft. The car proceeded up the hill, lurching and hopping, speeding up and slowing down. Twice Margot stalled the car. She had driven 300 miles the previous day but now she couldn't manage a hundred metres without stopping. After five minutes of this Germaine said, 'How far away are we?'

'I don't know.'

'Shall we walk?'

'Would you mind?'

They stopped on the empty mountain road and continued on foot. Margot looked back at the car. 'Do you think it will roll away?'

'We can only hope.'

With the mountains rising up before them Germaine felt a sense of liberation. There was no path to walk on, just a dusty verge dividing the road from the mountain scrubland. The air tasted clean and Germaine was glad now she had no rugged clothes to wear – no coat, no heavy boots; just her bag. She felt light and unencumbered. They were going to visit Tom Hannah and they might even get to talk to him. Everything was good. She looked at the scenery stretching out below.

'I like this,' she said.

'I hope Charles is all right.'

'He'll be fine. Englishmen like to walk.'

Germaine let the silence between the two of them grow into the spaces where a conversation might otherwise have taken hold. She was content to walk without talking. But then Margot said, 'I wish Charles would relax more. He gets cross about the smallest of things.'

'Does he?'

'It's not really his fault…'

'No.' Germaine refused to bite.

'Do you mind if we sit down for a moment?' Margot said.

Germaine sighed. Soul-baring – she could feel it coming. There was going to be soul-baring. Germaine loathed soul-baring. 'I think we should keep going.' But the road turned and revealed a wooden seat on the bend overlooking the sea below. Darn, Germaine thought. Margot must have known it would be there.

If Margot had wanted to tell Germaine about her feelings in relation to art, or any external entity, Germaine would have been able to listen with ease, to explore the topic, to empathise, sympathise, to connect in some way, to develop themes and arguments and points of view. But personal things? God, she hoped it wouldn't be personal things. She never knew how to behave in those situations. She didn't know how her face should look. What configuration her muscles should take. Would it be rude to put on her iLets?

'Oh look, a bench,' she said.

They sat down.

'This is nice,' said Margot.

'Yes. It is.'

'Lovely view.'

'Indeed.'

'Do you have… someone at home?' Margot perched on the edge of the bench and looked with determined openness at Germaine. Was that any of her business, Germaine thought? But she said, 'No. Not at the moment.'

In Germaine's relationships it was usually her partners who broke up with her, but only because she had lost all interest in them and could barely conceal it. She would be content to allow the aridness to persist for weeks and months, until her partners – who were perhaps more kind or practical, or just more willing to confront the obvious and deal with it – called a halt to the torment. The time would always come when they would look at her with a dreadfully serious expression and break the news that it was all over. And Germaine would sit and listen, wearing her own dreadfully serious expression, and try to nod at the right time and say the right thing at the right time, and feign some interest. Why did it always have to be so sombre? *Just go.*

'To be honest, I don't attach well,' Germaine said. 'My last affair, liaison if you like, was with Valerie Morin – La Jaune. The artist. Have you heard of her? It was a beautiful break-up. She came into our bedroom while I slept and painted my face yellow with a small, soft brush. It felt so nice, smelled so nice. And then she left.'

'How odd.'

'Not really. In her art, yellow represents the past. So, she literally coloured me out of her life. I thought that was so wonderful that I called her and asked if we could start again but she declined. She was more emotionally mature than I was, even if she did paint my face. Perhaps that is how it is with me. I am emotionally limited.'

'You don't seem limited at all. You seem… very complex.'

'Ah, but you see, I'm not. I am unadorned. An outline.'

'Oh.'

'May I ask, how did you and Charles come to be together? An English man and a Belgian woman. Were you an actress too?'

'Drama therapist. Facilitating personal growth and promoting mental health through improvisation, that sort of thing. I did a course in England and met Charles at a training day. He was helping out, earning some extra money. He was very handsome – he *is* very handsome.'

'And he moved to Belgium?'

'For the radio work. Europeans like funny noises.'

Germaine waited. It was coming. It would be the affair. It had to be the affair.

Margot plucked some fluff from her cagoule. 'I've never discussed it with anyone. I don't really know why I'm telling you. But it's such a burden. We don't have many friends, not in that way. Not in the confiding way. We associate with lots of people, of course, but, you know, there is never really anyone to talk to. I suppose…'

Just tell me or don't tell me. Get it over with.

'I had a thing…'

'An affair?'

'Well, it wasn't… Not, you know…'

'Sex?'

'I was going to say long term.' She laughed. 'God knows, I'm nothing to write home about. Charles used to call me his little cuboid.'

'That's nice.'

'He doesn't call me any names now. Just Margot.'

Germaine pretended to stretch her arms but really she was checking her phone. How long would this take? Say five minutes to tell the story, another five minutes for Germaine to say 'oh' and 'ah' and 'never mind', and then the wrap up. Fifteen minutes – twenty minutes, maximum. 'These things happen. Is it over?'

'Of course. Definitely. And Charles knows all about it. But he goes so quiet. I can't bear it. He won't talk. It's the trust, you see. Charles was away a lot, working on *Tuscan Fields* – a radio show. Have you heard it? I was at home and Charles's friend was staying with us. Robin Rix. They'd been at Bristol together. They specialise in yawns and coughs and sneezes – what they call non-verbal expulsions. Charles is very good. He can also do sniffs, snorts and all kinds of nervous swallowing – anything from a gulp to a full choke.'

'It's a gift.'

'But Robin was charming. He overdid the British accent for my benefit, of course, but that's what actors do. And Charles was doing well, and Robin was out of work, and I felt sorry for him. He was such a good listener and Charles, well, Charles is Charles. A quick phone call in the evening while he was away, working.'

'How did he find out? Did you tell him?'

'Robin did. I think I would have anyway, but Robin went to the set and told him. Poor Charles. He exploded. He punched Robin and lost his job and now Robin has got it instead, and he's doing well, and Charles is out of work. It was my fault. I made him lose his job – and everything, really.'

'It sounds like Robin did that.'

'I know it hurts him still. We can't seem to move on. We're stuck forever in that moment when he came home and his eyes were all red. I thought he was going to leave me, but he just sat in his chair and looked sad.'

'Have you seen Robin since?'

'Not *seen* him. Not in that way. Isn't life awful? In some

ways I wish Charles had been angry with me. His forgiveness is much worse. It's like being slowly killed with kindness. I can't bear to watch him sometimes. He says such dreadful things.'

Men, thought Germaine, always causing upset. 'Come on,' she said. 'Let's get to the house and see if we can get Charles an audition. And, tonight, we'll have a drink and find a picture of Robin Rix and you and Charles can colour it yellow.'

7

Another twenty minutes of walking and they reached the dirt track that led to Tom Hannah's property. Germaine felt a perverse disinclination to go any further. If things went wrong this was probably the end of her plans. She wouldn't get an interview; she wouldn't get a book deal; she wouldn't get her associate professorship. At least not this way. It would be back to visiting lecturer at the Université de Liège, articles in art magazines and an occasional *Kiecke in Conversation*. Not a bad life but not what she was working towards. Or what she was seeking to escape.

They walked up the track and then, as Borkmann had said they would, found it blocked by a pile of earth. They had to leave the path and skirt around it, walking through the scrubby brambles and shrubs until they could rejoin the track at the point it reached Tom Hannah's walled fortress.

It was quite a sight.

The walls, at least four metres high, were built from blue-grey rocks cemented into position by buff-coloured concrete, with the result forming art-deco geometric patterns. The massive wrought-iron gate was painted a similar blue.

'Now that,' Germaine said, standing back and looking up, 'is a boundary. Can you see a bell or a buzzer or an intercom or anything?'

Margot shook her head. 'No, but there's a camera.'

It was on the wall above the gate, looking down on them with its red light flashing. Germaine waved and then turned to Margot.

'Do I look as idiotic as I feel? This is so haphazard – oh.'

Three big dogs walked towards them on the other side of the gate. Borkmann had said he thought they might be a cross between a Great Dane and an African Lion Dog. Looking at them now, Germaine thought they might be a cross between a Great Dane and an actual lion. Or possibly a bear.

'The gate is locked, isn't it?'

The dogs came closer. Germaine stepped away but Margot walked towards them with her hand outstretched. They started to growl. Margot stopped and so did they.

'You weren't going to stroke them, were you?' Germaine said. 'Tell me you weren't going to do that.'

'Oh, I love dogs. The trick is not to be…'

'Eaten. I think someone's coming.'

The gate allowed a view of some of the driveway before it curved away. Now, coming into sight was Alta. Seeing her for the first time, it was hard for Germaine to put an age on her. She wore a faded vest and cut-off jeans. Her bare arms and legs were tanned and lean and her hair was uncombed and shapeless, growing in all directions and clearly self-cut.

The dogs turned and circled her like well-fed sharks. She made a clicking sound with her tongue and they sat in a line behind her. Germaine went up to the gate and the two women stood a metre apart, separated by the ironwork, looking into each other's eyes.

'*Hola*,' Germaine said. '*Mi nombre es* Germaine Kiecke.' She reached through the gate to shake hands and tried not to look as if she were expecting hers to be bitten off.

Alta took it, looked at it and then let it go. Her hand was warm and rough, but she didn't grip. It was a contact, not a handshake. She folded her arms and cocked her head to one side, smiling slightly. Waiting.

'¿Y usted es...?' Germaine said.

It seemed for a moment as if she wasn't going to tell Germaine her name but then she smiled more broadly and said, 'Altagracia Maria Rosario'.

Her voice had a pleasant sing-song intonation. Softer and warmer than Germaine had expected. More mature. Germaine had read that when a person says their own name something in their manner changes. Alta said her name with a mixture of pride and disdain. She added, 'Speak in English. I like to practise.'

'Altagracia. High Grace. That's a beautiful name.'

'Are you surprised?'

'At what?'

'That I should have a beautiful name.'

'No, of course not.'

'I let my good friends call me Alta.'

'May I...?'

'Where is your car? Did you walk up the hill?'

Germaine noted she wasn't to be included in the list of good friends. At least, not yet. 'Part of the way. We left it on the road.'

Alta nodded.

'I'm from Belgium,' Germaine said. She remembered Catharina's advice. 'From Liège. I was wondering if I could talk to you.'

Alta smiled and ruffled one of the dog's ears. 'To me?'

'Yes.'

'Not somebody else?'

'Well…'

'These dogs maybe?'

'I…'

'They're called Chico and Harpo and Groucho. But not Gummo or Zeppo. Would you call a guard dog Gummo? Not very scary.'

Germaine cleared her throat. She wanted to finish a sentence. 'I've come here because… because I'm writing an art book and I'm interested in the women who work with artists: muses, models… agents.' She waited, realising too late that if Alta had seen her emails to Tom then she would know that wasn't true. 'So, what do you think? Could I come in and talk to you?'

She felt suddenly weary. She had travelled a long way for this. She was thirsty too, and what she wanted most was to sit down. It was tedious conversing through a gate. She would much prefer to be in a cool café with waiters and menus and passing traffic, with a newspaper in her bag, talking to a reasonable person who was willing to participate in the conversation and not speak as if they were talking round a corner or some other acute angle that made communicating so difficult.

Alta shook her head slowly.

'I don't think you've come to see me.'

Germaine's energy was seeping out through her feet. She had expected to be rebuffed and, now it was happening, she wasn't sure if she had the stamina to protest.

'I'm sorry you think that,' she said. 'But I really would like to talk to you, and, yes, I'd like to talk to Tom Hannah too.' She laughed and winced when she heard how desperate she sounded. 'Could we start this conversation again?'

But Alta was already turning away, and the way she moved in that moment with her back arched and her neck straight told Germaine that this was no urchin. Altagracia Maria Rosario knew how to comport herself. Her English was very good, almost formal. She had been tutored. 'I don't think so. Goodbye, Germaine Kiecke from Liège in Belgium. *Adiós*.'

She was walking away when Margot called out, 'What about the audition?'

Alta stopped. 'Audition?' She looked at them both and smiled widely. 'What audition?'

Margot pressed her face against the gate and Germaine felt a pang of longing, a jealousy. What would it be like to have somebody in her life who was on her side, who would be her champion no matter how difficult life might be, who would press their face against a gate even though there were large dogs who might bite it off?

'My husband's an actor,' Margot said. 'Voice-overs. You should hear him. All kinds of noises. Coughs and sneezes, burps, sniffs – all manner of odd noises. And on cue. He never misses a cue.'

Alta smiled. 'I like your orange clothes and your fluffy hair, but I don't understand you.'

'Her husband makes noises,' Germaine said.

'He's very good,' said Margot. 'He's on the radio. Well, he was.'

'Does he do animal noises?' she said.

'Yes. I'm sure he would.'

Alta pursed her lips and her eyes flicked from one to the other while she thought. 'Too much talking,' she said suddenly and walked away with the dogs following. A moment later, they were gone, along with their opportunity, and Germaine and Margot were left on their own, still standing on the wrong side of the gate.

'At least she didn't throw stones at us.'

'Was that a yes or a no?' said Margot. 'I didn't hear a no.'

'It was a no.'

They walked back to the car from where they could see Charles coming up the hill carrying a plastic bag.

'I'm sorry about the audition,' Germaine said.

Margot smiled a sad smile. 'Charles is very good, you know.' Then she touched her head. 'Does my hair really look fluffy?'

8

Charles's face was red. He was grinding his teeth again. He looked, to Germaine, to be a bit unhinged and she was happy to let Margot investigate the problem, which quickly became clear as soon as he was in earshot.

'Rix!'

Charles said the name without parting his teeth, as a ventriloquist would, and Margot literally hopped backwards as if she'd been scalded. Germaine checked her phone. Was it Venus o'clock yet?

'What?' said Margot. It was a wail not a word.

'The bastard is coming here.'

Margot deflated in front of them while Charles seemed to grow in size. Germaine leaned against the car and lit a cigarette. Was Charles going to run amok? Would she and Margot be murdered, here on this lonely mountain road in Spain? The world was so beautiful; why did it have to include people? Human beings should not be allowed to run their own lives; they should be given a list of key events at birth and then chained to fate and kept out of her way.

'How do you know he's coming?' she said flicking ash onto a weed.

Charles stopped glaring at Margot, who remained locked in position, hands to face, horror-struck, and turned his bloodshot eyes on Germaine.

'Rodolfo asked if I knew a *Señor* Rix. Said he's got a booking for another Englishman tomorrow night. I said to him, "Do I know him? Do I bloody know him? Do I bloody bastard know him? Do I…?"'

'Did you manage to tell him you do?'

'Hyanh! It's the audition. He's got wind of it. We've got to do it now. Before he gets here.'

'But how did he get wind of it?' Germaine said. 'There's nothing to get wind of. There is no audition. This was meant to be a one-off just for you. You said so yourself, the idea was that I would try to set something up. How did Rix get wind of something that doesn't exist?'

'Well, he's coming.'

'Maybe. But…'

'I told him.' Margot's words rustled in their ears like leaves in a breeze. Both Germaine and Charles looked at her. 'I was proud,' she said. 'I thought this was a real audition. He sends messages. I always ignore them – I do. But this time… I said we were going to Spain. I wanted him to know that you were on your way up again.'

You know you can block people, Germaine thought. If you really want to ignore someone's messages, you can block them.

'You told him Las Sombras?' Charles's voice was flat. 'This place, here.'

'Yes.'

'You told him it was for the *Happy Family* thing?'

'Yes.'

'An audition?'

'Yes.'

He looked away. 'Shot from behind. Didn't expect that.'

'Charles…'

'Well, good luck to the lot of you, that's what I say. No, I don't. Bad luck to the lot of you. Bloody bad luck. Give me the car keys,' he said to Margot.

'No.'

'Give me the car keys,' he bellowed, and his voice echoed around the mountains.

Germaine stiffened. Men who shouted were not welcome. 'Give him the keys,' she said. 'We can walk back to the hotel.'

Margot handed them over and Charles got into the car, started it up and drove onto the verge. He wound down the window and shouted, 'Coming?'

'Coming where?' said Margot.

'To the gates of course. To the bloody gates of hell. I've come here for an audition, and an audition is what I mean to have.'

Germaine and Margot looked at each other. 'I'd better go with him,' Margot said.

'You don't have to.'

Margot smiled. 'I do.'

She got into the car and before she had time to shut the door Charles drove away, with stones and dust and bits of plant flying up into the air behind him.

Germaine shook her head. It was all getting away from her. 'Idiotic people,' she said. How could she let them go to where she wanted to be, without going too? She started trudging back up the hill following their trail of settling dust.

'Stupid, idiotic people.'

When she caught up with them, Charles and Margot were already out of the car and standing at the gate. Chico, Harpo and Groucho had returned and were watching him from the other side. There was no sign of Alta – or Tom. Just the dogs with their teeth and muscles and cool unblinking stares. The camera flashed every few seconds or so, but did that mean anyone was watching? Germaine didn't know.

'Are you sure?' Margot was saying. 'What if they're not hungry?'

'Shush,' said Charles. He was opening the plastic bag he'd brought with him.

'Is that meat?' Germaine said.

'Drugged meat,' said Margot.

'What?'

Charles looked at her and then shook the bag. 'Sleeping powder in the meat. Feed the dogs, dogs go to sleep, we climb over the gate, charm offensive on the Tash person, do audition, leave. Dogs wake up feeling refreshed and full of beans.'

Germaine was lost for words. In the end, 'You're joking?' was all she could say.

'He's not,' said Margot and if a voice could wring its hands, hers did.

'Well, that's insane.'

'You don't have to be here,' Charles muttered.

'Of course, I have to be here. Do you think Tom Hannah will be pleased you poisoned his dogs? Reward you with a job? This is illegal and foolish. And you'll ruin everything for me. This is my assignment, my interview, my book. Of course, I have to be here. To keep you from… messing everything up.'

Charles ignored her. 'It's not poison. It's sleeping powder.'

Germaine laughed. 'Sleeping powder? Are we in a nursery rhyme?'

'He got it from Rodolfo,' Margot said. 'He's got a sack of it in his storeroom. Helps him to sleep.'

'You knew about this?'

'A little bit.'

'A little bit? You might have mentioned it. You're both idiots. You can't drug the dogs and, if you did, the gate is too high to climb, and, if you could climb it, you'd fall off and then you'd be trespassing. Let's go back to the hotel and dispose of the meat – safely, without harming anyone. And then I'll buy you both a drink and we can get drunk and moan about Gerard Borkmann.'

'Later,' said Charles.

He had taken the three lumps of drugged meat from his plastic bag and was preparing to sling them over the wrought-iron gate.

'Charles,' said Germaine. 'If you do this I'll call the police.'

'Fine.' He threw the first piece of meat over the gate. It landed with a loud, fat slap. The dogs stood up and looked at it.

'Oh, for God's sake,' Germaine said. 'Come away now.' She led Margot down the scrubby slope, taking care not to slip or stumble, and got into the car.

'I can't leave him here,' said Margot.

'Yes, you can.'

They watched him throw the remaining lumps of drugged meat over the gate. Chico, Harpo and Groucho looked at Charles, then at the meat, and then, as if doing him a favour, sniffed it and began to eat.

'Oh God,' Germaine groaned.

'Coffee?' said Margot. She had a thermos flask in her rucksack with cups and plates for the sandwiches she'd brought.

'You have a picnic?'

'Just a snack. Keep the rumbly-tumblies away.'

Rumbly-tumblies? How far have I fallen? Germaine asked herself.

Charles stepped away from the gate and they all waited for the dogs to roll over and fall asleep. This did not happen.

What did happen was that the dogs became agitated and began barking at Charles wildly and violently as if they knew what he had done. And these weren't ordinary barks. These weren't the barks of a noisy dog in a neighbour's garden. These were sounds that dogs made in prehistoric times when they had enormous chests and throats and four layers of teeth and were bigger than people.

They ran at the gate throwing themselves at the iron bars again and again, with their eyes rolling in their sockets and their huge paws scrabbling at the gravel.

'What is that yellow stuff coming out of their noses?' said Margot.

'I don't know. Wind up the windows.'

Charles was backing away, and Germaine wondered how he felt, knowing his hands were smothered with the scent of drugged meat. The dogs were now biting the metal bars in their mad need to get to Charles. But, when they saw him stepping away, they jumped up, turned and vanished, galloping like a trio of insane, wild, savage horses. They almost fell over each other in their haste and didn't appear to be tired at all.

Margot opened her door. 'Get in, Charles. Before they come back. Let's go back to the hotel.'

Germaine thought they should go farther than the hotel. She thought they should take a fast plane to Kathmandu. She did not feel at all safe in their puny tin can on that lonely mountainside outside those tall and unwelcoming gates set in the wall of heavy stone.

But instead of getting into the car Charles stood on the slope above them and stared at the ground, listening as the barking grew fainter. Germaine opened her door and listened too. It seemed to her that the distant sounds of panting and running feet were becoming louder again. It probably occurred to all of them at the same time that the dogs had found a way out.

Germaine closed her door and locked it. 'Start the engines,' she said. 'Evacuate.'

'Charles, get in,' said Margot.

The dogs skidded around the corner of the wall. They saw Charles with what appeared to be a mad, unfettered, slavering joy. Germaine wondered what Charles was thinking. Dark thoughts, no doubt. There was no chance to cover the twenty metres or so and get into the car. All he had were a few seconds in which to cover the softer parts of his body with his meaty-smelling hands before the three-headed, multi-jawed, yellow-foaming monster engulfed him.

From where she sat, with the car doors locked and the windows tightly closed, Germaine could imagine they were all having great fun out there: getting up and falling down, running away, rolling on the ground, shaking each other, tearing off clothes, barking and shouting, being dragged through the undergrowth. She turned to mention this to Margot, but Margot had opened her door.

'Are you getting out of the car?' Germaine said.

'We can't leave Charles,' Margot said.

'What if you get eaten?'

'We have to rescue him.'

'We could chase them away with the car.'

Margot got back in, put her seat belt on, lifted the clutch and the car leaped forwards and stalled. 'Sorry. My one at home is much easier.'

'It's probably newer.'

'I don't use it much.'

'Shall we get Charles?'

This time the car bounced up the slope, its wheels spinning for purchase as they closed in on the dusty cloud that marked the spot where the dogs were burying Charles.

'Don't run him over.'

They pulled up and Margot pushed open the door, giving Groucho a hefty whack on his backside as she did so.

'Watch out for the yellow foam,' Germaine said. 'It might be toxic.' Margot climbed out, swinging her thermos flask backwards and forwards. 'Get off,' she said.

The dogs were reluctant to let go of Charles and tried to drag him away with them, but they were tired now and the fight had left them. And there can only be so many times even the biggest of dogs is willing to be clouted on the head by a coffee-filled thermos flask. They snarled and growled but gave ground until, after one last shake of Charles, they retreated around the corner of the wall, back, Germaine hoped, to the inside of the property.

9

Decisions. Always decisions. Would it be possible to never make a decision again? Just to be carried through life like a leaf on a river and be taken to the sea, swirling and splashing and gasping but knowing that a greater force was in control? That's all we are, Germaine thought, a decision-processing engine. People switched from one track to another; their lives a long trail of twists and turns laid out behind them like the slime left behind by a slug.

She could imagine in some celestial museum a large set of drawers that contained all of existence, and in each drawer on a black velvet cushion there were the lives of everyone who had ever existed, silvery squiggles arranged in ranks. And every day more lives were added, more squiggles, more tales each with its own beginning-middle-end, stored and locked away. And for whom, she wondered? Who would ever look at all those trillions of lives, and did it matter to the drawer-owner if one squiggle belonged to a sinner and another to a saint?

Germaine's immediate decision was whether or not to take Charles to a hospital. He didn't look good. He sat in the back seat of the car and shivered and stared at the windscreen. Margot was beside him. Germaine was driving.

'Are there any missing parts?' she said looking in her mirror.

'His trousers are ruined. There are twigs and things in his hair. And scratches. But I don't think they actually bit him. Just pulled him around a bit. More trauma than injury. Poor Charles, they were only trying to bury you for later, weren't they?'

'I could take him to hospital? Assuming there is one.'

'No. I don't think so. I think Charles would prefer a nice cup of tea and a sit-down. Wouldn't you, Charles?'

'Hyanh.'

On the way back to Las Sombras, Germaine thought about the decisions that had led her to be in that car with those people. A long time seemed to have passed since she had drunk three large whiskies and walked out on Borkmann because he had defined her as unadorned. A long time since she had found herself staring into a window in the rain. Decisions, decisions, decisions, and each with its own trail of consequences.

When they got back to the hotel Margot took Charles to their room and Germaine went to hers. She closed the blinds and lay down on the bed. She promised herself that when this was all over she would go to a mindfulness retreat somewhere high in the Alps, where talking during the day was forbidden and the rooms contained only the bare necessities of life. No technology, just natural light. A place that Tom Hannah might approve of. She would go there and find peace and quiet and serenity – which reminded her of the Garden in *Happy Family*. Time for my fix, she thought, even though she had the beginning of a headache and her eyes were tired.

She retrieved her iLets from the bedside drawer and sat on the bed with the pillows laid out around her, warm and secure and supportive, like an armchair. She pressed *Resume* and on either side of the bed grass appeared while the bed itself was overlaid with a fence. Mr Venus was still watching her, Mrs Venus was still not there and Harriet the Barn Owl was still descending through the ceiling. Sally and Anuj were making their way into her wardrobe – or a line of shrubbery as it now was.

A voice in her ear said, 'Your Dilemma has timed out. You have lost two hundred Game Privileges.'

A picture of Mrs Venus's face with a tear running down her cheek flashed in front of her and then vanished. Harriet landed on the bed. No options appeared, all Germaine could do was push back into her pillows and wait.

Harriet leaned into Germaine's face, her eyes filling the iLets like two burning planets. Germaine tried to see past her to where Mr Venus was standing. He was walking away. What age category was this version, she wondered? She checked: five to seven. Surely not.

But still she kept playing.

'Breakfast time,' Harriet said. And now the sky widened as she soared upwards, taking Germaine with her. Claws surrounded her like the bars of a cage and Harriet's flapping wings beat into Germaine's ears, her feathery proportions perfectly rendered as she took to the sky. Germaine was now both above and below: a small shape reclining on a hotel bed; a salamander nymph being carried away to a distant nest.

And then, as she waited for the *Game Over* message to flash, she fell. Germaine still had some Good Luck bonus points and Harriet had screwed up. Her grip had not been good. Through the iLets Germaine fell with her arms and legs trailing behind her. The rush of graphics all around gave the impression of immense speed. She clutched the bedclothes even though she knew she wasn't moving. She fell towards a house with a garden where a large white cat was lying on the patio. A flashing label above its head told Germaine the cat's name was JoJo. The iLets grew cold.

The ground rushed up in a whirl of colour and images and she landed on JoJo's head and then fell onto the patio. Now the perspective changed and so did the scene. The grass was gone and, in its place, concrete paving slabs covered the floor and rolled up across the bed. The bedroom wall in front of her was now the outside wall of a house with a back door, a cat flap and a kitchen window. On the floor, filling most of the available space, was JoJo. Her eyes, like Harriet's, enormous flaming orbs.

'Feedback on this game is not going to be good,' Germaine muttered. 'Five to seven, my foot.' JoJo came over, growing in magnitude until she was three or four times the size of Germaine.

'JoJo's treat-treat,' the cat said.

'Pssst.' The sound was so real that for a moment Germaine looked around to see who had come into her room. But it was Sally the Snail under a large leaf in the virtual shrubbery. 'She's not going to eat you,' Sally said.

'That's good.'

'She's going to keep you as her toy and play with you until you fall apart. Like cats do.'

'That's less good.'

'Then gift you to her owner.'

'Gift me?'

'And who knows what he'll do with you. But we have a plan. Shall we do it?'

The plan's title floated in the air above her bed: *Anuj's Meat.* Germaine shook her head in despair. Had the creative team been let loose without a grown up? A *Yes/No* option flashed and she nodded. What the hell.

'Anuj will distract her with his meat,' said Sally. 'When he does, leap to safety and hide in this shrubbery.'

'What about the "ant of the day" prize?'

'You'll lose some Goodwill points.'

Germaine watched Anuj crawl out from underneath the wardrobe. There was something wrong with his depiction, it was as if he were squeezing out of a tube. The scale was out; he was too big. He had too many legs. Surely this game was faulty.

JoJo sniffed the air and stood up. She walked across the bed, a giant cat treading carefully across the concrete bedcovers, nosing her way towards Germaine's little friends. JoJo's definition was flawless, each muscle flowing like lava beneath her skin, each hair in her fur looking more real than real fur would look. This was in stark contrast to the unfinished appearance of Anuj who was still crawling from the shrubbery. The game was too uneven to be a full release.

JoJo saw Anuj and hissed.

'Get back inside-side.'

But Anuj held firm which Germaine found touching. Here at least, in this software-generated fictional world, was someone willing to take a chance for her. Albeit an ant.

JoJo hissed again.

Anuj began to back away. They would be leaving the bedroom if he went any further in that direction.

'Naughty ant-ant,' JoJo said, following him.

'Now,' shouted Sally.

Germaine had forgotten she was participating. She stood up. 'Do I get inside the wardrobe?' She didn't know but it would have to wait. Her phone was ringing.

Germaine closed down the app and took off her iLets. The

sense of disorientation was stronger than it had been earlier, and she didn't know where her phone was until she saw she was holding it in her hand. Her battery symbol was flashing; she was low again. The game was sucking up energy in more ways than one, she thought. Her recovery time was longer; finding her way up through the maze game levels was more of an effort; reconnecting with her immediate past was more of a puzzle. Her head ached and she felt bunged up.

She looked at her phone and took the call.

'Hello, Catharina.'

Catharina's voice sounded different. More raw. 'Are you busy? Are you at Tom's house?'

'No, I'm back at the hotel.'

'How did the visit go?'

'Well, it didn't rain.'

'Oh. Not good, then?'

'No. Not good in any way. We didn't see Tom at all, but we did see the stone-thrower – her name is Alta – and she told us to go away. And then the actor who works for Borkmann showed up and tried to poison the guard dogs and they went mad and dragged him all over the mountain and buried him in a hole.'

'Oh, so…'

'In other news, the hotel owner's sister-in-law hinted very strongly that the hotel owner – his name is Rodolfo, by the way – murdered her father and probably her sister too. And the actor's wife's ex-lover is on his way to Las Sombras in order to attend a non-existent audition which is a toxic situation for the husband and wife team. Finally, and don't worry if you don't follow this part, something's gone wrong with my *Happy Family* game and I've been abandoned by Mr and Mrs Venus who are my parents. They're not meant to do that.'

'Right.' Catharina paused and Germaine didn't blame her. What was there to say in answer to all that? 'But it didn't rain?'

'No, it's quite sunny.'

'What is Las Sombras like?'

'Here? It's quiet. The whole place is like an empty film set. We're the only guests as far as I can tell – Charles, Margot and me. Of course, the lover will be here soon. Oh, and there's a son too, Rodolfo's son and Teresa's – she's the missing wife. His name is Claudio. It's all slightly unreal.'

As if to emphasise that, she suddenly felt very dizzy. Only once in her life had Germaine fainted. She could recall the feeling clearly even though she had only been ten or eleven years old. She remembered the sudden sense of mental clutching as if she were trying to get back inside herself, the black spots in front of her eyes that joined up, and then standing up and knocking over a glass. She must have fallen because, when her vision cleared, she was lying on the floor feeling sick.

Now, sitting on her bed and looking at her phone, she had that same sense of unreality, as if she had been made aware of herself and of her shape, her thoughts, her breathing and heartbeat. She wondered if she should call somebody. She was seeing double, triple images and her ears were buzzing.

'Hello?' Catharina's voice sounded a long way away. 'Are you still there?'

'Yes, I'm still here,' Germaine said. The feeling was subsiding. She took a deep breath. 'I think I need something to eat.' And that was true. She hadn't eaten since breakfast.

'Are there restaurants?'

'There's a bar and a restaurant in the hotel. Las Sombras is not much more than a village on a rock. No beach. No clubs. No casino. Just a glass bottom boat that doesn't move.'

Catharina said nothing for a moment and then, 'I enjoyed

that evening in your flat. It was fun. We should do that sort of thing more.'

'Definitely.'

'This may sound odd but, as I haven't had a break in a while, I was thinking I might come out – to Las Sombras. For a few days. Not to interfere with your work or anything. Just to visit. How does that sound? Would you mind? We could talk about the book. A business trip. What do you think?'

Germaine wasn't sure what she thought. 'It's a long way to come – and there really isn't much here at all. You'll find it very tame.'

'I like tame. It's been a long week. A long month. A long year. I need to get away from it all.'

Germaine wasn't sure about her agent coming to Las Sombras. She didn't want anybody to get between her and a Tom Hannah interview – not even Catharina. Charles and Margot she could deal with. She could handle Alta too, once she'd engaged with Tom. *If* she engaged with Tom. But Catharina was a more elemental force. Why would she want to travel all the way to a nowhere place where nothing happens? Unless she wanted Tom Hannah as her client? Was that it? But, despite her misgivings, Germaine couldn't deny the prospect of Catharina being in Las Sombras was appealing.

'I think if you want to get away from it all, this is the place to come,' she said.

'Good. I thought so too. In fact, I've already booked a flight. Can you sort out a room for me? I'll be there tomorrow.'

10

Germaine hung up and sat on her bed not moving and not thinking, at least not in terms of directing her thoughts. Finally, she stood up and undressed and went into the bathroom to run a bath. She ran it hot and deep, and lay in it, drowsy and sapped of energy. She lay with the water up to her chin and stared at her distorted reflection in the taps. The water clung to her skin, a hot and heavy liquid blanket that softened her flesh and turned her forehead wet with perspiration. It was too much effort to move and so she lay there until the water cooled and she could finally gather the willpower to wash and get out.

Afterwards, she stood in front of the wardrobe mirror and looked at herself. She was pink from the hot bath – scrubbed and flushed. She looked at the mirror for a long time, seeing a reflection of herself from many years ago.

A *vondeling.*

She raised her hand and put it across her mouth, her thumb upright and tucked into the outside corner of her eye. She started to squeeze her face, increasing her grip until her hand was a muzzle, pressing her thumb tightly against the side of her eye socket and cheekbone, pulling the side of her chin with her fingers. She took her hand away and saw a deeper red against her pink skin – the mark of her hand. She breathed deeply. One breath, then another, and then another. Five long beats in, ten short beats out. It was an old coping mechanism, a way of venting pain and anguish without making any noise. Why was she doing that now, she wondered? What pain and anguish did she need to release? Or was it just a way of trying to remember, to connect with her younger self. But why? Why connect with that unhappy child?

She looked again. Germaine Kiecke, academic and art historian, was back in the mirror and her younger version was gone; consigned to a time when horror had to be released into the palm of her hand, washed and thrown away. And so, as she had done as a child, she did then: she washed her hands slowly and thoroughly, shook them several times, shaking away any vestige of the sounds that had come from her throat. She checked her face again in the mirror. It was calm and serene, but her eyes were bloodshot.

She dressed, tidied her room and then went downstairs to find Rodolfo. He wasn't in the bar or by the desk at the hotel entrance, so she went outside and looked up and down the deserted harbour road. It was becoming dark, but she could see him leaning against the harbour wall, an angular silhouette. She joined him. The sea below was an empty darkness, a rhythmic breaking of waves against the rocks.

'*Hola*,' she said. 'A friend of mine is coming to Las Sombras. Arriving tomorrow. Do you have any rooms available?'

Rodolfo blew his smoke towards the sea. 'Of course,' he said. 'How long will they stay?'

'A few days. I'm not sure. Just one person. Her name is Catharina Caboulet.'

'It's no problem. You have told me. It's done.'

Germaine nodded. She walked down the cobbled street

towards the hotel entrance at the side of the building. Luisa was sitting on the bench drinking *razik*. Had she been there all day, Germaine wondered?

'*Buenas tardes. ¿Cómo estás?*' she said. 'It's cool out here.'

Luisa held up her glass. 'Not with this to warm the belly. Did you go to the house?'

'Yes, we did. No stones were thrown.'

'Ha. That's good. You saw her. Did you get your interview?'

'No.'

'I told you. *¿Mañana?*'

'Maybe.'

Germaine left her to her alcohol and went back into the hotel. She walked through the empty bar and poked her head into the kitchen where Claudio was stirring bubbling liquids in iron pots.

'Hello, Claudio. In case your father forgets, there is a new guest coming tomorrow. A friend of mine. She is nice. You'll like her.'

Claudio nodded. Germaine waited by the kitchen door, not wanting to invade his place of safety, wanting to say something but not knowing what. He must have been at least fourteen, but he looked younger. What was it with this place? Everyone looked either older or younger than they were. She cleared her throat.

'So… I just thought I'd let you know. About the new guest.'

Claudio nodded. 'I understand. Thank you.'

She wanted to say something more, to reach out to this boy whom she perceived to be lonely and uncared for; his mother missing; his father preoccupied and distant. But she didn't know how. She lacked the technique, the facility, the energy within.

In the end, we are what we do. Or don't do. And I suppose I don't do relationships.

'Okay, well, if you ever need to talk.'

What an inadequate thing to say. She left the kitchen and found Luisa waiting in the bar.

'Talking will never help him. His heart is broken.'

'Because his mother has gone away?'

'His mother is dead,' Luisa said flatly. 'You know that. Killed by that snake out there.'

'I don't know that,' said Germaine.

Luisa turned and looked beyond the bar to the dusk outside, to where Rodolfo was still lounging on his chair, and to the harbour and the rocks and the sea beyond.

'I do.'

Entering into the *El Tesoro Escondido* bar from the harbour street door, a visitor would step into a wide room with an unvarnished wooden floor, a high ceiling with two slowly revolving fans and walls decorated with the creative paraphernalia that an isolated fishing community usually generates: rough paintings, old photographs, dusty hanging drapes, framed articles, hooks, books, fishing props and a glass case with a long-dead, prize-winning fish, caught by Luisa's and Teresa's father.

A dozen or more tables with uneven legs and set with rickety chairs created an obstacle course between the entrance and the bar itself. On each table was a white tablecloth; a glass jar containing four knives, four forks and four spoons; a stack of curling paper serviettes; a salt pot, a pepper pot and a bottle of chilli sauce.

The bar was brickwork topped with a polished wooden surface lined with beer taps, towels, leaflets, charity boxes, menus and bottles. Two mirrors behind the bar reflected the windows and the outside beyond – which created an uplifting sensation of space during the day and a claustrophobic awareness of the encroaching darkness at night. Between the two mirrors were three shelves of liquor with dusty, colourful and sticky labels, and no optics. Alcohol was always splashed without measure into the customers' glasses. It was the adult way.

Beyond the bar on the left there was a door that led to the hotel reception area, the cobbled street and the staircase to the rooms above; and on the right of the bar were the double doors with their round porthole windows which separated the customers from the kitchen.

Perhaps on this particular evening the visitor would have been tempted to come in, but, then again, perhaps not. There was an atmosphere in the bar, a tang of metal in the air that suggested an incoming storm; a certain stillness in the attitudes of the people who sat there; a brittleness to their words as if they might crack and fall to the floor once they had left their speakers' mouths.

The visitor would see that, on the left of the room, Germaine, Charles and Margot were sitting at their table, and, on the right of the room, Rodolfo was at his table staring moodily at his newspaper – and, in the middle of the room, like a tightly twisted knot, Luisa was huddled at her table.

The visitor, who was no doubt a sensible traveller, might conclude that the evening would be better spent elsewhere. They might decide that it would be prudent to close the door and leave Las Sombras forever. They might be right but, of course, there was no visitor. There seldom was.

Germaine was too preoccupied with her own thoughts to notice much about her companions' mood when she sat down. It was only when Claudio served them that she gave Charles and Margot her attention.

'Are you two all right? You're quiet.'

'Charles is upset,' said Margot.

'I'm not surprised,' said Germaine. 'Those dogs…'

'It's not that. It's… you know,' Margot whispered although everyone in the room could hear her.

'It's that bloody bastard,' Charles clarified. 'We're leaving. In the morning.'

'What about the audition?'

'Stuff the audition.'

'Charles.'

'Will you take the car?' said Germaine.

'Stuff the car.'

'Charles. Please.'

Germaine was aware of some other activity on her right. She saw Luisa half-standing, leaning on her table, hissing something at Rodolfo which Germaine couldn't hear. Rodolfo ignored her and concentrated on his paper. Claudio came with her food, distracting Germaine's attention and then a chair fell over. It was Luisa's. She had stood up and was pointing a wobbly finger at Rodolfo.

'*Asesino*,' she growled.

'Go to bed,' Rodolfo said in English. 'Sleep it off.'

Claudio, on his way from the kitchen again, stopped halfway across the room with two bowls of mussels in his hand. Charles waved. 'Over here.'

'*Asesino! Diablo.*' Luisa shouted.

'They'll go cold,' Charles said.

Germaine looked at him and then at the room in general as if she were seeing it all for the first time. Again she had that feeling of dislocation – the remote village, the moody owner, the pale son, the avenging in-law, Rix, Charles, Margot. It all seemed too staged. She was gripped by an urgent desire not to be there – not to be in this scene.

And then, as if events were determined to move her yet further from reality, the door leading to the harbour road flew open and a small thunderstorm blew in. It was Alta, accompanied by a large, shambling, black and white dog. She caught sight of Charles and marched towards him with a fire blazing in her eyes that could melt skin.

'Monster,' she said. She swung her knapsack onto the floor, rummaged through it and took out a plastic bag. Badger set off towards the bar and the intoxicating scents emanating from the slop bucket, while across the room, in the rival altercation, Rodolfo was standing up, glaring at Alta.

'Out,' he shouted.

But Luisa wasn't to be ignored. '*Asesino*,' she shouted at Rodolfo.

'Monster,' Alta shouted at Charles, holding up the plastic bag.

'Out.'

The shouts interleaved and created a hypnotic percussive beat. Germaine felt dizzy. Now Alta produced a faded blue towel from which she pulled her dagger.

'You poisoned my dogs.'

It all seemed to be happening in slow motion. Charles opened his mouth as if to say something. Rodolfo pushed Luisa away from him. Claudio dropped his bowl of mussels and hot garlic sauce ran free across the floor. Alta moved towards Charles with her dagger in one hand and the bag of meat in the other. Margot put her hand to her mouth.

In the old-style Hollywood westerns where cowboys wear colourful neckerchiefs and native Americans dress up in feather headdresses and tailored buckskin trousers, people have a great time fighting in barrooms. They hit people with bottles and swing on light fittings, and glamorous, fun-loving sex workers appear from mezzanine rooms and push people down the stairs while their clients pull up their trousers and jump into the fray with excited shouts.

Germaine sometimes watched those films on wet Wednesday afternoons and tried to relate those cartoon images to the violence she had witnessed at Chateau Giselle, where a relentless series of punches delivered by a large, heavy man usually resulted in a swollen and broken face and a lifetime of nightmares, rather than a comical expression.

And now here she was in her own barroom brawl.

'Put your knife down, Alta,' Germaine said. 'Please.'

Alta ignored her. 'You're going to eat the same poison that you fed to my dogs,' she said to Charles. She took a lump of half-chewed meat from the plastic bag and dropped it onto the table. 'Eat,' she said. 'Eat your poison before I stuff it down your throat.'

On the other side of the room Luisa was now shouting: 'Murderer.' Her fists were raised above her head as if she intended to beat on Rodolfo as she would beat on a closed and locked door. Claudio rushed over and stood between his aunt and his father.

'No, *Tía*.'

Luisa ignored him and began slapping at Rodolfo with flailing hands while he fended her off. Claudio was caught in the middle and now he wrestled with his aunt while she held onto Rodolfo. All three became a single uncontrolled ruck that knocked over tables and chairs.

Not to be outdone by the melee on that side of the room, Alta pushed the meat into Charles's face. His chair tipped backwards and he fell onto the floor, sending a table sliding across the room towards Rodolfo and his revolving pack of relatives.

The two fracas were becoming one.

Again, time slowed down for Germaine. She watched as Margot shouted 'no' in slow motion and seized hold of Alta's fingers and bent them backwards. Alta yelped and snatched her hands away. She picked up a chair and threw it at Margot, missed and hit Charles on the side of his head.

'Enough,' Germaine said and surprised herself by standing up, pulling the tablecloth from the table and sending knives, forks, spoons, serviettes, salt, pepper and a bottle of chilli sauce onto the floor where they joined the mussels and the garlic sauce. She threw the tablecloth over Alta's head and then hugged her, pinning Alta's arms to her sides.

'Let me go,' Alta said. 'Or I'll kill you, too.'

11

This was the scene that greeted Tom Hannah when he walked into the hotel bar. On one side of the room Alta was wrapped up in a tablecloth, and locked in a tight embrace with Germaine, amongst upturned tables and fallen chairs; Charles was lying on the floor in a small sea of mussels and sauce, his face smeared with meat, with Margot kneeling beside him looking dazed. On the other side of the room, Luisa was trying to gouge out Rodolfo's eyes while Claudio struggled to pull her away. To top it off, Badger emerged from behind the bar and was quietly sick on the floor.

Tom cleared his throat and said, 'Hello?'

All movement ceased. And then Claudio released his aunt and ran out of the bar, into the street and into the night.

'Claudio,' Rodolfo called after him. But Claudio had cut loose.

Luisa sat on a chair, looking small, drawn and diminished in the bright lights of the bar. It was as if her violence had used up some of her physical being. Rodolfo, his face scratched by Luisa's nails, picked up tables and chairs and put them back in their correct positions. Margot helped him. Germaine stood by the open door, smoking, having released Alta who had tried to tear the tablecloth to shreds and was now sitting, fuming, at a table away from the rest of them with a sleepy-looking Badger, watching Charles who was sitting alone at a table.

The poisoned meat had been tied up in the plastic bag and thrown into a bin. Alta's dagger was once again wrapped in its towel and stored safely in her backpack. Order was being restored and only Claudio was still out of position. Rodolfo kept looking at the door through which he'd run.

Tom Hannah – cartoonist, artist, creative director, recluse and object of Germaine's visit – leaned on the bar. He made for an unorthodox sight. Six feet four inches tall, rangy after months of eating very little, thick curling eyebrows, big tangled beard, big moustache, long, coarse greying hair. Big hands, big feet, big bones and too little flesh. He was wearing baggy shorts, sandals, a t-shirt and what had probably been an expensive jumper once, but was now torn and frayed with twigs and leaves stuck to it.

Germaine finished her cigarette and returned to the bar and sat on a stool next to Tom.

'Hello,' she said.

He looked at her and nodded. 'Ms Kiecke.'

'I've come a long way to talk to you.'

'So I see.'

'I don't suppose you've read any of my emails? Heard my voicemails? I'm writing a book about… I wanted to…' She stopped. 'Oh, it doesn't matter. Do you want a drink?'

Tom shook his head, smiling. 'No, I'm fine thank you. I just popped in to pick up Alta. She's a bit wound up, but I can see you know that. She does love her dogs.'

Germaine doodled a circle in some spilled beer with her finger, and then said, 'I was speaking to Gerard. He says you've dumped him.'

'Is he here?'

'No. He came to Belgium, though. We had lunch. He's paying for my trip. He wants me to remind you of who you are.'

'Does he? Well, you'd better do that.'

'Right now, I don't think I can. I'm not even sure who I am any more.'

They watched the clearing-up operation and Germaine nodded towards Alta who was kicking mussels towards Charles. 'She's very intense.'

'You don't know the half of it.' He stood up and stretched. Badger licked Germaine's ankles and also got to his feet.

'Are you off?' she said.

She felt strangely relaxed, as if she had been studying for an examination that was now over. All the scheduling and planning, reading and researching, the lists of things to do and the guilt of not doing them, the late nights and the early mornings, the putting off of this and the not doing that, the compartmentalising of her life and the control and order and rigidity of everything she did – it had all gone away. Something had happened to her – had been happening and was still happening – and whatever it was, now in the afterglow of the evening's events, she liked it. Somewhere, a long way away, was a place called Liège where she had a life and work and decisions. But that was elsewhere, a place she called home, and was still home, but which no longer seemed to be the tight-fitting uniform she had wanted it to be. For the moment she felt content to sit in the bar while everyone cleared up around her and do nothing. She didn't even want to talk about her book.

'I'm pleased you're here. It would be good to catch up properly,' Tom said. 'I enjoy our little chats.'

'You mean my carefully researched and highly structured interviews?'

'Yes, those.'

Tom looked at Charles and Margot who were hovering nearby, avoiding close contact with Alta but not wanting to be too far from Tom. One last chance at an audition, Germaine thought. Good for you.

'This is Charles Cubberley,' she said. 'He's a voice actor. And this is his wife, Margot. They drove seven hundred miles to bring me here.'

Charles stepped forwards and said, 'Bodily functions. Sounds. Sneezes and things.'

Tom shook Charles's and Margot's hands. 'Pleased to meet you. Well, you should all come over some time. Visitors in Las Sombras are rare.'

'We're free tomorrow,' said Charles.

'Charles.'

'Perfect. You know where it is, of course.'

'That's so kind of you,' said Margot.

And so very easy, Germaine thought.

'Great,' said Tom. 'Tomorrow, then.'

With a last look around, a nod to Rodolfo and a small bow to Luisa, Tom left the bar and walked into the night with Alta and Badger on each side like patrolling watch scouts. As she left, Alta looked back at Germaine and their eyes locked. Alta drew her fingers across her throat.

Germaine went to her room. It was nearly midnight and her mind was fizzing with the images and experiences of the past few hours. She made no attempt to collate her thoughts and moved slowly around the room, opening the window, pulling down the blinds, switching on her lamp. She locked her door and checked her phone for emails and social media updates but the wifi was poor and her signal was weak. She got undressed and stood naked in the room on the rug, feeling its coarseness through her toes.

Only then did she begin to think in any purposeful way. She stared at her bed and breathed deeply. A draught from the window moved the blinds and blew across her shoulders. Her flesh became taut as the temperature dropped and goosebumps appeared on her arms and legs. Soon she would put on her dressing gown and lean out of the window and smoke, but for now she wanted to stand still and think – to be only a body and a brain.

Charles, Margot, Rodolfo, Claudio and Luisa – they were the background to all this, she thought, whatever 'all this' was. A colourful mixture of paint to be studied in slow time. She put them to one side. Borkmann, Tom Hannah and Alta. If this were a painting they would be in the foreground. She had come to Spain to interview Tom Hannah, struggled across a mountain and been rebuffed at a gate. And now Tom had appeared in the hotel and invited them all up to his house. Just appeared.

'Restart,' she shouted at the ceiling and laughed as if she were drunk.

She moved to the bed and lay down. How long had she been in Spain? Two days? Three? Time was getting away from her. Her thoughts were getting away from her. Where was her precision? She remembered that soon Catharina and Rix would be joining them. She smiled at the thought. And then Alta's angry face floated into view. Alta. What was she in all of this? A genuine runaway? She had felt real enough. Germaine had held her body, felt her squirm like an eel and struggle in her grasp. Germaine swung her legs off the bed, stood up and went to the window where, instead of smoking, she breathed in the cool night air. Lights from the hotel and bar below lit the cobbled street, while off to her left the Atlantic Ocean rumbled in the night.

'I fought,' she said shaking her head. 'I fought.' She went back inside, picked up her iLets and plugged them into her phone. If ever there was a time to earn some bonus points, it was now.

An hour later Germaine was dressed and creeping through the hotel bar wearing her iLets. She was in the game – in the shrubbery. She had leaped. Now she was following Sally the Snail and the semi-formed Anuj. The hotel lights were switched off, with the residents and staff in their rooms. Wherever Claudio was, and whoever was looking for him, they weren't downstairs. Germaine pushed through the kitchen's double doors and switched on the kitchen lights.

'What am I looking for?'

Sally was close beside her. 'Be careful, Germaine.' Anuj went ahead to the far side of the kitchen and stopped by the sink. He reared up and leaned against it as if he were about to do some washing up. Germaine was aware that her iLets were now very cold. She moved carefully, not wanting to miss anything or wake any of the hotel's residents.

'Let's go,' she whispered. Sally nodded.

Anuj turned around from the sink.

He had the face of Tom Hannah.

Germaine caught her breath. She swayed.

The hair, beard and moustache were shorter than she had seen on Tom in the hotel bar. This was not a recently created avatar. He, or it, stared directly at Germaine and, although she knew that the character was being displayed on her iLets, she was nonetheless shocked by the directness of the gaze.

'Hi,' it said.

It wasn't Tom Hannah's voice. The lip-sync wasn't working either. Germaine could hear the words, but Tom's mouth wasn't moving. The intonation was Germanic. One of the Bird brothers, she wondered? If so, it would mean this was a cuckoo. She pulled off her iLets, closed down the game and switched off her phone. Whatever it was that had just happened, her game was now infected and no doubt her device was too. Why was Tom Hannah appearing as a character in his own game? The whole thing had the feel of something that wasn't fully developed. A beta-version. One that could evade the *Coyote* upgrade?

There was no point in trying to make any sense of it so late in the night. She went back to her room and lay in her bed and stared at the ceiling. She was overdoing the iLets. Her eyes felt like dried-up raisins, even her eye sockets seemed to hurt.

Tomorrow she would visit Tom at his house. That at least was a success. Except, of course, it wasn't. She hadn't succeeded in getting an interview. He had come to her. And he had invited the Cubberleys.

She switched out her light and waited for sleep. It took its time in coming but when it did it was deep. She dreamed of cries and muffled voices, and Charles and Margot and Rodolfo and Luisa processing through the bar in a sleepwalking conga line, and Alta's grin, floating in the air like the Cheshire Cat's smile, was leading them to the door. But in the morning she remembered none of it.

12

The following morning Tom sat at the table on his patio drinking coffee, Alta lay on the grass with her head on Badger's back and in a semicircle in front of them were Chico, Harpo and Groucho, recovered from Charles's drugged meat, panting and waiting patiently for new instructions.

Through half-closed eyes Tom surveyed the landscape. The lawn was weedy and pockmarked with yellow patches where the dogs urinated. The shrubbery was tangled and overgrown. The whole garden looked untended, which it was. A strong smell of honeysuckle and herbs drifted on the air. Nature was reclaiming her land.

'They'll be here soon,' he said. 'Be nice.'

Alta plucked at the grass. 'I'm always nice.'

'Be more nice.'

It was quiet on the hilltop behind their high walls. Only insects and rustling leaves and the panting dogs. Sometimes a bird cried from high above, gliding on invisible air currents. Alta watched them as they drifted above.

'Is he coming today as well?' she said.

'Not today. But soon.'

'I don't like him.'

'You don't like anyone.'

'I like Badger.' She leaned back and gave her dog a hug. He grunted, semi-asleep. Chico, Harpo and Groucho looked up but didn't move. In the distance, a car could be heard, its engine straining as it came up the hill. It stopped and faraway doors slammed.

'They're early,' said Tom. He finished his coffee and then opened his laptop and looked at the camera feed. 'It's them. I'll open the gate. Will you collect them?'

'If I have to.'

She stayed where she was.

'Well, go on then,' said Tom. 'They're in.'

'All right. I'm going.' Alta reached back onto the lawn, raised her hips as high as she could and then flipped upright, like a gymnast. She set off across the grass: a skinny waif with a scruffy haircut and a jaunty gait; her dagger strapped to the back of her belt, looking like a religious cross. Chico, Harpo and Groucho bounded on ahead. Badger stayed where he was, soaking up the sun.

Tom watched her disappear down the driveway and then suddenly sat forwards and shielded his eyes, staring not at Alta but at the path she had taken, as if there were something trailing behind her.

'Did you see that?' he said. But Badger yawned like an old soldier who had seen and done it all before.

At breakfast Germaine had found Luisa standing by the doors to the kitchen like a lost soldier – armed and ready to fight, but alone and in the wrong battleground.

'Is Claudio back?'

'No. He has been gone all night. We have called the *policía*.' She shook her head. 'This family is cursed.'

'The police will find him, or he'll come back on his own. I'm sure he's all right. We're driving up to the house now, the artist's. We'll keep an eye out for him in case he's up there.'

Germaine hadn't been sure what else to say. She didn't know enough about the mountains. Presumably they were dangerous at night.

They took the car and struggled up the winding incline until they reached the mound of earth that blocked their path and then walked the rest of the way. None of them looked at the shallow hollow that lay off to one side, the site of Charles's dog-fight the previous day. They stopped at the gate, waved at the camera and waited.

'I thought it might be too early,' Margot said after a while. 'Should we come back later?' But as she spoke the entire gate swung open. They looked at each other and at the open entrance and at the sweeping, tree-lined driveway beyond it.

'Shall we go in?' Germaine said. 'It is why we're here.'

'The dogs,' said Charles. 'Might bear a grudge. That sort of thing.'

'If you want to audition, you have to go in.'

They went in and the gate closed behind them. The driveway led them through the outer layer of woodland that surrounded the house, sweeping in curves, the land rising as they approached the house.

'Big place,' Charles said as they walked.

The woodland fell away and now, on either side of them, was a thick band of overgrown, flowering shrubbery, each plant growing into the next, a cloud of insects buzzing above the tangled flowers. It formed a second square around Tom's house, which was now visible, wide and low like a ranch, set in the centre of a large shingle surface. A huge swathe of neglected, unmown grass lay between the visitors and the shingle. The driveway continued in a straight line up to the front door, a depiction of perspective that might have come from one of Tom Hannah's own cartoons. The air tasted clean at that altitude and a warm breeze ruffled their clothes. It was very quiet.

'Peaceful,' Germaine said.

They walked on. So, was this really it, she wondered? An audience with Tom Hannah? The last time she had interviewed him was on her late-night television show, *Kiecke in Conversation*. That was before he'd moved to Spain. She should have brought the transcript with her to refresh her memory with their last official conversation.

'Oh no,' Margot said, interrupting Germaine's thoughts. 'Here they come.'

Germaine looked up and saw Chico, Harpo and Groucho racing into view from behind the back of the house, crossing the shingle and now galloping across the lawn. Margot stepped behind Charles and Charles stepped behind Germaine like a well-drilled comedy troupe.

'They look well enough,' Charles said. 'Where's that bloody girl?'

'There. She's coming.'

The dogs ran up to them and Germaine closed her eyes and stood still. If she couldn't see them, they couldn't see her – another coping mechanism. Strange how stress returned her directly to her childhood. She felt one of their muzzles push against her hand. She felt Margot or Charles bump into her and, when she opened her eyes, she saw that they were standing in a tight group of three with the dogs in a triangular formation around them. She and Charles and Margot had been corralled like sheep. They really were big dogs. She could smell their hot, wet breath rising up from their hanging tongues. Alta ambled up, wearing a t-shirt that read 'Binned & Beautiful', skinny jeans and old battered sandals. She circled round the dogs and rubbed each of their heads in turn before stopping in front of Germaine.

'So here you are,' she said.

'Yes,' said Germaine. 'Here we are.'

Alta looked at Charles. 'Hey, dog-poisoner, can you make animal voices?'

Charles looked down at her with some surprise. 'Can I what?'

'Can you make animal voices?' she said again. 'Can you talk in animal languages? Your fluffy-haired wife said you can.'

'I don't know. Never tried. I'm an actor, not Doctor bloody Doolittle.'

Alta laughed and then clicked her tongue. Chico, Harpo and Groucho broke ranks, turned and began to lollop back towards the house. 'Come on,' she said. 'You're early but we're ready for you.'

She led them up the driveway and then round to the back of the house and onto a wide patio. A door on the left, the door from which Tom had once fallen onto his knees, led to the kitchen. On the right were two tall and wide sliding patio windows that led into a conservatory. The dogs stayed outside while Alta ushered Charles, Margot and Germaine into the conservatory, bowing extravagantly as if she were their servant.

Beyond the conservatory was the living room where Tom was waiting for them. This was the room in which he had once lain on his face on the cherry wood floorboards, draped in his dressing gown with grass and earth up his nose and a deep-purple furrow around his neck. But today he was wearing a linen shirt, white shorts and sandals. His long hair was tied back and his beard hung like tangled wool from his face.

'Welcome to *El Callejón*,' he said. 'A pleasure to see you all.'

Germaine smiled. 'Thank you. I think the pleasure is mostly ours.'

Tom shook their hands while Alta curled up on the sofa and watched. Badger came in, jumped up and sat with her. She pulled him close as if he were a cushion.

'Charles and Margot, isn't it?' Tom said. 'Delighted you could make it. You're going to let me hear some of your sounds?' he said to Charles. 'I have a scenario you might be interested in. A few words. Do you do words?'

'Hyanh.'

Charles beamed and Margot gave his arm a squeeze.

Tom pointed at the spiral staircase that led up to the mezzanine level where a table was laid with food and drink. 'I thought we might eat. Then I could show you around.'

They followed him up the staircase and gathered around the table. The food, Germaine noted, was ready prepared and shop bought – and not from Las Sombras. It couldn't be cheap to have it brought in. There was plenty of wine and, while Tom refrained from alcohol, Charles and Margot loaded up on the Rioja. Germaine restricted herself to water. Booze and business, she had learned, did not mix. They took their food and drink onto the patio where they sat at the wrought-iron table.

'Nice place,' said Charles. 'You like the isolation, I take it?'

'I do. Although sometimes it's enforced. The roads become difficult in the winter. Sometimes villages are cut off from each other for days on end. Power goes down. The infrastructure is variable. Phones are out. No network coverage.'

'I wouldn't like that,' said Margot. 'What do people do?'

'I don't know. Tell stories? Fight? Make love? Like all remote communities, this is a place filled with myths and folktales. Legends and rumours. Lies and gossip.'

'And fairy tales,' Charles said. 'Like that Santa Claus Rodolfo was talking about.'

'Santa Claus?'

'He means the *Santa Compaña*,' Alta said. 'Don't you, dog poisoner?'

'Superstition,' Charles said. 'Facts – that's what we need. More facts, less fairy tales. Goblins and elves and gnomes and things. Tchah.'

'Is that one of your sounds?' said Alta.

'What?'

'That.'

Charles looked lost and Alta grinned.

Tom watched them all and when they had finished eating he said, 'Charles and Margot, would you mind waiting here while I borrow Germaine for a moment or two? Help yourself to everything. There's plenty. Alta will keep you company. Germaine, there's something I want to show you.'

Perhaps it was the reappearance of Chico, Harpo and Groucho but Germaine heard Tom's words more as instructions than an invitation. She had a strong feeling that Charles and Margot were being detained and that she was being escorted to whatever Tom had planned for her – because he had clearly planned something. Before they went Tom looked back at Alta and gave her a look. 'Remember.'

'I know. Be nice.'

13

Tom led Germaine back into the living room and up a second set of stairs to the first floor.

'So,' she said. 'This doesn't feel like a visit that you thought of only yesterday.'

'How do you mean?'

'It feels like you've been expecting us for a while. Preparing for us.'

'Well, perhaps I have. I did read all your emails, and listened to your voicemails, and read your texts.'

'But you didn't reply.'

'No. I didn't reply.'

They walked along a hallway and then through another door that led onto a short flight of steps, another door and then out onto the roof terrace where they had a 360-degree view of the sea beyond the trees, the sweep of the shoreline and the mountains rising up behind them.

'Sea and mountains,' Germaine said. 'You're very lucky.'

'I thought you'd like it. On a clear day you can see the Azores.'

'Really?'

'No, not really, but it's nice to think we might. It must be good for our health to gaze upon beauty. There must be some physical benefit. Life-prolonging – if you want such a thing.'

'I agree. Natural art. It's the environment into which our prehistoric ancestors were born. Our DNA responds to it. And I think you're right, it's good for the mind and the body. We should exercise through all our senses.'

At the far side of the terrace was Tom's studio, the door now repaired after Alta's forced entry eighteen months before. They went in.

'Home from home,' Tom said. 'Welcome to my world. Studio Hannah.'

Germaine sat by the desk and Tom dropped into a boxy leather sofa against the far wall. There was a table to one side with a laptop on it.

'To be frank, I don't visit my world much,' he said. 'I used to spend a lot of time getting drunk and that can take up a big chunk of the day. There's the time it takes to get drunk; the time spent being drunk; and then the recovering from being drunk phase. Very labour intensive.'

'But now you're on the wagon,' Germaine said. 'You have reclaimed your days. That's a good thing.'

'I owe it to Alta. She's an elemental force. She saved my life. Did you know that? Literally saved my life.'

'No, I didn't know that. She's quite young.'

'Older than she looks.' Tom studied her. 'Are you wondering what our relationship is?'

Germaine returned his gaze. 'Yes. But I'm not going to ask.'

'It's platonic.'

Germaine shrugged. 'You didn't have to say. I was wondering, not judging.'

'It's a teacher–pupil thing – and don't ask me who is whom, because I haven't worked it out yet.' He paused. 'You look tired, Germaine. Are you all right?'

Germaine frowned. Did she look tired? She felt fine. 'Was there something you wanted to show me. Because I'd like to talk to you too, about a book I'm writing…'

'Do you know anything about existentialism?'

Germaine gave up. She couldn't remember the last time she'd completed a sentence when referring to her book on new art. Maybe she should just hand out a leaflet. But Tom was watching her, apparently interested in hearing her answer, so she refocused. 'Existentialism. I only know the headline. Humans make sense of themselves in a senseless universe. There is no God; just get on with it and try to be nice.'

'I call it the horror of deciding to be what we're not.'

'Right.'

'I had an existential crisis after my mother died. My mother was the most honest person I ever knew. She truly experienced life. She didn't try to change it or shape or judge it or do anything with it. She just let it come to her. The good luck, the bad luck, the iniquities, the anomalies.'

His mother's dead. You should bear that in mind when you meet him.

'I interviewed her once,' Germaine said. 'She was a lovely person.'

'Yes. She died as she had lived: honestly, bravely, knowingly and without any fuss. She didn't try to make sense of it at all. Just blew with the breeze. I was there. I saw it. I would not have died in such an honest way. I always tried to make sense of it, and now the man I have become is not the man I am; is not the man I want to be; or should be.' He looked up at her. 'What do you think: are we what we are, or what we do?'

'Or what we say we do?'

Tom laughed. 'Neat. You and Alta are very alike – although she hates words. She says that as soon as people start talking they lie.'

176

'But she talks.'

'And she lies too. But she's been teaching me to feel life like an animal would, to follow my instincts and strip away the artifice. I am in the process of simplification. I am a work in progress. I am removing the artist – the profession, the occupation, the baggage – from Tom Hannah. Peeling the meat from the bone.'

Germaine shifted in her chair. Had he brought her to his studio to have a metaphysical discussion on the value of his life? If so, she was happy to engage. Maybe then she could slip in a word or two about her book. 'But we're not animals. Humans are fantasists – imaginers, dreamers. Capturing imaginings and hopes and aspirations is what we do. It's important. It's art. It's how we invent things. Animals don't do that – at least not to the same extent. Yes, we have occupations; things that we do. If you can paint, why wouldn't you paint? And why wouldn't somebody call you a painter if you did? It doesn't mean that's all you are. We are all lots of things; and we can be lots of different things at different moments.'

'I want to be just one thing: me.'

'Okay. I'm just saying there is not necessarily just one you. It depends on the moment and where you are and who you're with – and how you're feeling.' She smiled. 'We're complicated creatures.'

'And that's the problem. We can become too complicated. And I have. I have become defined by what I do. I am measured and graded and categorised in terms of my output. I am a commodity and my value is based on other people's perception of that commodity.' Tom leaned forwards. 'When you look at me, you don't see *me*. You see the Tom Hannah you want to see. The person who fits into your model of the world. That's not the real me.'

Germaine didn't want to sound rude, especially not to Tom

Hannah, but she was becoming bored with this conversation. 'I think that's just fame. Nobody sees the real anybody. You can always get off the grid for a while. You have the money.'

'I have been, and it doesn't work.'

He rummaged in the back of a drawer, produced a set of iLets and handed them to her. 'I have to hide them from Alta. She doesn't want me to use them. I'd like you to watch something. It's a personal thing and you don't have to if you don't want to. Alta's seen it. It might help explain what I'm talking about.'

'What is it?'

'It's my mother's death.'

Germaine looked at the iLets. They were newer than her standard version with more sensory pads than she had seen before. 'No,' she said. 'I don't want to see that.'

Tom was already typing something on the keyboard. 'Not even in the spirit of research? What makes an artist tick? It's not something I show to everyone. This is about as personal as it gets. But I'd like you to see it.'

Germaine put on the iLets. There was the normal moment of synchronisation and then she saw, in preternatural clarity, as if in the same room as they were, a hospital bed in which lay a woman she recognised – Barbara Hannah, Tom's mother. She recognised her, but only barely. Barbara looked very ill, her face was sunken, her hair pulled back in a way it hadn't been when she was well. She could hear her rattling breath and smell the odours in the hospice room.

'No.' Germaine took off the iLets. 'Thank you, but no.'

Tom looked at her and then nodded. He closed the laptop. 'I used to watch it every night. Again and again. And all the while I'd drink myself into unconsciousness. It became a habit, a comfort, an escape – a connection. A closeness to my mother and her precious last moment. Respect for the body – you ever heard that saying? It's what soldiers say at funerals. I don't know how many times I woke up downstairs on the sofa or on the floor or in the garden. Alta said she used to watch me. She was living in the garden. Does that sound weird? It should. Anyway, I used to watch my mother slip into nothingness every night. One moment alive, the next not alive. Alive, not alive. Alive, not alive. Not gone, not elsewhere, not in another room, not on her way to heaven – just stopped. Alive and alive and... stop. My sister calls it a dot. I call it a full stop.' He studied her, deciding how much to say next. 'I wanted that. I wanted that moment, that natural passing from one state to the next. I wanted not to be. I tried to kill myself. Properly. Not a cry for help. I meant to do it. But Alta saved me – or cursed me. I'm not sure which.'

Germaine let his words float around her mind. More soul-baring. There were too many bare souls in Las Sombras for her liking. 'You were grieving. In shock. It's natural to want to be with someone you love. Even if they've died.' She wondered if that was true. After all, she had no point of reference.

'Is it? I don't know if I knew how to be natural. That's why I want to get back to basics, to the essential me. I want to shed my skin like a snake. Slough off this thing called "artist" and rediscover Tom Hannah. And then become a new me; a simpler person I can recognise and someone my mother would recognise.'

Germaine sighed. 'This is all preamble, isn't it? To something.' Once again, the purpose of the meeting wasn't to talk about her project. She was being used for something else. She felt as she had in the restaurant with Borkmann, only this time she was sober. She suddenly wanted to go home, to return to her world, her life, away from the bruising contact with other human beings. Perhaps Alta was right. Words were levers to manipulate.

'Germaine, I want you to document my transition. The paring back. I think you, of all people, will appreciate it.'

'What are you going to pare back?'

'I'm going to erase the originals of all my work, including all my notebooks and diaries.'

'Erase?'

'Yes. And I'm going to release a virus that will delete as many instances of *Happy Family* as possible. I've had Richter Bird up here. One of the *Bird of Prey* people. Nice man. Bit sombre. Likes his Bauhaus and football. He's going to play around with stuff.'

'Richter Bird. So, that's who... Rodolfo mentioned someone. You're playing with fire working with him, Tom. He's a money-grabber. A hacker for hire. It won't just be about deleting your game. He'll rob all your users in the process. Is that what you want? To work with a criminal?'

'He won't do that. He's being paid more than enough to do exactly what he's been asked to, and only what he's been asked to do.'

'Really? In my opinion you're wrong. I think I have some of his "stuff" on my phone already.'

'He's testing, that's all. On a limited basis.'

Germaine nodded. 'Yes. On Rodolfo's wifi. He was down there. Now I have a cuckoo in my game. *Your* game that I have bought and paid for.'

'I can get that fixed. Look, forget Richter Bird for the moment. Seriously. The "how" is not important. It's what I want to do, that matters. The outcome. So, tell me, what do you think?'

'About what? Getting rid of all your work? The originals? Your masters and safeties? Why would you do that? I don't see the point. If you've had enough, just walk away. Why be so dramatic?'

'Is that how you see it? Dramatic?'

Germaine hesitated. 'I don't know. I don't mean to down-play how important this is to you – and to me. And to all your fans and followers. But you've sprung this on me. I don't know what I think.'

'You need to understand, it's like an anchor dragging me down. I can't stay afloat. It's like life is drowning me, with everything clinging to me like wet clothes. I've got to break free and the only way to do that is to throw it all away.'

'Did you tell all this to Gerard when he came to see you?'

'Yes.' Tom looked at her. 'So, again, what do you say?'

Germaine looked around his studio. What did she say? She should say 'no' or 'stop' or 'for goodness sake, don't be such a fool'. But for the moment she felt curiously disengaged. Perhaps she really was tired, too tired to feel anything. She shook her head.

'I don't know, Tom. It all seems so unreal.'

He frowned. 'But it's not. It's as real as anything has ever been in my life. I mean that. Come on, let's go and talk to Charles, I'm hoping that he's going to be the voice of the virus.'

14

Back at the patio Alta was lying on the grass. She looked up when Tom and Germaine returned. 'I was nice,' she said.

Tom nodded. 'Good.'

'Alta was telling us an interesting story about how she likes to walk through the villages at night and look into people's windows,' said Margot. 'Apparently she sees all sorts of things.'

'I'm sure she does. Shall we walk and talk – take a stroll to the rose garden?'

Alta jumped up and collected the dogs around her. 'I'll lead,' she said.

Germaine stood off to one side. Her mind was running through the implications of what Tom had told her. Destroy all the originals? That would mean the entire collection of draft *Scraps* cartoons, published and unpublished, all his notes and other art work, the *Happy Family* cartoon strip (never published), the roughs for the *Happy Family* game graphics, detailed layerings, technical notes, colour palettes, working scenarios, photographs and who knew what else.

It was a nihilistic act and she wondered if, in itself, it could be described as an act of art. Perhaps new art. Was that why

Tom wanted her to document his 'transition'? As a piece of art? However he saw it, Tom was a fool to involve Richter Bird.

The group was on the move. They strung out in a procession – Alta and Badger in the lead, Harpo and Chico either side, Groucho at the back, Tom, Charles, Germaine and Margot in between. They followed Alta across the lawn, through grass that was long and meadow like, and it might have been a peaceful and innocent walk but for the sense of menace created by the dogs.

'We're like school children,' Margot said as they wound through the obstacles. 'Take a partner and form a crocodile.'

'At my school,' said Germaine. 'We had real crocodiles.'

They reached the shrubbery and then tracked along its border, circling the house until they came to another path which led through the bushes, which in turn led to a concealed rose garden. The bushes were tall and woody and thorny, and needed pruning and deadheading. But the scent was rich and intoxicating and the plants aggressively entwined with their neighbours. Germaine thought it looked like a floral orgy.

Alta stopped by a bench and Tom turned to face them as if he were their tour guide. The wind died down in that part of the garden, unable to penetrate the tall shrubbery on either side of them and the wood beyond, leaving the air flat and quiet.

'I thought we might do your audition here, Charles,' Tom said. 'I like the natural acoustics.'

'Right-ho.' Charles's tone said he'd do it anywhere Tom liked.

From his pocket, Tom took a folded piece of paper. 'I'm introducing a new character into *Happy Family*,' he said. 'It's a character that will appear in every game, no matter what level you are at, or what scenario you have chosen.'

'Oh, Charles,' Margot said sitting down on the bench, and

Germaine knew that what she really meant was, *'Oh, Charles, maximum exposure. Think of all the royalties and the spin-offs.'*

'It's a kind of authority figure,' Tom continued. 'Part of the game's infrastructure. A metacharacter, if you will. Imagine that the executive control in your brain had a voice. That sort of thing.'

'What does he look like? I assume it is a he?' Charles said.

'He looks exactly like you.'

'Me?'

'Yes. Or me. Or Margot. Or anyone. It's an amorphous character.'

'Hyanh.'

'Exactly. There are not a lot of lines and no body noises, I'm afraid. And for today I want you to say just one word.' Tom handed Charles the piece of paper. 'And I want you to say it with a big smile on your face. I want to hear your big, big smile in that word.' He sat down on the bench next to Margot.

Charles read the piece of paper. He looked back at Tom. 'Just this?'

'Just that. With a smile. Big smile. When you're ready.'

Charles cleared his throat and looked around at them all. Germaine and Alta drew away, giving him his stage. The dogs were quiet. Alta sat on the path. A bee buzzed. A bird called. A grasshopper hopped.

'I haven't really warmed up,' Charles said. 'Probably should do a few vocal exercises.'

Tom spread his arms wide. 'It's your show.'

Charles opened his mouth wide, then closed it tight, and repeated that manoeuvre several times. Alta laughed.

'Alta,' Tom said.

Charles stuck out his tongue and waggled it up and down, making a lapping sound. The dogs looked up with interest, possibly wondering what Charles was drinking in mid-air.

'Me-me-me, mo-mo-mo, muh-muh-muh,' Charles said. 'Bo-wubba, bo-wubba, bo-wubba. She sells sea shells on the sea shore. Peter Piper picked a peck of pickled pepper.'

Charles placed his hand on his diaphragm. He took a deep breath. He shuffled his feet sideways, spreading his legs. He looked at the ground.

'Just do it, you idiot,' Alta shouted.

'Alta.'

Charles took another deep breath, let it out slowly and then, with an enormous beatific smile on his face, he looked up and said, '*Goodbye*'.

'The voice of the virus,' said Charles. 'Well, I've played worse parts.'

They were in the car and Margot was driving them back to Las Sombras. 'It's marvellous,' she said. 'It's a job, Charles. An opportunity. You'll be famous.'

'Or infamous,' said Germaine.

'How so?'

'Your voice will be the last thing a player hears before their game is wiped out. Is that good?'

'It's only a game.' Margot said.

'Only? Mrs Cubberley, you have no idea.'

'It doesn't matter what they bloody hear,' Charles said. 'I've got the role.'

Germaine didn't say any more. Charles would go back the following day to sign a contract for the shortest role of his career. Would she go back to begin her role as witness to Tom's act of artistic nihilism; the destruction of his work? She wasn't sure she could.

They pulled up along the cobbled street near the hotel. The

earlier layer of milky white clouds had burned off and the sky was blue, the sun was shining and there was a crisp, clean, salty breeze running up from the harbour. Germaine wanted to lean on the harbour wall, inhale the sea air and decoke her lungs. She noted with interest that for once she didn't want a cigarette. Perhaps the sea air was good for her. She should move to the coast, she thought. Buy a straw hat, open a shop and sell local art. Hang washing on a line and carry baskets full of fruit and flowers and buy freshly baked bread every morning. Have a bicycle and a dog – no, a cat and…

'Look out.'

Margot took Germaine's arm and guided her back onto the pavement. A taxi was rumbling down the hill, but it was hardly surprising that Germaine had been caught unawares – who would expect traffic in Las Sombras?

'It's him,' Charles said.

'It might not be,' Germaine said. 'I'm expecting a visitor too.'

They waited and watched the taxi pull up outside the hotel.

'Bloody, bloody bastard.'

'Charles, please.'

The door nearest to them opened and Catharina stepped out. She stood up like an exotic plant that had suddenly sprung free from its container. A cloud of perfume sweetened the air. She looked around, got her bearings, saw Germaine and smiled.

'Thank God,' she said.

'Welcome to Las Sombras.'

They hugged while the taxi driver took Catharina's luggage from the boot and took it into reception.

'This is Charles and Margot,' Germaine said. 'And this is Catharina Caboulet. My agent – and my friend.'

'Hello and hello,' Catharina said. 'Excuse me.' She turned and paid the taxi driver, waved away the change and watched him drive away. Then she smiled at Germaine. 'Yes. Your friend.'

But Germaine was now staring beyond Catharina. And so was Charles.

'Hyanh.'

He must have slipped out of the passenger side of the taxi nearest the hotel, unnoticed and without ceremony. Catharina followed their gazes and said, 'Oh yes. And this is Robin…'

'Rix!' Charles said with a half howl, half yip.

'We shared a taxi from the airport.'

'All the way from Madrid?' said Germaine.

'Good God, no. We flew to A Coruña Airport. Madrid is miles away.'

'Oh, of course. You weren't on a Borkmann budget break.'

Germaine looked at Robin Rix. Until that moment, she had imagined he would be a similar type to Charles, whose faded good looks and buried charm aligned with her impression of what a middle-aged actor should look like. She had assumed that Rix would be cast from the same mould but perhaps with a more roguish look, a devilish twinkle in his eye, a twirling moustache. A cravat, even.

No.

Robin Rix looked like a tortoise. Or rather his head did. Germaine peered at him more closely and yes, there was no doubt about it, the overall impression from the neck up was that of a tortoise. Without the shell, of course. Was it the skin, she wondered? Or the eyes? Those wet rheumy eyes that met hers and then slithered over her body, charting and recording her dips and curves. Or the mouth? Yes, the mouth definitely played a part. She wanted to examine him more closely but there was no time to do that. A movement of heat and air beside her indicated that Charles Cubberley was in motion, striding at full speed towards the hotel's entrance.

'Charles,' Margot called but he took no heed. He entered the hotel and was gone.

They all waited but no other sounds were heard. No slamming of doors, no shouting, no explosions. No loading of rifles.

'Have I missed something?' said Catharina.

'The entire first season,' said Germaine.

Robin Rix detached himself from the wall. 'Hello, Margie.'

He had exactly the right voice for a tortoise, Germaine thought. Small yet fruity.

'Oh, Robin.' Margot shook her head and walked past him into the hotel.

15

'They wear lipstick, you know,' said Catharina.

They were sitting at a table outside the hotel bar, sharing a bottle of Cava. Across the road was the harbour wall. Rodolfo's plastic chair by the glass bottom boat mooring was empty. Margot and Charles were nowhere to be seen, nor was Robin Rix. In fact, there was no one to be seen at all. No Luisa, no villagers, no stray animals – only gulls waiting for a rubbish bag to tear open.

'Who do?' said Germaine.

'The seagulls. See? The red marks on the end of their yellow beaks. They look so prissy.' She sat back and studied Germaine over her glass. 'You seem different.'

'In what way?'

'I don't know. Sunnier.'

'Tom Hannah said I look tired.'

'More womanly.'

Germaine laughed. 'I'm not pregnant.'

'Happier. That's the word: happier. Perhaps a bit tired too, but in a nice way.'

'Happy? Well, I wonder if I am. I shouldn't be. This is the dark night of my soul. Tom Hannah has no interest in my book. He's focused on destroying all his art and being reborn like some hairy phoenix rising from the ashes. All the originals – worth millions – are to go. And he's going to infect *Happy Family* with a virus – some variant of the *Bird of Prey* thing – which I think is almost certainly illegal. So, all the things that give me joy in this world are about to be taken away: my career, Tom's art, Mr Venus. Puff: up in smoke. Probably, literally up in smoke.'

'Mr Venus?'

'A salamander.'

'I see.' Catharina poured more wine. 'Let's come back to that one.'

Germaine laughed. 'So, there you have it. All of it. I do feel happy, but I don't know why. Being here – in this place with these people – it should be everything I detest. But, it's not. I feel good. You know I have no family. I don't bond. I don't attach. I am a product of the Motherhood. All I have ever had – and all I have ever wanted to have – is my brain and my body and art. Nothing else. Well, my apartment. And my phone. But that's it. Oh, and distance, of course.'

'Distance?'

'From everything. The past, people, the awfulness of life. But now, annoyingly and against my better judgement, you're right. I find myself in a happy state. It's galling. I can't bear the thought of what Tom is about to do, yet at the same time I find myself enjoying the sun and the breeze… and sitting here with you.'

'I'll drink to that.'

'Or I'm thinking about Charles or Margot, or Claudio who's run away, or Luisa who is broken and bitter, and even Rodolfo who is like someone who was born inside out. Why do I even care about these people? I've known them less than a week. And Alta – she is so fascinating. I would love the chance to speak to her properly. Honestly, Catharina, what is going on? I've become a people-person and it's driving me nuts.'

'Not to mention your pet newt.'

'Salamander. But, yes. Mr Kevin Venus and Rachel. I used to play *Happy Family* every day but now all this other reality is getting in my way – and I like it.'

'Kevin and Rachel are...?'

'Game characters.'

'Not pets?'

'My parents, actually.'

'Right...'

'I used to be interested in people purely in terms of their creative ability. It meant I didn't have to think about them as human beings so much as... as artists. I could focus on what they did; not what they were. I didn't want to know about their messy emotional stuff – or if I did, we could talk about it through their work. Like a cipher. La Jaune said she knew the way to have sex with me was to paint my portrait. I thought she meant I was an art-slut but now I know she meant that I needed an abstraction – to be one step removed from reality; keep looking at the art and ignore what's going on underneath it. Does that make any sense?'

'Not really.'

'Good.' Germaine picked up her glass and drained it. 'But now here I am, down in the mud. And on top of all that, I think I might have accidentally given up smoking.'

'I have never heard you talk so much.'

'I know, it must be the sea air. Everybody's at it – revealing their innermost thoughts.'

'I like it.'

They sat in silence for a moment and then Germaine said, 'So. Why have you come to this remote, rocky outcrop when you could be somewhere a lot nicer?'

'Why do you think?'

'I have been wondering. Do you want Tom Hannah as your client?'

Catharina put on her sunglasses and looked out to sea. 'Wrong – well, I would like that, but that's not why I'm here. I know you hate hearing about people's private lives, but six weeks ago I asked my partner of five years if he would move out. He's a film producer; I'm a literary agent. We're a match made in heaven, but I broke us up. He couldn't believe it. I'm not sure I can, either. Not yet. Not fully. But it's done. I made a decision and now I'm single. What do you think of that?'

Germaine thought she was becoming used to these confidences. 'I am an outline, colour me in,' she said.

'Pardon?'

'I was thinking about something Gerard Borkmann said. About life and art. About people. About me.' It used to be so simple. Art was good; reality was bad; keep the two apart. Vivid and clean; dull and dirty. A good place and a bad place. But now she had to wonder, which was which? She smiled. 'Anyway, what do I think? I think you had your reasons and you made a choice. That's all any of us can do. And I think it will be all right. You'll both be sad for a while, but time will go by and things will be different, and then – who knows? Nothing is written. Anything is possible.'

'That sounds very wise, Germaine. You have become a people-person. Now, the next thing you must say is that there are plenty more fish in the sea.'

'Well, you are by the ocean. Is that what you want? To find a new fish?'

'Would that be wrong?'

'Not at all, but I'm not sure this is the place…'

'Germaine, I'm going to say something, and you mustn't laugh or look at me in a funny way or go quiet and not

192

say anything. But especially you mustn't laugh. You have to be kind.' She leaned forwards and took off her sunglasses. 'Remember, don't laugh.'

'I won't. But at what?'

'At me.' She opened her eyes wide. 'Look. What can you see?'

Germaine leaned forwards, too, and peered at Catharina's face.

'What am I looking for?'

'Just tell me what you can see. In my eyes. Don't mess this up. I've rehearsed it a hundred times.'

Germaine looked into her eyes and then leaned back with a half-puzzled smile on her face.

'I can see me,' she said.

'Thank God for that. Good. Yes. Then you can see why I came all the way to this remote, rocky outcrop when I could have been somewhere a lot nicer.'

It took a moment for Germaine to understand. And when she did, she couldn't help but laugh.

'Oh. Am I a fish?'

'You are *the* fish. I'll paint your portrait too,' Catharina said. 'If it will help.'

In his bedroom at the top of the hotel, Rodolfo was packing. He had spent most of the day with a local policeman trying to organise a search for his son. Now he zipped up his bag, slung it on his back and went down the stairs, through the reception area and out onto the cobbled street – only to find Luisa blocking his way yet again.

'Where are you going?' she hissed at him. 'You can't run away.'

'I'm not running away. I am off to find my son.'

'You won't escape the gallows.'

'Gallows? What century are you living in? I have to find Claudio. I'll find him and bring him home and then we'll find Teresa.'

'She's dead and you know it. If I had the strength, I would kill you myself.'

'Fine. I wouldn't have to hear your voice again.'

'You'd hear me in hell.'

Rodolfo pushed past her and set off up the hill while Luisa fumed and bristled and seethed until Germaine tapped her on the shoulder and said, 'Excuse me, could I get the key to my room?'

And in another part of the hotel Charles and Margot were talking in hushed, urgent tones in their room while Robin Rix listened at their door.

'What were you doing even talking to him?' Charles was saying.

'He accosted me in the corridor.'

'Accosted you? I'll accost him. Did he touch you?'

'No, just a peck on the cheek. I couldn't stop him. He's very quick.'

'Bloody bastard. A peck on the cheek? I'll peck him on the cheek. I'll peck his bloody head off. Did you tell him about the audition? Did you tell him I had already done it? That he's too late?'

'Yes. I told him all about it.'

'What did he say?'

'When?'

'When? In the corridor. How many "whens" are there? He's only been here an hour.'

Outside their room Rix's snooping was interrupted by Germaine and Catharina on their way to Germaine's room.

He looked at them and his lips parted and created a gap in his face. It was a smile. 'I wasn't sure if this was my room or not,' he said. 'Probably not.' He slipped past them and Germaine noticed a greasy mark where his forehead had been pressed against the door. She raised her eyebrows at Catharina who said, 'We were on the same flight. Adjacent seats. It was a long journey.'

Back in the room Charles curled up on the bed and Margot cradled his head on her lap.

'Let's go home,' she said. 'Let's go home and forget all about this nonsense.'

'I'm going to kill him.'

'No, you're not,' she said, stroking his head. 'No, you're not.'

'He'll never go away. Even if you tell him, he'll never go away. He's that type.'

'Shhh.'

Margot closed her eyes and carried on stroking his head but if she thought she was lulling Charles into a state of tranquillity, she was wrong. He stared at the wall as if seeing a scene projected onto it and his eyes grew wider and wilder as he watched.

Outside, looking down on the hotel from the hillside were Tom, Alta and Badger. They watched Rodolfo argue with Luisa and then set off up the hill. They saw Germaine and Catharina talk to Luisa and then go inside. They saw Germaine close the curtains of her bedroom window. They saw Rix emerge from the hotel and sit on the bench, open a map and refer to it while looking up the hill.

'Who are these new people?' Alta said.

'I don't know,' Tom said. 'But it's getting busy down there.'

'The pale boy, Claudio, he's run away.'

'Rodolfo and Teresa's son. Do you know where he is?'

'Badger will find him. When is the other one coming?'

'Soon…'

'I don't like these people. I'll be glad when it's only us again.'

'I know. We should go home now.'

Alta looked down at the harbour wall and the waves rolling over the rocks beyond. From where they stood the sea looked deep. 'Thomas Arthur Stevenson Hannah,' she said.

'Yes?'

'I was saying your name.'

'I know.'

She turned and looked up at him. 'I'll always find you,' she said.

'Will you? That's nice. When?'

'When I need to.'

'Are you going somewhere?'

'No.'

Tom nodded. 'Good. Well, I don't know what you're talking about but thank you. Anyway, we have a big day tomorrow. An end and a new beginning.'

Alta nodded but her smile made her look sad.

Germaine and Catharina lay on Germaine's bed at an angle to each other, looking up at the ceiling. It was getting dark outside. They had lain there a long time, dozing, blonde and black hair mixed up, skin merging into skin.

'You remember when you came to my apartment?' said Germaine.

'I do. But, before then, I had a feeling…'

'I ran to the bathroom…'

196

'I wasn't sure, you know, I'd not really thought in that way…'

'And washed my face with soap…'

'But you kept looking so… so something.'

'That's my tip. Nothing smells nicer than soap on skin.'

'It was… new. The feeling. Whatever you call it. The attraction. For me. I mean…'

'I suppose I was hoping.'

'For a long time I'd imagined… us.'

'Imagined what?'

'Situations…'

'When we'd…'

'The things we've done and said. You'd be amazed.'

'Would I?'

They looked at each other.

'This would make a good game,' Germaine said.

'I don't do newts.'

'Salamanders. Don't tease me. *Happy Family* is my safe place, my happy place. I don't want Tom to take it away – for selfish reasons. It's part of my,,, barrier.'

'You don't need a barrier. The real world can be your happy world.'

'Maybe. I don't know how I feel about what Tom's going to do. What he's taking away. There's a snail in my game and I sometimes wonder if that's a coincidence. Because I'm like that. I hide in my shell.'

'I don't like to think of you as a snail. And *Scraps* and all the other artwork Tom has? Is that part of your shell too?'

'Yes. All the published editions will remain, but the original artwork and the sketches will be destroyed. Or so he says. Lost forever. Tom will be killing himself as much as his cartoon characters. I suppose that's the idea. But he'll take a piece of me too. I'd rather see them in a museum.'

'How will he destroy it?'

'Burn it, I imagine. With Alta dancing around with a pitch-fork.'

'Starting tomorrow?'

'I think so. He's asked me back.'

'Is it really worth millions… and don't look at me like that. It's a lot of money to put on a bonfire. Could we call the police?'

'I doubt it.'

Catharina stretched. 'Why is he doing it?'

'It's existence versus essence.'

'Oh, that old thing.'

'He wants to just be a man called Thomas Arthur Stevenson Hannah – that's his base existence – and then start again. The thing that he is now, the artist, that's the essence he wants to get rid of. It's Sartre-speak. I think Borkmann had already thought this through when I met him in Liège. He said, "treat it as an exercise in existentialism". He wanted me to bring Tom back from the brink. I should have listened more closely. Instead I got drunk.'

Germaine sighed and sat up. 'It's ironic. I was disappointed in Tom because I thought he was thinking about himself at the expense of others, but I'm just the same. He's hidden inside himself, as I am – just on a bigger, more physical scale. The walls, the woods, the shrubbery, the house – I thought they were meant to symbolise a cartoon frame, or even a screen on a smart phone, but they're not. It's a bubble he's put himself in. He's on the inside looking out and I'm on the outside looking in. We're both alone in our bubbles, our thoughts bouncing off the sides, the echoes getting louder and louder, bigger and bigger…'

Catharina put her arms around Germaine. 'Hey. I'm in your bubble now. If this were a game, the *Happy Family* game, what would we do? I don't mean now. I mean what would we do to stop Tom doing what he's about to do tomorrow?'

'If this were a *Happy Family* game? I'm not sure. I thought I wanted a book deal, a new job, some validation of… of what I do. But right now, I don't know. If Tom goes ahead the world wouldn't stop turning. Nobody would die. It would just be some drawings and a game that were lost. But…'

'But?'

'But the world would be a poorer place without them.'

'So, in the game we'd save the art and get a book deal. And you'd get the girl, of course.'

Germaine laughed. 'Of course. I always do.'

They sat in silence, thinking, and then Germaine said, 'You know that nice thing you did outside with me? When you made me see myself in your eyes? Tom talked about something similar, but he got it wrong. He thinks I see him as something he's not – but actually, I think I reflect what he is. Borkmann said I'm Tom's context. He said I authenticate him. Perhaps that's what I should do: let him see himself as I see him. Not as an artist, but as a man. A great man. Or, as Borkmann put it bluntly when I met him in Liège, be Tom's shock of realisation.'

16

Night had come to the mountains. The sky was cloudless, moonless, and a thousand, a million, a billion specks of light were scattered across its darkness. More stars than not, it seemed. Below, the mountains were mostly silent. A few large mammals moved quietly and furtively, intent on their purpose. Insects scavenged and bred and multiplied. Birds slept or took to the wing, sharing airspace with bats, in search of smaller animals who had been foolish enough to forget that death can come suddenly and violently from above.

But mostly the mountains were dark and silent and gave the impression of emptiness. These were lonely places at night. Familiar dusty trails became black gaps on the ground. Trees and woodland that by day were comforting landmarks became shapes of fearful anticipation when the sun went down. Twigs underfoot that snapped unnoticed when the sky was bright exploded like rifle shots in the dark.

Claudio was huddled in a combe, hiding beneath hard, prickly foliage away from the main road – a long way from the main road. He had strayed from the path and now in the dark he was lost, halfway through the second night away from his warm, safe bed. His pale skin was luminous and shone from behind the broken bush. He had been crying. His face was damp and greasy. His clothes were becoming a home for ants and earwigs and spiders and other small, wriggly, invasive creatures that saw no difference between him and the shrub beneath which he shivered. But there were other predators in the night who would see him as easy meat, who would sense his fear, his vulnerability, his willingness to give up and roll over. Foolish Claudio, because just a few hundred metres away, on a higher slope, his father, Rodolfo, who was seeking his lost son, was also settling down for the night.

Rodolfo: a man reviled and loathed by his sister-in-law. He seemed to have his own fears this night. He had drawn a circle on the ground along with a chalk-drawn six-pointed star. It was the Seal of Solomon and he was in a Solomon's Circle. If he had had a black cat with him, no doubt he would have tied it to a nearby tree. Was he dreading the appearance of the *Santa Compaña* whose visitation would imply his death was due? Almost certainly. The All Souls Procession; the *Estadea*; the Ancient Host. How the myth of spirits of the dead walking on the haze of darkness searching for the lonely, the lost and the unfortunate thrust dread into his heart. Rodolfo planned to spend the night lying face down. No scouts from the *Estadinha* would look on his face. The cruel leader of that procession would have to find her recruit elsewhere. Rodolfo was a more seasoned camper than Claudio. He had blankets and provisions, but his eyes were as wide as his son's and they both stared into the night with fear on their faces.

At the base of the mountains, where the land met the sea, in her house on the corner of the cobbled street, Luisa lay on a hard, narrow bed, her long black hair pinned up beneath a hairnet and her face lathered with harsh-scented cream. She gazed at her ceiling, listening intently for any unnatural sounds

– such as a sweaty slap–slap–slapping of feet on her wooden steps. Her lip was curled in its habitual expression of contempt and her hand moved to the heavy metal candlestick she had waiting beside her bed. Should anyone be tempted to find her in the night and smother her bony face with a pillow they would find they had a fight on their hands.

Across the road in the hotel, Margot lay on her back, her arms spread out, taking up three-quarters of the bed, breathing heavily but not yet at the point of snorting and snoring which was her nightly habit. Next to her Charles lay awake on his side, clinging to his slender space on the bed. He too watched the darkness, his lips moving with his thoughts. He had the look of a man beset with a fever. He no longer looked like the Charles who had arrived in Las Sombras with such high hopes.

Perhaps the object of his thoughts was Robin Rix, who slept like a baby in his room along the corridor. He had had a profitable day. A free ride to Las Sombras; a stolen kiss from Margot; and the promise of a lucrative contract in the morning. He had already scouted the landscape, found the fastest route to Tom Hannah's house, and if his dreams turned to Charles and the harm he would do him by taking his job (and, who knew, perhaps his wife), then they must have been amusing dreams because he, of all the people in the hotel that night, had a smile on his face and slept with contented sighs.

Further along the corridor Germaine and Catharina were asleep together in Germaine's bed. Catharina had scarcely been into her own room. No walk of shame for her in the morning – her cases and toiletries were next to Germaine's. She was wearing a t-shirt with the words 'Binned & Busted' printed on it. Their legs were tangled together, and they shifted and moved against each other, still unused to their new proximity, their rhythms, their ways of sleeping. They turned frequently and muttered, reaching out for one another, pushing the covers away and then pulling them closer. Germaine hadn't smoked for more than twenty-four hours. Now she was dreaming. A shifting mosaic of images and scenes and half-formed story-lines. But the theme was an approaching event. Something unpleasant. Something nasty. Where were Mr and Mrs Venus when she needed them? Were her dreams of reality now more vivid than her waking imaginings?

Out into the night and back up the hill, back to *El Callejón* where Chico, Harpo and Groucho lay on their padded rugs on the patio. It was warm enough outside and they had no fear of dark things in the night. They had no fear of anything. They lay as they had lain as puppies: a single furry mass of breathing meat and muscle. Inside, the creature called Badger slept on the sofa, also snoring. The mountains were not silent at all if all the snoring were to be taken into account. What failure in natural selection allowed prey to signal its defencelessness by snoring?

Above, in his bedroom, Tom Hannah was wearing his secret iLet-Inserts which made his eyes ache, but Alta had found his standard iLets again and broken them, so he had no choice. He was watching in high definition 3D augmented reality the moment his mother died – again and again and again. Like Claudio, his face was damp. He had a bottle of whisky by his side. Old habits die hard and some people die harder. He had spent the evening preparing for his transition to a new, unencumbered Tom Hannah, sitting in his garage amongst all his original artwork. He had arranged for it to be brought to Spain in a stack of especially constructed fire-retardant boxes. There were sixty-three boxes, stacked in seven tiers of nine. They were on a pallet on the power-assisted flatbed trolley.

Alta – who Rodolfo had called the devil, the *intruso*, the thief, the pusher-in, the mother bitch, the witch – kept watch. She had left the house and prowled the garden, too quiet to disturb even her guard dogs. She walked through the shrubbery and into the woods and climbed the walls and entered the country-side beyond, walking up the hill, passing Claudio and Rodolfo and all the other sleeping creatures. Alta had learned long ago how to tread silently through other people's dreams. After an hour of walking she reached a small plateau, a place from which she could look both down on the village and up to the long sweep of the mountain road and the point it disappeared over the horizon. She looked intently at that point as if, like Germaine in her dream, she sensed something was coming. Something unpleasant. Something nasty.

Gerard Borkmann bounced along the treacherous mountain roads in his hire car. It was long after midnight and he had been travelling for many hours. Soon his headlights would appear as a tiny star on the point on the mountain ridge at which Alta had been staring, and he would begin the long descent towards Las Sombras. But that was an hour away and Alta will have returned to her bed by then. In the meantime, Borkmann battled on.

Despite the warmth of spring turning towards summer he was wrapped in a heavy overcoat. He coughed and spluttered and popped painkillers. He had changed since Germaine had last shared a meal with him. There was less of him. He had always been spare and lean, in the same way that a polished hardwood baseball bat is spare and lean, but now his skin had lost its sheen, it was sallow and papery and looked as if it might split. His face had sunk, his eyes seemed larger, his teeth more prominent. It was as if he was burning away, like meat on a stick, until all that would remain would be the bone.

His journey was windy and dangerous and he drove badly. His windows were wound up and misted over. He hit every pothole and lump and bump along his path. He weaved from one side of the road to the other, taking bends too fast, slowing when he didn't need to, accelerating when he shouldn't. Frequently his tyres were off the road and on the sloping scrubland that led to ravines and valleys. He jerked the steering wheel this way and that, his teeth clamped together, as if passing responsibility to fate. He would either make it or he would not. So far, he was making it.

He crested the ridge, the top of the mountain and began the zig-zagging descent. The sky lightened and he could have seen, had he opened his window to clear the condensation, the lower slopes of the mountain silhouetted against the broad expanse of sky and sea. But he didn't open his window and so he missed it. He missed the calls and cries of rising birds wheeling high above him. He missed the scents of the plants as they opened their heads ready for a new day. He missed the taste of the distant sea on the breeze and the damp odour of drying dew. He missed it all as he nearly missed every turn of the road.

At just before five o'clock in the morning, with the new daylight still tinged with a touch of the night and Las Sombras less than twenty minutes away, Borkmann stopped at the turn to Tom Hannah's house. His car came to a messy halt on the rough, dusty scrubland. He switched off his engine and sat back in his seat, closed his eyes and breathed as slowly as he could. He sat there for some time, neither asleep nor fully awake, until he was startled back into life by somebody tapping on his window.

It was Rodolfo.

Rodolfo stood back and waited respectfully while Borkmann clambered out of his car. Tall and skinny though Rodolfo was, he was shorter by several inches than the cadaverous Borkmann who emerged onto the road encased in his overcoat like a grub still in its cocoon. Neither man said anything at first. Borkmann stared down the road towards the village and the sea beyond, while Rodolfo continually scanned his surroundings. But at last, as if by mutual consent, they took stock of each other.

'Are you thirsty?' Rodolfo said. 'I have some water if you want.'

Borkmann shook his head. 'I'm tired. I'll get some sleep soon.' He coughed. It was a small cough, but it shook his body. 'Do you have it?' he said, wiping his mouth.

Rodolfo put his rucksack on the ground, opened it and took out a rectangular wooden box. It was scuffed and worn, and the catch and hinges were cheap metal. It looked like a box that a compendium of games would be kept in; a box handed down from one generation to the next.

'Have you checked it?' Borkmann said.

'*Sí*. It is as it should be.'

Borkmann put the box on the bonnet of his car, opened it and looked in. He studied its contents for a moment and then closed it again, glancing around as he did so, as if he expected to see someone looking over his shoulder. He put the box onto the back seat of his car and took an envelope from his inside pocket and gave it to Rodolfo.

'This is as it should be too.'

'*Gracias*.'

'Thank you for coming out so early. I appreciate it.'

'I am here already. I am looking for my son. He has gone. Run away. So, I am out here looking for him.' He shrugged. 'Teresa, she has gone too. I don't know where. She hears about her father and she goes. Maybe. I don't know. Her crazy sister thinks I have… you know.' Rodolfo mimed slitting his own throat. 'So, we argue all the time. And now Claudio. It's not good.'

'I'm sorry. I'll keep an eye out. If you need anything. Money. Help. Let me know.'

Rodolfo patted Borkmann's arm. 'I will find him today. If not, then I will ask.'

'And everyone else? They are all here?'

'The nice blonde lady and the actor and his wife. And the tortoise man, *tortuga*, and the glamour one.'

'Glamour one?'

'*De moda*. Very nice.'

Borkmann sighed. 'I don't know who they are. Are they with Ms Kiecke?'

'The woman is. More than with her. *Amantes*, I think.'

'Really?'

Rodolfo slung his bag back onto his back. 'I have to go now. You sure you're all right? You don't look good.'

'I'm fine. Tired. Good luck. I hope you find Claudio soon.' Borkmann looked at his watch. 'Is your truck ready? Come back at lunchtime. I'll make sure the gate is open.'

Rodolfo walked up the hill and Borkmann eased himself back into the car, pushed his seat back and looked at his watch. 'Time for a nap,' he said. He dropped the seat and reached across to the back and lifted the box onto his lap. He was asleep as soon as he closed his eyes.

17

It was barely two hours after Borkmann fell asleep that Alta shouted, 'There's a man at the gate.' She was sitting next to Badger on the sofa, feeding him cheese and watching the CCTV on Tom's widescreen television.

'Who is it?' Tom was making coffee in the kitchen; he was tired and his eyes were puffy.

'One of the new people.'

Tom came into the living room and looked at the screen. Waiting by the gate was Robin Rix. From where the camera was situated his image loomed upwards towards them like a face in a bath tap. They would soon learn that was how he looked in real life.

'What does he want? I don't want things to go wrong today and he looks like something that could go wrong.'

'I'll make him go away.'

'Take the dogs but be polite.'

Alta went out into the garden, clicked her tongue and ran down towards the gate with Chico, Harpo and Groucho trotting after her. She slowed and strolled the last fifty metres with her hands in her pockets, her signature cool and unconcerned look. Rix peered at her.

'Hello there,' he said.

'We're closed.'

Rix pressed his face against the gate. 'Oh, that's all right.' His voice might have been a feather in her ear. 'I've come to give Thomas Hannah a message.'

'You can give it to me.'

'I should tell him myself.'

'No you shouldn't.'

'If you wouldn't mind…'

'I would.'

Rix looked at the gate and gave it a rattle. 'Things get lost in translation. It wouldn't be your fault.'

'Just tell me.'

He stepped back and looked at the camera. He waved. 'You're a good gatekeeper,' he said, bending down and peering into the lock. 'Very good. Are you related to…?'

Alta folded her arms and waited.

'Just interested to know. Is there a way you could let me in? I could pay you. Perhaps.'

Alta laughed. 'I'm bored now. Goodbye.' She turned to go.

'Wait. Charles Cubberley is not going to do the job,' Rix said. 'Tell your boss that – but tell him I can.'

Alta stopped and looked back. 'He's not my boss.'

'Whatever he is. Tell him. I'll wait here.' Rix reached through the bars as if he were trying to pull himself through the air towards her. The dogs growled and he dropped his hand. 'Tell Tom Hannah that Charles Cubberley has let him down. And then tell him I can do the job. Tell him that Robin Rix the actor is here.'

Alta stared at him. 'I'll tell him,' she said at last. 'You can wait or go. It's up to you.'

'What does he sound like?' Tom asked when Alta returned to the house.

'Like leaking gas.'

'That's a good sound for a virus.'

'I don't like him.'

'But maybe we should hear him.'

'He's a liar. The message isn't true.'

'Probably not. It's a cut-throat business.'

'Don't let him in.'

'All right. Not in the house. We'll keep him outside. But let's see. Just for twenty minutes.'

'Ten minutes.'

'All right. Ten minutes.'

Tom released the gate from his laptop and they waited outside on the front steps until Rix appeared, accompanied by Chico, Harpo and Groucho.

Tom stepped forwards and shook his hand.

'Alta's told me about Charles.'

'Yes, bad news. But to be honest, it's an ill wind and so on. One door closes and another etcetera.' He handed Tom a card. 'Robin Rix. Voice actor. Nice place you have here. Lovely pets.'

'They're not pets,' said Alta.

'Oh, I don't know.'

'I do.'

'This is Alta,' Tom said. 'My very good friend. So, Charles Cubberley has definitely pulled out? He told you that?'

'He did. Dreadful let down. He wasn't going to tell you but I said he must. It's only professional. But that's Charles. He's always been the same. He lets people down. Not his fault, it's how he is. I said, "If you won't tell them, Charles, then I will." I came straightaway. He's going. He's leaving today. He won't be back. So, if I can help in any way, here I am. So to speak. Literally.'

'I'm surprised. He seemed very keen. And no call, no text…'

'No phone signal. He tried but Charles and technology – well, they just don't – you know. Get on. Margot's no better. A bit dinosaurish. Nothing wrong with that but then they don't know the games scene, do they?'

'And you do?'

'Always at it.'

'Really. Well, it's lucky you're here. What are the chances of two actors being in Las Sombras at the same time?'

'I know. Like buses. Wait for weeks and then – here I am.'

'And you want to try out for the role?'

'Yes.'

'Okay we could do it now? It's just one word. It's…'

'"Goodbye." I know. Margot told me.' Rix rubbed his hands together. 'Where do you want me?'

'It's unorthodox, I know, but how about out here?'

'I don't…'

'Charles did his audition outside.'

'Outside is perfect.'

'Take your time, warm up, vocal exercises, whatever you need to do, and then let me hear a few variants. Do you want some time alone to prepare?'

'No. I'm ready now.' Rix cleared his throat. He said: 'Goodbye.'

'Goodbye.'

'Goodbye.'

'Goodbye.'

'Goodbye.'

'Goodbye.'

'Good…'

'Got it. Thank you,' said Tom. 'You certainly got the word.'

He looked at his watch. 'Hey, look, I'm sorry, I don't mean to be rude, but I have guests arriving soon. So again, thank you for coming all this way. I'll be in touch. I've got your card. Would you like a drink before you go? Tea? A coffee? A sandwich?' He was conscious of Alta's glare. 'Outside? To take with you?'

'I was wondering…'

'Bathroom? Through there, on the…'

'No, not that. I'm not really Spain-based, you see, and I was wondering…'

'Two times you were wondering,' Alta said. 'What were you wondering?'

'I was wondering… expenses. For the audition. Some help with the fare back? And the hotel. That sort of thing. Only if I get the job, of course. Maybe a bit up front?'

Alta looked at Tom and grinned. 'See?'

Tom laughed. He was not an unkind man. 'Well, I did ask you to do it. I'll pay for a taxi back to A Coruña Airport. How's that? You arrange it and ask them to call me for payment.'

There was a moment when it looked as if Rix would press for more, but then he relaxed and smiled. 'Wonderful. Thank you.'

'Good.'

To Alta's disgust Tom made coffee and a sandwich for Rix, and allowed him inside to use the bathroom, and chatted pleasantly to him all the while, and then showed him politely to the gate, rather than having the dogs drag him there as she had suggested.

Beyond the gate, and on his way down the track, Rix passed a tall, frail, stick-like creature walking up to the house.

'The auditions have closed,' Rix said. 'The role's been taken.'

Borkmann looked at him. 'What?'

'The role. If you're going to the audition, it's gone.'

'Has it? Thank you.'

'Are you...?'

'Goodbye.'

Borkmann carried on walking and Rix continued down the track, ruminating on the fact that Borkmann's 'goodbye' had been delivered with a chilling finality he had failed to capture.

Left to his own devices Badger stirred on the sofa, looked around, yawned, scratched and rolled onto the carpet. There was uneaten breakfast food on the mezzanine level but instead he walked out to the patio and stood with his legs stretched straight and his head erect, experiencing the day. After a while he walked across the grass and through a gap in the shrubbery and then into the section of the woods that ran parallel with the side of the house.

He paused here and there to smell tree trunks, roots, plants and small stones, to urinate on them, and occasionally to roll on them. Sometimes he ran forwards, disappeared into a bush, only to return empty-pawed, or he ran a few metres back the way he had come before turning and resuming his journey. It looked like random meanderings but there was a general trajectory towards something – and that something was where the ground dipped into a narrow, earthy channel which extended under the wall, through its footings and into a prickly, thorny bush on the other side.

It was the route that Alta and Badger had taken when they had first come to Tom's house on a chilly autumn's evening. It was also the route Chico, Harpo and Groucho had taken when, driven insane by Charles's sleeping draught, they had broken free of their mental restraints, abandoned their posts and charged off in a semi-hallucinogenic delirium to bury him.

Now, with the entire Galician Massif available to roam, Bad–

ger bounded upwards and away from the house. For him, the mountainside was not a bare, barren expanse of rock and scrubland. For him, it was a mosaic of scents; a forest of odours; a lake of fragrances; a river of aromas.

He ran uphill, moving diagonally across the mountain slope away from the house. He crossed the road that led to Las Sombras and disappeared into the dips and hollows where the land became less of a slope and more of a steep, jagged incline. A dangerous place for humans to walk without sturdy boots and a stick.

Claudio, who had no sturdy boots or a stick, was at that moment setting off across the slope. Fear, hunger and a lack of sleep may have cured his urge to flee because he was heading down the hill, back towards Las Sombras. He had walked fifty metres in the direction of the sea when he stopped and listened.

In the high, clean air, Badger's running feet and panting breath could be clearly heard. Was it a wolf or a bear? Claudio turned and ran back to his den, scrambled in and pulled the bush over him. He whimpered and moaned as Badger bounded up and wormed his way in too.

'Oh God, no,' Claudio cried. 'Help me.' He wriggled out and ran away.

Half a mile away, on the other side of the road and at a higher altitude, Rodolfo stopped and listened, his head jerking from one side to another like a hungry parrot or Charles saying 'Hyanh', and then he turned and started to make his way downwards, towards the distant cries of Claudio.

'Claudio. Claudio,' Rodolfo shouted.

Claudio was running as fast as he dared, and now someone else was calling from a long way away. At first the sound was barely audible, a cry on the wind that might have been a bird or some other animal. But it grew louder and more insistent and more human-like.

Badger watched Claudio running away from him below, and Rodolfo running towards him from above.

Rodolfo had the longer legs and was gaining on his son who in his panic was running into rougher and rougher terrain. 'Claudio, it's me.' He whizzed past Badger.

There must have been something in his voice, some familiar tone, because Claudio stopped running and turned and faced his oncoming father. It might have been that, or it might simply have been that, like a rabbit scared of the fox, he would rather face his pursuer than escape it.

'Papa,' he shouted.

'Claudio.'

Running fast down a steep slope covered in loose scree is an act of faith. Rodolfo ran faster and faster. Surely, he had never run so fast in his life. His legs were a blur. He shot past Claudio and it seemed possible that he would continue running right off the mountain and into the sea.

Badger watched. Rodolfo was now a diminishing figure on the mountain – and then suddenly he vanished in a puff of dust. Badger looked away and studied a seagull circling high in the air until, at length, he stood up, yawned, stretched and followed Claudio down the hill towards the scene of the accident. It was as if he had foreseen this moment; as if he had come to this point in time and space specifically to be on hand to help these two useless human beings.

18

Germaine and Catharina walked from the front of the hotel to the point where the harbour wall ended and became a jumble of piled-up stones, and then leaned against the wall and surveyed the village with its cluster of tiered houses and the mountains that rose above them.

'The mountains look like they want to push us into the sea,' said Catharina.

'Perhaps they do. Perhaps they're bored with us and our games.'

'Does anybody other than the hotel people live here?'

'I haven't seen anybody. It's like a ghost town. When I arrived I thought it was a film set. It reminded me of being young – a child. In the Motherhood I used to pretend I was someone else, anyone else, but usually characters from a book. I'd always pretend I was one of the minor characters, though. In the background. Or sometimes I'd imagine I was outside of me, narrating my life. It helped.'

'Did they let you read in that place?'

'Oh yes. They were very strict on learning. *Very* strict. They saw no incompatibility between a good education and daily abuse.'

'Horrible. How long were you there?'

'Fourteen years. From a baby until the police broke in. It was all I ever knew – how to hide myself – as if I were hiding myself from myself. I used to watch my reflection in a window or a mirror and will it to run away. It was like it could escape if it wanted to, but it always stayed with me.'

'You must hate those people.'

'I do. I think. I hate what they did. As individuals. Yes, I do. Of course I do. But they were all we had. Some of us actually sought out the abuse. We wanted to be noticed. Or to have the attention. I know. It doesn't make sense. But if they weren't… doing things, to you, then you were discarded. Not wanted. And that could be worse. Much worse. Some of us loved them even though they were so evil. We all knew it was wrong but none of us really knew what *right* was. It's frightening what a human can get used to. We normalise excesses and life just trundles on. There's always another day. Until there isn't.'

'Children died?'

'Sometimes. Not as often as people think or the news stories make us think. But yes, sometimes. More often they disappeared. That was our norm. To be sold on like livestock.'

'It's unbearable.'

'The children they kept became more like dolls to them. Toys. Dressing us up, teaching us to read, throwing us away, swapping us around. They wanted to make us like them, too. Make the abused the abuser.'

'Did you, you know…?'

'Hurt the younger ones? No. I was lucky, or unlucky. I always looked younger than I was; I didn't mature physically like the other girls did – I wasn't really noticed as much. They were so used to me I think sometimes they didn't see me.'

Catharina turned and looked down at the waves rolling over the rocks.

'I don't know how you came out of it so sane.'

Germaine laughed. 'Assuming I am. I think children can be very fragile and very robust at the same time. I knew I could think clearly; I've always known that; and I tried to think my way out of the misery, to detach myself from my surroundings somehow. They had a book of religious art – all the horrible pictures depicting the death and torture of saints and martyrs. Some of them are truly graphic. But I saw more than the grisly side of it – I saw the *art*. The skill, the technique, the craft. And suddenly I wanted to see the real pictures, to see how the oils had been applied, to touch the texture. I wanted to see for myself that the horror had been contained in the paintings' frames, trapped on the canvases. It was an epiphany. I wanted all the pain in my life to be put in a frame too, something I could look at, that was mine but couldn't hurt me, where I could be safe in some room looking at all the screaming madness of the world on a wall. I more than loved art – I needed it. I sought sanctuary in it. I used art as rocket fuel, a way of getting as far away from childhood as I could. I lit the blue touchpaper and used all the fear and loathing to propel me as far away from that frightened little girl as I could. And I'm still rocketing. Or trying to.'

Germaine's voice caught and she frowned, unwilling even in that intimate moment with Catharina to be that person she detested: the soul-barer.

'Anyway, that was then, and this is now. Tom Hannah does the same. He used to wrap up his life in a cartoon strip; now he keeps it all in the iLets. I wonder what will happen to him when he lets it run free.'

They stood in silence. Finally, Catharina said, 'What time are you due back at Casa Hannah?'

'Lunchtime.'

'Can I see his house from here? Could you wave to me?'

Germaine shielded her eyes and then pointed. 'Not really. It's behind that ridge up there. And anyway, I hope you'll come with me so there will be no need to wave.'

'I'd like that, but he might not want an interloper there.'

'I shall insist. And I'm going to call Borkmann too. He needs to know about all this. And his sister. Could I use your phone? I don't want to switch mine on in case the game is genuinely infected. Would a phone call spread it? I don't know how these things work.'

'Me neither, and of course you can use my phone, but if Tom has only just auditioned for the virus's voice he can't have released the virus yet. Can he?'

Germaine sighed. 'I really don't know. Perhaps the character I saw is the old cuckoo and the Tom-face is part of the new virus. A test or a prototype. Or a hybrid. Something I shouldn't have seen yet. If Richter Bird is behind it, whatever it is, it's wrong.'

Robin Rix packed his bag and left it in the hotel reception area while he sat outside on the bench with his legs stretched out and his hands folded across his pot belly. A breeze from the sea lifted his wispy hair. In a kinder world his taxi would have arrived and taken him over the mountains and far away. That world would have turned, the sea would have ebbed and flowed, the breeze would have blown and the day would have passed without any further incident in his particular direction. He would have been, as he always had been, a minor character of little narrative value.

But it was not a kinder world. This was the Las Sombras version which turned light into dark, and where shadows crept across the floor, up the walls and over the faces of sleeping children. And so, as Rix sat in his seat and bathed in the morning sunlight, Charles and Margot came down the stairs from their room and stepped out onto the cobbled street and Charles stumbled over his outstretched legs.

'Oh,' said Margot.

Rix made no effort to move. He looked at them and smiled. Charles's face turned red. Margot put a hand on his arm and turned him away, taking him up the hill, away from Rix and his legs.

'You haven't seen a taxi, have you?' Rix called after them. 'I'm leaving, you see. Job done. Thought you might be pleased about that. Get out of your hair.' He sat up and shouted, 'I did the audition, by the way. The virus thing.'

Charles stopped. He didn't look like a normal human being any more. He looked more like a portrait of a man whose paint had run in the sun. He breathed heavily and it was possible there really was steam coming from his nose. He was becoming something that might once have been Charles Cubberley but was now just a human-shaped clenched fist.

'Well, you don't mind, do you?' said Rix. 'Fair contest. I popped along this morning. Lovely walk. They asked me to stay for breakfast. Made me very welcome. They even arranged a car to take me back to the airport. Lovely dogs too. I've always got on well with dogs. Do you get on well with dogs, Charles?'

Charles's head twitched from side to side. His dials were in the red zone.

Margot said, 'Come on. Let's go for a drive.'

'I did a few sound tests,' Rix continued. 'The usual sort of thing. Not much of a stretch but what an opportunity – global audience, all sectors. Massive. Quite a career-changer. By the way, I hear there's a Dutch comedy troupe looking for a man who can belch if you're interested. Have you had breakfast? Had mine up at the house. Fabulous.'

'Come on, Charles.'

But Charles shook Margot's hand from his arm. This was the moment when, in yet another world, Robin Rix would be vaporised by a heat ray. But in Las Sombras, red-faced and almost beside himself with fury, Charles merely strode up the hill and disappeared round the bend.

'He'll make the airport before I do at that rate,' Rix said. 'Did I see him with a cigarette, Margie? I thought he'd given up.'

Margot looked at the empty road where Charles had once been and then said to Rix in a matter-of-fact way, 'Don't call me Margie'.

She walked back into the hotel and Rix jumped up, followed her in and caught her by the arm at the bottom of the stairs.

'I've got some time before my taxi arrives,' he said.

'Go away, Robin.'

'Come on, Margie.'

'Let go.' She pushed him hard and he bumped against the wall. She carried on up the stairs while Rix blinked several times and then followed her.

'Don't be mean, Margie.'

She reached her room, went in and slammed the door. He tapped lightly.

'Margie.'

'Go away.' Margot was leaning against her side of the door. 'I mean it, go away.'

'I only want to say goodbye. A friendly goodbye between friends. That's all.'

'Go away, Charles will be back.'

'I doubt it. He'll be gone for hours, huffing and puffing and making that silly noise of his. One goodbye and then I'll be gone. Promise.'

Rix leaned against the door and it moved enough to reveal that it wouldn't withstand much pressure. He leaned harder.

The door bent. He stepped back and then hit the door hard with his shoulder. The lock snapped and the door opened. Margot tried to push it back, but Rix got an arm and a leg and a shoulder and part of his face into the room, and then he slipped in entirely, filling out like a cartoon.

'Don't be like this,' he said, pulling his jacket straight.

Margot put the bed between her and him. 'Get out. I mean it.'

'Do you, though? It's just a little kiss goodbye and then I'll be gone. Am I that awful?'

'Yes.'

'Margie.'

He walked around the bed towards her.

Margot backed herself into the corner of the room. Her face was set. She picked up a bedside lamp.

'Look at you,' Rix said. 'It's only me.'

Greed and lust are dangerous playmates. A wiser, more careful Rix might have noticed Margot's expression grow harder as he approached her. He may have wondered why her eyes flicked over his shoulder for an instant before returning to his face. But then again, perhaps not. It's not possible to tell with people like Robin Rix. He did pause, though, as if sensing a change in the atmosphere – a movement in the air that couldn't be accounted for by their presence alone. Did he have time to wonder about that? If he did, then it's unlikely he wondered for long. Much more likely he became immediately preoccupied with the after-effects of Charles hitting him on the back of the head with a fire extinguisher.

Rix frowned, put his hand to his head and looked round. Charles hit him again and Rix fell awkwardly at Margot's feet.

'Got him,' Charles said as if he had finally dealt with an elusive mosquito. 'I bloody got him.'

18

Margot looked at him, looked at Rix, looked at the fire extinguisher and then fled the scene.

19

Catharina and Germaine were walking briskly back to the hotel. Germaine looked determined. 'I'll call Borkmann, send an email to Caroline, find Charles, try to persuade him not to take the part – that might slow things down, and then you and I can head up to the house and see what we can do – although I don't know exactly what.'

'Disrupt and distract.'

'Exactly.'

Catharina passed over her phone. 'You make your calls and emails. I just want to go to my room.'

At the hotel entrance they met Margot coming down the stairs.

'Margot,' said Germaine. 'Is Charles around?'

Margot looked at Rix's bag in the reception area. 'I don't know,' she said and ran out of the hotel.

Catharina looked at Germaine and raised her eyebrows. 'Running from or to something?'

'I'm not sure.' They watched her run down the cobbled street towards the sea. 'I'll just check she's okay.' Germaine hurried after Margot. 'Margot, wait.' But Margot didn't wait. She reached the harbour wall and ran down the steps that led to the rocks and a narrow stone jetty. Germaine followed. Margot had nowhere else to go other than the sea or the glass bottom boat. She looked left and right and then sank to the ground.

'What is the matter?' said Germaine rushing up. 'Are you all right?' She sat down next to Margot. 'Has anything happened?'

'Nothing,' said Margot. 'Just nothing.' She shook her head and let her chin fall to her chest. 'Oh God.'

Germaine looked at her and then out to sea. Unsure of what to do, she put her arm around Margot. 'Is it Charles? You know, he mustn't do the voice-over for Tom Hannah. It's really important that he doesn't.'

'He's not going to.'

'Oh. Good.'

Margot took Germaine's arm from her shoulder. 'I have to sit here for a while, if you don't mind. Alone. You get along. I'm fine.'

Germaine stayed where she was – sitting by the rocks, hidden by the wall, with this woman she hardly knew. She wanted to say something, but she didn't know what. Close contact with strangers and their tangled web of moods and emotions was hard work. In the end she spoke about herself, as people usually do.

'My parents let me go. One or the other, or both. Oh, it's possible they had good reasons; some distressing story which meant it was their only course of action. But the plain truth, the outcome, the indisputable fact, is they gave me away – their gift from God, their little bundle of joy. They gave me to some people, to the worst people imaginable. They gave me to monsters. I'm saying this only to establish my credentials: I don't have any experience of love. And I'm fine with that. It's like somebody else's toy. I never had it, I don't miss it and I'm not sure I even want it. Desire, I get. Fondness. Even caring. But anything more? *Nada*. Anyway, despite all that, and my inexperience in these matters, I think Charles loves you and you love Charles. Whatever that means. So… so there you are. That's my contribution.'

Germaine stopped talking and thought about what she might say next. It probably wasn't the best tête-à-tête Margot had been part of, but interacting with humans was difficult and Germaine still wasn't very good at it. Words: better out than in but did they really capture her intent, her meaning? Did they really articulate the images in her mind that she wanted to share with Margot? What would Catharina have said? Would she have hugged Margot and let it go at that? Or Alta, what would she have done? Germaine smiled. Alta would have pushed her into the sea. 'I sometimes feel there's another me in another life, watching all this and being glad they're not here. I watch my reflection to see if it's laughing at me when I'm not looking.'

Margot closed her eyes. 'I just need a long sleep, I think. That's all.'

They sat in silence and watched the sea rise and fall below them and the glass bottom boat bob up and down, and seagulls drift across the water and land and float and look pleased with themselves with their prissy lipstick.

Behind Germaine and Margot was the harbour wall, the other side of which was the harbour road, and across that road was the hotel. Looking at *El Tesoro Escondido* from the front, an observer would see an alleyway on the right that led to the back of the building where Rodolfo kept his truck and where all the assorted hotel detritus was stacked and stored: bins, boxes and bags; pallets, crates and cartons. Most of the plastic bags had been vandalised by the seagulls and pigeons, and ancient rotting food and waste littered the ground. It was a place where rats and mice and cockroaches and other hungry creatures could come and feast.

A greasy white wall provided a private enclave between the back of the kitchen and this rubbish. Within the enclave there were two doors – one led into the kitchen; the other into a long, thin, dusty and cluttered storeroom. A single opaque, cobweb-strewn window allowed some light into this room, but it was a dark and dingy place even when the flickering fluorescent bulb was turned on.

Having watched Germaine hurry after Margot, Catharina walked through the empty bar and into the kitchen. There were plenty of cupboards in the kitchen and she opened them all but didn't find what she was looking for. She stood in the middle of the room and drummed her fingers, her lips pursed in an attitude of thought. She scanned the room and saw the back door. She opened it and went outside, found herself within the enclave, and saw that the adjacent door which led into the storeroom was open. She was about to go in when Charles Cubberley walked out. He stopped when he saw her. He was carrying a large potato sack and some rusty metal chains.

'Hyanh,' he breathed, and his head twitched to the left.

'Oh,' said Catharina. 'Hello. We haven't properly met. I'm Catharina. I'm with Germaine. I'm her agent and... things. Well, thing. Singular. We're each other's things. Thing.' She smiled brightly. 'Let's just go with "I'm her agent".' She looked at the sack and chains. 'Are you wrapping something up?'

Charles squinted at her warily. 'Just packing up. Getting rid of a few things.'

He seemed poised to push past, but Catharina said, 'It's Charles, isn't it?'

'Yes.'

'While you're here – Charles – I've been having trouble sleeping. Germaine said there was some sleeping powder somewhere. She mentioned that you had found some. You know… the dog thing.' Again she looked at the sack and chains. 'There's no need to bother Rodolfo with all this, is there?'

Charles held the sack and chains closer to himself. His head twitched as the cogs turned. Finally, he cleared his throat and said, 'At the back, on the right, third shelf down. Cloth bag.'

'Thank you.'

'Word of warning: yellow froth. From the nose. Not pleasant. I wouldn't recommend it. Cup of warm milk might be better.' He started to close the storeroom door but Catharina stepped forwards with a smile.

'I'll try some anyway,' she said. 'Just a little; just to see. About a tablespoon, do you think?'

'Teaspoon.'

'Heaped?'

'Quarter.'

'Thank you.' Catharina squeezed past and Charles clanked off into the kitchen and the hotel beyond. 'Good luck with your packing,' she called. She waited until she was sure he was gone and then kicked a brick against the storeroom door to make sure it didn't close behind her. She found the cloth bag, held her nose and filled a small, dusty beaker with the coarse ochre-coloured powder and put it in her bag. Then she left, closed the door, made her way to the bench outside the hotel and waited for Germaine.

'They're at the gate,' Alta said. 'Blondie and her girlfriend.'

Tom looked at the CCTV displayed on the television screen and nodded. 'Good.'

He was sitting next to Borkmann on the sofa who was still in his overcoat and nursing a cup of coffee. His hand trembled.

'Catharina Caboulet,' Borkmann said, looking at the screen. 'After your business, I expect, Tom.'

'I'm not so sure. They're holding hands.'

'That's as maybe, but don't underestimate an agent. I'm just saying.' Borkmann stretched out his long legs and winced. 'Germaine has been trying to call me all morning. And texting. She's contacting your sister, you know.'

'She wants to stop me.'

'Of course she does. She's a fan as much as a critic. Which is why I think it's fitting that she will be your witness. She's devoted a lot of academic energy to your work over the years. She deserves to see the entire cycle. I notice you don't set the dogs on them, though. I thought that was your normal welcome, friend or foe.'

Outside, Chico, Harpo and Groucho sat on the patio with their ears up, no doubt aware that visitors were at the gate. Ousted from her usual spot on the sofa, Alta was curled up in a reclining leather chair.

'Where is Badger?' Tom said. 'This picture's not complete without Badger.'

'He's out,' said Alta. 'He'll be back later.'

'What is he doing? Visiting friends? Doing some shopping?' said Borkmann.

Tom laughed. 'You two are exactly the same. Do you know that?' He stood up. 'Two curmudgeons. Let's get ready for our guests.' He paused and looked down at his old mentor. 'And, Gerard, before it begins, I want to say thank you for helping me. Really. I know you don't agree with any of this, but I appreciate your coming round to my way of thinking and not making it more difficult for me – and for fixing it so Ms Kiecke could be here, and the two voice actors.'

'Two?'

'And also for you coming here. I know how hard that will

have been for you. But you were the first person to see my work, and you'll be the last. It's symmetrical. Neat. I like that.'

Borkmann shrugged and carefully shifted position. 'I'm here for you, as I have always been – to best represent your interests. Personally, I think you're a damned fool. And I wasn't going to help you. Not after that first visit. It was a shock seeing you like this…'

'Like what? Happy?' said Alta.

'Different. But I was uncharitable in my outburst that day.' He glanced at Alta. 'You were a bigger shock.'

She grinned at him. 'Good.'

'Anyway, Tom. I'm pleased to see you're looking better since last we met. I wish you could say the same of me.'

Tom patted him on the shoulder. 'It's been a long journey for you. For all of us.'

Alta stood up too. 'I'm going to let them in.'

'No, I'll do it,' said Tom. 'You start getting things ready.'

'So, this really is it?' said Borkmann.

'Why not? Germaine's here. You're here. We're all here. It's time.'

20

Germaine and Catharina watched Tom approach the gate. Chico, Harpo and Groucho trotted behind him. The morning sun reflected off their short black fur, accentuating every movement of muscle – a visual exposition of youth and power. Tom, by contrast, shambled along like an aging prophet from a Hollywood epic; his hair, beard and moustache lifting in the breeze – his shirt loose on his rangy frame.

'Impressive,' Catharina said.

'Tom or the dogs?' Germaine said.

'Both.'

'He's lost weight. Too much.'

'I don't know. He looks good on it.'

'He doesn't.'

Tom used a remote control to open the gate and let them in. 'Ms Kiecke,' he said. 'And…'

'Caboulet. Catharina Caboulet.' Catharina held out her hand. 'I'm a literary agent. Specialising in art books.'

Germaine thought that at that moment she too looked a formidable force: tall, athletic and confident. They were titans meeting for the first time and Germaine felt like a hobbit. 'I asked Catharina to come along,' she said. 'Is that all right?'

'It's perfectly all right. I think you'll find, Catharina, that I curate my work in an unusual way.'

'I'll be frank,' said Germaine. 'We've come to talk you out of everything you told me. I've also called Borkmann and I've emailed your sister.'

Tom nodded slowly. 'Well, the paint will run where the paint will run. Let's see what happens. But I should tell you now, Gerard Borkmann is here.'

'What?'

Catharina laughed. 'That sly dog.'

'I'm telling you now because... because he's not well. He looks ill. Diminished. And if you haven't seen him for a while the change is noticeable. He's a proud man and you'd be doing me a favour if you didn't let any shock you might feel show in your eyes.'

Germaine took a deep breath. So Borkmann was in Spain. In Tom's house. All the deceit, the magnitude of it, seemed to weigh her down, and her stupid naiveté in believing anything Borkmann had said to her. She felt a fool. Was there anything he had told her that was true? Or was it all an inscrutable joke in which she was a helpless stooge. And looking at Catharina swinging along with her backpack and sunglasses and sunhat, as if she were on a holiday outing, Germaine wondered who else was in on the gag.

'I'm sorry to hear that,' she said.

When they reached the house it was clear that Tom and Alta had prepared for their arrival. Tom led them round to the back of the house where Alta had laid out drinks and cold tapas on a table. She was already eating some of it.

Tom had understated the change in Borkmann since Germaine had last seen him. He looked as if he were fading out of existence. It was clear that he wasn't just unwell; he was deeply ill.

'Gerard,' she said. 'I didn't expect to see you. I've been calling.'

'I thought I'd surprise you.'

'You have.'

'You old fraud,' said Catharina more directly. 'You said you couldn't be here.' And then added, 'You look beat.'

Tom dispensed drinks. '*Salut*,' he said and then passed Germaine an AR camera which had been waiting on the table. He said, 'Do you know how to use this?'

Germaine had seen similar cameras before, but this was a more sophisticated device. 'Point and shoot?' she said.

'It has three one-hundred-and-eighty-degree lenses and there are additional multisensory inputs too – smell and air movement. And sound, of course. It's all editable. It's for you. You can film everything, make a commentary and say whatever you like. Use it for notes, as a recorder, it's a device to capture your feelings. Anything. Ask any questions. It's your documentary. I trust your expertise on this.'

'To document what I don't want to see? A witness to an execution?'

'Imagine it's an arts project – a living exhibition that you're recording.'

'Can we talk about this? Privately?'

Tom laughed. 'No. Talking time is over – and you'll have to excuse me too. I need to get the props.'

He looked over at Catharina and Borkmann. 'Help yourself to drinks.' He gave Alta his look that said 'be nice' and then went indoors.

Germaine turned to Borkmann.

'Gerard. Surely we can't let Tom do this? You know what he's going to do, don't you? He's going to destroy it all. Everything. All those years of creativity coming to this. It's wrong. This isn't what should happen. And he's going to put a virus in the *Happy Family*. A virus. That's illegal, isn't it? That's your product, Gerard.'

'It is, indeed.'

'Well… stop him.'

She was aware that Alta was watching her, her eyes narrowed as she followed her words. As for Catharina, she seemed to be unnaturally docile, more concerned with fixing herself another drink – and clumsily at that.

'Oh shit,' Catharina said, knocking a glass onto the chair. 'Sorry, everyone.' She knelt down and started fussing with the glass and a cloth. 'That was Tom's glass, too. Top tip, Germaine: never knock over the host's glass if you want to be invited back.'

Frustrated, Germaine turned to Borkmann again. 'Don't you have any responsibility to Tom's legacy? To the future?'

Borkmann laughed. 'The future?'

'Gerard Borkmann has no future,' Alta said. 'He's dying.'

That put a crimp in the conversation. Nobody said anything.

'Are you too stupid to see that?' she added amiably.

Catharina looked up from where she was kneeling on the ground, partially obscured by the table, opened her mouth, but said nothing.

Germaine looked at Borkmann but said nothing.

Alta dipped some cheese in honey, looked at them all, but, having already spoken, now said nothing.

Finally, Borkmann broke the silence. He said, 'Well, somebody say something. I am still here.' He pulled a chair to him and sat down, closed his eyes for a moment and then sipped some Cava. He shivered. 'As one gets older,' he said, 'one finds that instead of life being an open park, with limitless horizons, it becomes a minefield. I have trodden on one. That's all. Let's move on.'

Germaine watched him as he spoke. Gerard Borkmann:

ancient and leathery Englishman. *Always be on your guard with Gerard Borkmann. Nothing was nothing with him. Nothing was always something.*

'I'm sorry,' she said.

'Thank you, but don't be. The game's not over yet. I have time.'

'Not much,' said Alta.

Borkmann looked at her and smiled. It wasn't something that normally happened, and he wasn't particularly good at it, but at least he'd tried. 'Thank you, Miss Altagracia, for bringing your usual clarity to the table.'

'And Tom knows?' Germaine said.

Borkmann nodded.

'Is that why he changed his mind? You told us that he wouldn't see you.'

'And he wouldn't. Tom did tell me what he intended to do, that time when I visited, and he did tell me that I wasn't to come back. His little Rottweiler here,' he nodded at Alta, 'is an effective deterrent. So, I wasn't deceiving you. Not completely. And when we met in Liège, I genuinely thought that if you came here you would be able to change his mind. I thought it was a phase, one of Tom's dark periods, and he would emerge the same old Tom if we gave him time and encouragement. You were to be that encouragement. And I still hope that will be true.'

'I haven't made any difference to Tom's plans at all. In fact, I'm now part of them. There's not much time left in which to change his mind.' Germaine felt a dull ache of disappointment in her throat. She knew that Borkmann was ill, but she couldn't help but speak her mind. 'You knew before I came here that Tom wouldn't be interested in an interview. You knew when we were finalising the arrangements there would never be a book on new art.'

Borkmann looked at her and, ill or not, his eyes were hard and the fire behind them burned as fiercely as ever. 'I gave you an opportunity – and it's not over yet, Germaine. You never know what's around the next corner.'

Germaine shook her head. She turned to Catharina for support but she seemed unperturbed by the entire conversation and was sitting back in her chair with a slight smile on her face.

'I agree,' she said. 'Corners are surprising things.'

21

Tom came back, not through the house but around the side, dragging the power-assisted flatbed trolley stacked with the sixty-three large document boxes – the same trolley that Alta had once used to bring him back from the dead. Tom wiped his brow.

'Art is heavier than you'd think,' he said and reached for a drink. He looked hot and Germaine wondered how much exercise he'd been getting recently. She thought again he looked like he'd lost too much weight.

'Have some water,' Alta said to Tom as if reading Germaine's mind. 'Save your bubbly wine for later.' She handed him a pitcher of water and a glass and took his wine as if she were a schoolteacher confiscating cigarettes.

Germaine looked at the boxes. They were white cardboard and she could see the fire-retardant symbol on their sides, which gave her some hope. They seemed out of place in the harsh sunlight. Gardens were not where these containers belonged. They looked too office-like, too corporate, too mundane to be outside where grass and plants and trees grew, and a breeze blew, and clouds drifted past a blue infinite sky.

They were meant to live in a dusty archive building or a warehouse storeroom.

Tom sat down and sipped his water while Alta hovered by the table looking from one person to the next with her always-ready-to-be-aggressive eyes.

'So, there it all is,' he said. 'Everything. It took me six months to gather it all together. From doodles to overlays, drawings to animation cells, it's all there. Even my school stuff. Sixty-three boxes. It doesn't seem much, does it? For an entire career. But paper packs well.'

'Don't you have any originals?' Germaine said to Borkmann, but he shook his head.

'Sadly not. At least, nothing substantial. I have a couple of framed originals, gifts from my grateful client, but that's all.'

'Think how much they're about to go up in value,' Tom said. 'The higher the flames, the higher the price of what's hanging on your walls.'

'You're really going to burn it?' said Germaine.

'Yes.'

'Isn't that – crude? Unimaginative? A bit obvious? A bonfire on the lawn?'

'Not on the lawn.' He still had the remote control he'd used to open the gate. He fiddled with it, muttered to himself and then looked up and at the centre of the lawn. At first nothing happened, and then Germaine became aware that the grass was moving, the turf tightening and stretching – and lowering. An area of perhaps nine square metres dropped and then separated into four quadrants, with each quarter rolling under the remaining grass.

'That, I like,' said Catharina.

'It's a firepit,' Alta said.

'It was actually designed to be a hidden, sunken hot tub,'

Tom said. 'But it does work equally well as a firepit for barbecues and songs around the campfire. And bonfires.'

'I'm sorry,' said Germaine. 'But I can't take this seriously. It's so surreal. In fact, it's so banal. So… ridiculous. I can't get my head around what I'm seeing. Your life's work is being pulled along on a trolley and you're going to burn it in a converted hot tub like a two-dimensional James Bond villain? How can this be? Tom, you are much better than this.'

'Imagine it is a form of surrealism. Or better still, a cartoon.'

'But it's not, Tom. It's vandalism. Arson. Stupid and pointless. What a waste of time and money and imagination. It's puerile. I could cry.'

Alta came over to her, leaned on the table and peered into Germaine's eyes with mock seriousness. 'Oh, I see what the matter is,' she said. 'Do you want it to be a game to make it more real? He's only going to burn some pictures.'

'Alta,' said Tom.

Germaine smiled at Alta. It was a genuine, sad smile. 'What you don't understand, Alta, and I doubt that you ever will, is that what is in those boxes *is* real life. It makes it real. It records it, interprets it, and sometimes, just sometimes, it changes it. Art touches real people's real lives. And if I don't cry for it all, who will? And what sort of world would we live in if nobody did? I'm sure you are free thinking and wild and living in the moment and in touch with your natural self. But people were making art from day one. We need art. It's what we do.'

Alta laughed and skipped away before returning to lean in towards Germaine again. 'I wish I could speak like that. Then I could make my life to be however I want it to be. Pretend that things aren't what they are. I could say, "Oh, that drawing is real life because it makes me sad, and sad is real, isn't it?" Or how about, "I know I hurt you, but I'm kind really." Or, "Do what I tell you, but it's your choice."'

She looked into Germaine's eyes. 'Words are just bubbles of air that pop out of your mouth and then disappear. You use words to make other people think you are something you're not. Those pictures are only pictures and if he wants to burn them then let him. They're his, not yours. If you want to cry about something, then cry about your own empty life – because you don't have anything to burn, do you? Nothing. Nothing precious in your life at all except words that don't mean anything.'

'Would anyone like a drink?' Catharina said.

'I'll do it,' said Alta. 'You hold your girlfriend's hand in case she sees more reality.'

Alta passed everyone their glass.

'The paper and canvases may be Tom's, but the art isn't,' Germaine said. 'The art belongs to everybody.'

'Technically speaking, there's an argument it belongs to me,' said Borkmann, piping up from his seat across the patio. 'Contractually speaking, that is. Copyright is yours, Tom, of course. But these artefacts might belong to me.'

'Might?' Catharina said. The conversation had moved to her territory now.

Borkmann looked at her, as one professional to another. 'I don't know if it would stand up in court,' he said. 'I was younger then. Less precise. My lawyers have been over it and it's ambiguous.' He glanced at Tom. 'Might delay things, of course. Tom, would you consider a moratorium until we can get some clarity on who owns the contents of all these boxes?'

'No.'

'I didn't think so.'

'What about the virus?' said Germaine. 'That's definitely illegal. I've got an ant on my phone with Tom's face on it.'

'Tom's new project,' said Borkmann. 'Tom, you may have Richter, but we have Holst. Goth-Ungoth as they say.' He

240

glanced at Germaine. 'The *Bird of Prey* Brothers. They fell out. They loathe each other. Holst is on a mission to cleanse the world of his brother's shadow. If you think you're infected, would you mind lending me your phone? There are some excellent technicians back at the ranch who would love to see what Tom and his gothic friend have been working on.'

It was some relief to know that Borkmann was at least working to protect *Happy Family*, although Germaine would have to think about whether or not she wanted to hand over her phone with all her private messages and phone numbers. Even if he were ill, Borkmann was still Borkmann. She became aware that Catharina was tugging at her sleeve.

'What?'

'I don't feel very well,' Catharina whispered.

'What do you mean?' Germaine whispered back.

'I mean...' A thin string of yellow foam ran out from Catharina's nose. 'Oh God.' She pushed her chair back and bent over. 'Quick. My hair. I'm going to be sick.' She spat out some of the yellow foam onto the patio. Chico, Harpo and Groucho, sitting nearby, saw it, jumped up and ran away.

'Oh, I must have given you the wrong glass,' said Alta. 'Sorry.'

'What have you done?' said Germaine.

'I didn't do anything. It was your friend who put the powder into the glass. I saw her. I just moved them around.'

'Catharina?'

'I thought – I wanted – I thought he would fall asleep and not – Oh Christ.' She hobbled, bent over, across the patio and onto the grass where she knelt down in the weeds and buttercups and dandelions. 'Don't look,' she said and then vomited. Again, insects that had been minding their own business looked up to find they were covered in bile, and then scurried away.

'Can we get her inside?' Germaine said. 'She's been poisoned. We need to call an ambulance.'

Tom looked at Borkmann and then at Alta. 'Is this real?'

'Come on. Help me.'

They half-carried Catharina into the living room and laid her on the sofa. The vomiting had stopped and now she was dozy. She looked up at Germaine with her face a mess of ruined make-up, grabbed her head and tried to kiss her.

'Sorry,' she said. 'I – Am I going to die? I feel like I'm going to die.'

'Maybe if she sleeps it off?' said Tom.

'No,' said Germaine. 'Call an ambulance.'

Tom rubbed his beard. 'We can try but it won't be quick. It would be better if you drove her to the village and met a doctor there. They come by boat from a town up the coast. It's faster.'

'We haven't got the car. We walked.'

'I have a car. You can take that.'

'I'll need help. Please, Tom.'

'No, Germaine. I'll help you out with her, and you can take the car. But I'm staying here to complete this. Alta will help me with the boxes and Gerard can film…'

'Just a moment.'

It was Borkmann. He came into the living room carrying the worn wooden box given to him by Rodolfo. He put it on the mantelpiece, opened it and took out a long-barrelled revolver. It looked like it might have last seen service in the Spanish Civil War, and perhaps it had. It appeared to be more a piece of heavy metalwork than a weapon that might hurt someone.

'That's a gun,' said Germaine and to her ears her voice sounded as if it were spoken in an empty room. 'Why have you got a gun?' Later, when she replayed this scene in her mind, she would wonder why she had said such a ridiculous thing.

242

21

Borkmann pulled back the hammer while Tom and Germaine and Alta simply stared, as if they were watching Borkmann insert a cufflink into his shirt. Catharina snored quietly. The hammer clicked into place and Borkmann pointed the revolver at Tom, holding it with two shaky hands.

'I'm sorry to be so overly dramatic. This must look very corny,' he said. 'But Germaine's right. I can't let you do this.'

Germaine sat down on the sofa and put Catharina's feet on her lap. She had never seen a real gun. It looked both ludicrous and terrifying.

'Gerard,' said Tom.

The gun wobbled erratically. It must be difficult to hold a heavy revolver for any length of time, especially when the person doing the holding was tired and frail and trembling in the first place.

'We need to get some help for Catharina,' Germaine said gently. 'We need to drive her to the village.'

Borkmann nodded. 'Of course,' he said. 'This won't take long. Alta, would you sit down please. And you, Tom. Could one of you open the gate? I presume you can do it from here?'

'You want to open the gate, then you do it,' said Alta. She joined Germaine and Catharina on the sofa and then clicked her tongue. Chico, Harpo and Groucho came into the house. Borkmann gave a short, sharp laugh. 'I won't hesitate to shoot those,' he said. 'Trust me on that. In fact, if you don't open the gate, that's exactly what I'll do. One at a time.'

'I'd kill you before you could pull the trigger,' Alta said.

Tom sighed and ran his hand through his hair. 'Let's not turn this into a soap opera. I'll open the gate.' He used the remote control and on the television screen they could see the gate slowly opening inwards.

'Can I get the car ready, at least?' Germaine said. 'Please?' She looked at Catharina who was smiling in her sleep. 'She's ill.'

'I know what you're thinking,' said Borkmann looking at her. 'That this is about the money. But it's not. And it's not about art for art's sake either. It's about a legacy. My legacy. God knows I can't create anything but through you, Tom, I made all this. And it's not going to go up in smoke on a damned bonfire, I promise you that. My success, our success, will live on, in a museum or a gallery, even in a private collection. I don't care. But *live* it will. And it will have our name on it because, while you were sitting in your studio conceiving and creating, I was making it happen. I was out there. Being Gerard Borkmann. Working. Negotiating.'

'You're not going to shoot us.'

'I hope not.'

'Just put it down.'

Borkmann closed his eyes for a moment. He was sweating. 'Don't... try to do anything. This thing might go off anyway. Just, please, sit still. And wait.'

'Wait for what?'

'We're going to sit tight and wait for Rodolfo to show up with his truck. We're going to put the boxes on it, and then he and I are going to drive it away and leave it somewhere safe while my lawyers sort it all out. And trust me, they will sort it all out.'

Germaine knew that Borkmann would never pull the trigger. He had spent his career protecting Tom Hannah, why would he change now? This would be forgotten. The only danger was that the gun would go off accidentally, and that was why nobody moved. Cynically, she thought that if they waited long enough, Borkmann would probably topple over. He already looked unsteady on his feet.

She understood what Borkmann was doing, and she was sure

Tom did too. This was another game they were playing. The artwork was Tom's. All Borkmann's lawyers could do would be to delay the destruction. It was the moment that was being hijacked, not the art. Borkmann had given his life to Tom's work, and, yes, he'd made a lot of money too, but, in a way, he was no different to her, or to Tom. They all craved a meaning. Only Alta seemed indifferent to such a thing – and she wasn't taking any notice of their exchanges. She was watching the television screen.

'Here comes Badger,' she said. 'He must have smelled trouble. Oh, and look who else is coming.' She turned and smiled a sweet smile at Borkmann. 'I thought he was bringing his truck. It doesn't look like he's going to be doing much driving. That ankle looks painful.'

They all looked at the screen where, limping into view and coming through the open gate, being supported by a stout branch on one side, and Claudio on the other, was Rodolfo.

Borkmann shook his head and sighed deeply. 'One job,' he said. 'All he had was one job: bring the truck. You simply cannot get the staff any more.'

He looked at them all, shrugged, gently let the hammer down on the gun, put it on the table and sat down.

'I don't know why I'm being so careful,' he said and coughed heartily as if to make sure that no one should forget that he was ill. 'It's not loaded.'

Perhaps it was the release of tension, or perhaps she was going insane, but Germaine started to laugh. 'You've got to let the paint run where the paint will run,' she said. 'Now, please, can you help me get Catharina back to Las Sombras?'

22

Margot came in from where she'd been sitting by the harbour wall and stood at the hotel reception desk. She looked around and then walked into the bar, cocked her head like a bird and listened. It was quiet. Her footsteps echoed on the wooden floor as she walked across the bar to the harbour-side door and looked onto the road. No familiar faces turned to greet her. Luisa was indoors. Germaine and Catharina were still at Tom Hannah's house with Alta and Borkmann, and Charles was nowhere to be seen. Only gulls and pigeons turned to look at her.

'Charles?' she said and waited, as if by saying his name he would appear on the street in front of her. He did not. She went back into the bar. 'Charles?' Still nothing – or was that a thump? Muffled and distant, but still a thump. 'Charles?'

She walked to the bar and peered over it. Another thump. It was coming from the kitchen. She went to the swing doors and looked through the porthole windows. No one was working by the ovens or the hobs or the sinks. No one was in the kitchen. She pushed open the doors and listened.

Thump.

She walked into the kitchen and stood amongst bare stain-less-steel surfaces, dormant grills and rows of unused pots hanging on their hooks. There was an absence of sound, of hustle and bustle, of shouts and sizzlings, of crashes and clatters. No steam, no smoke, no food. No Claudio. No Luisa. No Rodolfo. No Charles.

Again: thump.

What could be making that sound? The plumbing? The wind? A rat?

Thump.

The thumps were coming from a tall cupboard in the far corner of the kitchen. Margot went to the cupboard door and listened. Something was moving inside. She put one hand on the door handle, hesitated, and then pulled open the door. It was indeed a rat. A big rat called Robin Rix, tied up with the tasselled cord from their bedroom curtains and gagged with a serviette.

'Robin. Where's Charles?'

'Mnnnn.'

She pulled down his gag.

'Margie!'

Margot got up and fetched a bread knife.

'I meant Margot,' he called. 'Margot. You saw it. He hit me, Marg – Margot. Dragged me here. Locked me in this cupboard. In the dark. He's insane.'

Margot came back and knelt down in front of him. 'He's very cross.' She looked at him and shook her head slowly, as if she were imagining a scene that didn't make sense. In an abstracted way she pressed the blade against the tip of his nose.

'You should go before Charles comes back. And, Robin...'

'Yes?'

'Don't come back. Don't call me or try to see me again. Ever.'

She sawed through the cord and stood up. It had none of the

symbolism of La Jaune's yellow paint but, as goodbyes go, it did the job. A cut cord is a cut cord. Rix scrambled to his feet, looked at her for a moment, looked at the knife, and left the kitchen, limping and hobbling where the rope had cut off the flow of his blood.

She watched him leave and then put the knife back in its rack. She looked around the kitchen one more time, perhaps in case Charles was watching from under the sink or behind the dishwasher, or from inside a drawer, and then she left too. She went out to the reception area. Rix's bag was gone. Absently, she picked up a pile of out-of-date tourism leaflets and arranged them neatly on the table. Then she returned to the empty bar, poured herself a large gin and tonic and sat on a stool dangling her legs.

'This is an obvious distraction,' Tom said. 'It won't change anything. It's a temporary delay, that's all.' He was less than happy as he drove down the mountain road to Las Sombras. Crammed into his car were Germaine, Catharina, Rodolfo, Claudio and Borkmann. Alta was still at the house.

'Nothing personal,' Tom had said to Borkmann, 'but I'm not leaving you alone with the pallet loaded with my life's work.'

'How can that not be personal?' Borkmann had said. 'You trust that wretch of a runaway but not me.'

'You had a gun.'

'I was making a point.'

'Yes. You were pointing it at me.'

'It wasn't loaded.'

'You were going to take it all.'

'Not for me. For posterity. To put it somewhere safe. What if she takes some of it? Or burns it anyway?'

'She won't. She knows it has to be me.'

So, Alta had stayed at the house with the dogs while Tom transported the broken Rodolfo, the concerned Claudio, the poisoned Catharina and the worried Germaine to the village, to where a local doctor was already on his way arriving by motor launch. In that region where villages clung to the land and fringed the mountain foothills along the coastline, it was often easier to get from one village to the next by boat. The nearest medical centre was a two-hour journey by road, whereas a waterborne ambulance could be there in thirty minutes, if the waters were calm and the wind was right.

Tom pulled up outside the front of the hotel opposite the harbour wall. Claudio jumped out and he and Tom helped Rodolfo limp into the bar where they installed him in his favourite seat by the window.

Margot, sitting at the bar, waved and watched. 'Is Charles with you?' she said. Nobody heard her.

'The doctor is on his way,' Tom said. 'Wait here.'

'Claudio, fetch me a drink,' Rodolfo said but Claudio shook his head.

'If they have to operate they won't be able to give you any anaesthetic if you've had a drink.'

'Operate? It's a sprained ankle.'

Tom left Rodolfo muttering darkly with Claudio holding his arm. Since finding him on the mountain he had not left his father's side for a moment. On his way back to the car Tom saw Luisa marching out of her house and heading towards the hotel. It was proving to be a challenging day. He helped Germaine take Catharina into the bar and sat her at a table on the other side of the room to Rodolfo.

'It might be more peaceful over here.'

Luisa was already trying to prise her nephew from Rodolfo's arm. Tom was pleased to note that Claudio was having none of it, and clung on stubbornly.

'*Tía*, he came to rescue me,' Claudio said. 'Don't shout at him.'

'Yes, don't shout at me,' Rodolfo said.

'No shouting,' Margot sang from the bar.

'Ask the neighbours to turn it down,' Catharina murmured and lay forwards on the table with her head in her arms.

Tom surveyed the scene, nodded and went to the door. 'The doctor will be here soon. Gerard and I will go back to the house, now. Good luck.'

'Tom.' Germaine stood up and went to him. 'Please don't do this. Wait and let me come to the house once the doctor has been and everything is calmer.'

Tom took Germaine's hand. 'No.'

'But why? Who says this has to happen now? Why can't you leave all your art where it is, or put it in storage, or hide it? And then walk away from it all. Start your new life anyway. Why do you have to destroy it?'

'I don't have to. I want to. I *choose* to. That's the point.'

'I can't process this. I've studied your work, collected it, reviewed it, enjoyed it, interviewed you, read about you, talked in depth to you – but I don't know you.'

Tom let go of her hand. 'Precisely.' He looked around and saw Borkmann in the doorway with his hand to his forehead. 'Gerard, are you coming?'

'Stomach cramp,' he said. 'Anyone got any painkillers?'

Rodolfo looked up and called to Borkmann through the shimmering air that Luisa's presence created. 'Behind the bar, or look in the kitchen.'

'I'll go,' said Tom.

'No, no. It's all right.'

While Tom waited at the door, and Germaine returned to Catharina, and Claudio stuck to his father's arm, and Luisa sat at Rodolfo's table and glared at him as if daring him to continue to exist but unwilling to further upset her nephew, and Margot sat at the bar and got quietly drunk, Borkmann went in search of painkillers.

He found none behind the bar and went into the kitchen. It was gloomy and poorly lit, but that must have suited Borkmann with his stomach pain because he didn't switch on any lights. He looked around and saw the cupboard in the corner which had, until recently, been the place where Charles had stored Robin Rix. Borkmann opened the door and stepped in, looking through the kitchen miscellany on the shelves for painkillers.

He didn't hear Charles come in from the rear door.

'Hyanh.'

A sack was dropped over Borkmann's head.

'Got loose, did you?' Charles said, wrestling Borkmann onto the floor and wrapping him up with chains and padlocks. 'Well, get out of that.'

Unmoved by the muffled cries that Borkmann was making and his meagre struggling, Charles dragged him across the floor towards the back exit and the alleyway beyond.

At that precise moment, Rix himself was climbing into a taxi that had arrived at the side of the hotel. He had been hiding behind the parked cars, waiting for it to come. Nobody saw his departure except Margot, whose position allowed her to see through the open bar door and the hotel reception area, and onto the cobbled street.

She waved and poured herself another drink.

23

For Catharina things were taking a downward turn. The sleeping powder was still working its way through her system and she suddenly reared up in her seat and spat a large amount of yellow foam all over the table.

'Oh no,' said Germaine.

'Oh God – sorry,' said Catharina. And then she did it again. 'Oh Christ.'

She pushed herself away from the table, turned and staggered out of the bar, surely destined to fall flat on her face but somehow remaining upright. She lurched across the road to the harbour wall, which provided physical support, and then, again, she threw up a good proportion of everything that was inside her. Tom and Germaine ran to her side, and to her credit Margot, who had been a good way into her fifth gin and tonic, dropped off her stool and followed them out.

'Shoot me,' Catharina said.

'It's okay,' Germaine said.

'This is the opposite of okay,' Catharina gasped. 'I'm environmentally disgusting.'

'The doctor will be here soon,' said Tom looking out to sea.

'Hello,' said Germaine. 'Is that Charles? What is he doing?'

It was not so much a question as a means of capturing everyone's attention because it was obvious what Charles was doing. Charles was scrambling onto the glass bottom boat, dragging with him a long sack covered with chains which contained a struggling human being.

'That's not right,' said Margot. Hadn't she just seen Rix get into a taxi and leave?

There's only so much dragging an old sack will take before it starts to come apart at the seams. The polished kitchen floor wasn't too bad, but the cobbled street, tarmac, pavement and jetty was proving too much for the fabric. The sack was disintegrating and revealing the outraged red face of Gerard Borkmann. He was not a man who liked to be dragged onto a boat wrapped in a sack and chains.

'That's Gerard,' said Tom. 'What the hell…?'

'Oh my God,' said Germaine. She let go of Catharina who sank to an untidy heap on the ground and fell asleep.

Charles was struggling to complete the job and had no time to verify who it was he was about to toss into the sea. No doubt he felt that only one person would be in a kitchen cupboard, and, in fairness to him, that would normally be the case. His mission now was to get Rix into the water as quickly as possible. Later, Charles would explain that what he was doing wasn't so much drowning a man as simply making him 'be gone'.

He dropped Borkmann into the sea, chains and all.

'Hyanh!' he cried, partly with the effort, partly in triumph.

'Oh no,' said Germaine and she clutched Tom's arm. 'Oh no.'

Tom said nothing. He simply removed Germaine's hand, swung over the harbour wall, jumped down to the rocks and dived into the sea.

This is what Germaine saw. She saw her hands gripping the wall, pressed against the rough stonework so hard that the tops of her fingers turned white. She saw a small boat in the distance chugging through the water on its way to Las Sombras with a doctor on board. She saw Catharina sitting at her feet with her back against the harbour wall and her eyes closed. She saw a seagull gliding on the wind high in the sky. She saw Tom in the water by the rocks and suddenly he didn't look so big. He swam with heavy, clumsy strokes, a man unused to swimming or any form of exercise and weighed down by his saturated clothes. A man who had lost too much weight and, with it, too much strength. He swam towards the glass bottom boat where Charles was on his knees leaning over the side and trying to free himself of something.

'The chain's caught,' Margot said. She was right. Part of one of the chains in which Borkmann was wrapped had caught on a fender.

And then Borkmann broke the surface.

'Oh my God,' Germaine heard herself say again.

Borkmann's face seemed to be mostly wide eyes and open mouth. She saw Tom adjust his course and make slow progress towards his friend, while in the distance the launch with the doctor on board came ever closer.

Borkmann thrashed hard in order to keep his head above water, the white heat of his willpower temporarily overcoming the world around him. He shouted at Tom. 'Go back. Go back. Go back.'

'Shut up,' was all that Tom could manage as he ploughed forwards.

All this Germaine saw and heard. She had no inner awareness at all. No reflective thoughts, no consciousness of herself. She was receiving input on all channels, alive to the moment, responding to the moment, part of the moment.

Charles looked up and he must have seen Borkmann and realised the terrible mistake he'd made. When a person is turned mad by the existence of another, and makes the decision to extinguish that existence, what new insanity must be spawned when he sees the wrong person wrapped up in chains? He ceased to function. He stopped and flopped and stared.

'Pull him in,' Margot shouted at him. 'Pull him in.'

Germaine saw the error of that instruction just as Charles blindly acted on it. 'No,' she cried but it was too late.

Charles hauled on the chains that were still wrapped around Borkmann's legs and in doing so he took Borkmann back underwater. The weight was too much for Charles and he let go, and now, free from the fender, Borkmann, complete with sack and chains, sank.

Tom stopped swimming for a moment and stared at the empty surface that had once contained a Borkmann. He was less than five metres away. He bobbed for a moment and then thrashed and splashed and pushed his way under the water.

Germaine waited and her fingers turned from white to blue. It seemed a long time before Tom appeared again, bursting through the water as if he were sitting on a rocket, his heavy hair and beard and moustache flattened and pulled downwards. He snorted and coughed and floundered and looked directly into Germaine's eyes.

She saw him and she knew that he saw her. And she imagined that in his eyes she could see herself, as in her eyes he would see himself – a man in the water trying to save a friend who was already terminally ill; witnessed by her, a woman watching by a wall; lives authenticated and validated. I am the other, she thought. Mine is the look.

And then Tom wasn't there any more.

It wasn't clear to Germaine whether he dived again or simply sank. But the seconds ticked by while Germaine watched and waited, and Charles knelt on the side of the boat, and Margot began to cry.

How long can one hold one's breath before the desire to inhale is overwhelming, even if it means sucking in lungfuls of cold, salty seawater? Two minutes, three? Not five, surely, and certainly not ten. What does it feel like to breathe that one last breath? To begin that short transition from somethingness to nothingness. And never to know it has all stopped.

Germaine stared at the sea. Had Tom and Borkmann found each other down there and had time to know that, as in life, they had been there for each other in death. Arguing and bickering and begrudging, but together – through the necessity of life. What were they without each other? And what, she wondered, was she without a Tom Hannah in the world? It occurred to her in a macabre way that Alta's assertion that words were no more than bubbles of air was literally true when calling out underwater. She felt a stirring in her mind, a shifting of perspective. Things were changing.

The doctor's boat approached and now it seemed to Germaine that his original purpose for being there had diminished to the trivial. What were a damaged ankle and a little light poisoning compared to this?

Death; the dot; the shadow; the normality. Under the water Tom had joined his mother and his father and all the others who lay in the lake of tar, forever in their final moment between one second and the next, *all the way until the world ends, and then until the universe ends, and then for all the ever and ever that comes after that.*

Germaine turned her back on the sea and looked up at the mountain where, on one of the lower slopes, a flickering girl-woman and her dog, who had watched it all, turned and walked away.

I'll always find you. And it will be all right.

24

The deaths of Tom Hannah and Gerard Borkmann meant that for a short while Las Sombras was overwhelmed by the world's media – and, being the only hotel in town, *El Tesoro Escondido* did good business. Better even than when the so-called Las Sombras mermaid had been sighted.

The police commandeered the glass bottom boat and used it as part of their search for the bodies. Rodolfo didn't complain, he was in hospital with a broken ankle, accompanied by Claudio who never left his side, much to Luisa's annoyance. Fortunately, she was too busy accommodating the numerous hotel guests and the even more numerous requests for interviews.

The news stories got bigger when three bodies were pulled out of the sea: Tom, Gerard – and the picked-clean skeleton of Luisa's and Teresa's father. When Luisa heard that news she nodded with grim satisfaction.

But instead of going immediately to the hospital and placing Rodolfo under arrest, as she demanded, the authorities took the view it was more likely that his father-in-law had fallen off his boat when he'd been working on it, perhaps due to a heart attack, and spent the next fifteen years or so drifting with the tides while his daughters searched for him only a few hundred metres away.

Of course, no one could say for sure what happened as there were no witnesses, and there were no signs of foul play and if there had been any such signs, any traces of yellow foam for example, they would have disappeared long ago.

As for Teresa, she really had boarded a bus and left town, despite the bus driver saying he hadn't seen her. This was probably because she was leaving to move in with him and for the past six months they had been living happily in a village on the other side of the mountain with the firm intention, or so she claimed, of letting everyone know where she was as soon as she had 'sorted things out'.

There never had been any letter with news of her father – she just didn't want to have a row with Rodolfo. But the news of Tom Hannah's and Gerard Borkmann's deaths with all the attendant publicity had reminded her she owed her sister a call – not to mention her husband and son. Germaine had thought she looked a jolly woman in her photographs and couldn't blame her for seeking a life of her own beyond the shadows of Las Sombras.

Rodolfo and Claudio certainly felt that way because Claudio joined his mother and Rodolfo moved further up the mountain, away from Las Sombras, to the low-slung, sprawling wooden cabin once visited by the Victorian adventurer Joshua Waite – *a place for the* Santa Compaña *and the harsh* Nuberu *to rest their feet and await the passage of unsuspecting mortals*. But he turned it into a traveller's rest for ordinary mortals – particularly mortals who liked to drink and gamble and make use of the ambiguous regulations that exist on that narrow tract of no man's land, without local jurisdiction.

Who would Luisa berate on a daily basis now? People who knew her well, and there were precious few of those, thought she would cut a tragic figure running the hotel on her own. Once the media storm was over they imagined her alone at the bar each night, drinking *razik*, looking across the empty tables and playing host to the ghosts of what-might-have-been.

But it turned out that wasn't the case at all. After a year she sold up and moved to Seville and bought a modern, spacious apartment along a tree-lined avenue. She joined a flamenco class where her harsh angles and superior distain were met with great approval. She developed a small fan base of men who enjoyed being insulted and accepted with gratitude the rota she set out by which they each had a monthly opportunity to take her for dinner.

None, however, ever crossed the threshold of her front door – although they often tried. She had other fish to fry. A well-wisher from Belgium had sent her the latest set of iLets and at night Luisa, now a convert to augmented reality, sat on her sofa and became a young girl again, playing *Happy Family* with her mother, father and younger sister, Teresa.

Caroline, Tom's sister, arrived in Las Sombras and took possession of Tom's house and his artwork – as well as Chico and Harpo and Groucho. Of Alta and Badger, there was no sign. She had a long talk with Germaine and Catharina, about what had happened and what might happen in the future. Before they left to return to Belgium, Germaine said, 'What will you do with this house?'

'I don't know yet. I'll probably sell it. It's too big for me.'

'And the dogs?'

'Oh, I'll keep them. Bring them back to the UK if I can. Aren't they lovely?'

'Ye-es,' said Germaine. 'Big.'

'Bitey,' Catharina said.

'Nonsense. They're gorgeous and they're coming home with me.' She looked at Germaine. 'Who was that man who was working with Gerard? The composer.'

'You mean Holst Bird. He's a hacker.'

'Do you have his details?'

Richter Bird sat in a small hut on the outskirts of a village in northern Albania. Outside, partially concealed by stunted, stubby bushes, were two satellite dishes. At the back of the hut was a generator with an illegal line to Albania's national energy grid and another to an array of solar panels set further up the hill. Inside the hut there was very little to see other than Richter Bird himself, in his underpants. He sat on a beanbag with a ruggedised military laptop balanced on a tea tray. In another room there was a camp bed, a suitcase full of clothes and a poster of Bauhaus pinned to the wooden wall.

Richter sat back and put on his iLets. The hut became filled with the slippery images of multiple half-formed cuckoos. He was still working on the virus. He needed to get it right if he was going to enter, unnoticed, the worlds of hundreds – no, think big, Richter – thousands of highly experienced and bug-savvy game players. He selected one of them and began to run the beta-game, looking for flaws in their design to improve, for ways to…

'Ahem.'

Richter looked up. At the doorway to the hut there stood a tall, stick-like, leathery-looking old man. Richter lifted his iLets but really there was no one there. He put them back on and carried on with his work. That happened sometimes, a character from somebody else's game tried to talk to him. He ought to fix that, he thought.

'Hey, bro. How you doing?'

Richter looked up again. The avatar with Gerard Bork-mann's face and body had his brother's voice.

'Holst? Is that you? What are you doing here?'

'I'm cleaning up, man. Getting rid of bugs and microbes and nasty little virus things.'

It took less than a moment for things to click in Richter's mind. 'Shit.' He pulled off his iLets and slammed the lid of his laptop. 'Shit, shit, shit.' He took his phone, switched it off and pulled out the SIM card. Too late. He stopped and listened: he could hear distant sirens. He grabbed his suitcase and the poster of Bauhaus and ran out, still in his underpants. As he scrambled down the hill, he couldn't shift the image of Gerard Bork-mann's face laughing at him.

SUMMER 2024

1

Charles released an enormous yawn, stifled it and then turned it into a deep, hollow hiccup followed by a rasping cough. It was a master class in non-verbal expulsions and when the red light switched off all the other actors applauded spontaneously. Charles took their tributes with a modest smile and a slight nod of acknowledgement.

'Hyanh.'

In the Green Room Margot was waiting. 'Bravo, Charles. Oh, bravo.'

She gave him a big hug. 'You were wonderful. What a performance.'

Charles beamed. 'Still room for improvement, of course. It's taking a bit of time to get the backstory worked out, but I think I've got the measure of this character all right.'

'Come and have some tea. We can go to the little café they have here.'

'Can we? I mean… me, as well?'

'It's all right. I've checked.'

Charles relaxed and together they walked down the corridor of the occupational therapy unit to a small room that served decaffeinated tea and coffee, unsweetened biscuits and cakes.

Margot fetched their drinks and they sat opposite each other at a table by the window. Outside was a small courtyard where people were talking, sitting, reading or otherwise peacefully passing the time. No one was wearing iLets of any type – they weren't allowed in San Ramon Secured Psychiatric Hospital.

'It's good to see you,' Charles said. 'Are you staying over?'

Margot put her hand on his. 'Do you mind if I don't this time? I have such a lot to do back at the house.'

'Of course, of course. You know you always can...' he trailed off and looked at her, smiling. 'Anyway, it's good to see you.'

They had this same exchange every time she visited. 'You were wonderful in there,' she said. 'Just wonderful.'

'It's good to be back in the saddle. They want an endless variety of sounds you know. I'm really building up my repertoire.'

'That's good. I'm so proud.' Margot sipped her tea. 'You're looking very well.'

'Lots of exercise. Sleeping soundly, too. You won't know me when I come home.'

'No. I won't.'

'Of course, I'm smoking again. Sorry. An actor's life and all that. Lots of... just waiting around. Calms the nerves.'

'It's all right.'

'I'll give up when I... you know.'

'I do know.'

Charles licked his lips. He looked around before leaning forwards. 'You haven't heard from *him*, have you?'

'No, Charles. Absolutely not. You know I'd tell you. That's what we do now, isn't it? We tell each other everything. Talking is good, that's what they said.'

'Hyanh.'

'We mustn't bottle things up.'

'No. You would tell me, though, wouldn't you?'

'I would.'

'You're sure?'

'Charles, yes. Absolutely. Nobody in the business has heard from him. He's out. You're in.'

Poor Robin Rix. He never got his chance to be the voice of the virus. He carried on as a bodily functions voice actor when he returned from Spain but his work on *Tuscan Fields* dried up after the actor who played Bill Flapp started producing his own sneezes. Such are the ups and downs in an actor's life. Rix was last heard of working with a Dutch comedy troupe making belching noises.

'If you do see him, kick him hard.'

'I will.'

'I mean it.'

'I promise.' Margot smiled. 'You know you mustn't keep thinking about him. He's gone, Charles. Gone from our lives.'

'I should have hit him harder. Cracked his bloody skull open. Somebody let him out, you know. Swapped him for that other fellow. Devious.' Charles looked up at the camera that was in the corner of the room. 'He's got friends, you know. Everywhere. That little shit.'

'Charles. Please.'

'Kick him hard.' Charles's mood seemed to have darkened and he sat in silence staring at the table. 'Bloody bastard.'

'Charles. Look, I've brought these.' Margot took from her bag a small stack of old newspaper clippings. 'Some of your past reviews. Shall I read them to you?'

Charles looked at them and then at her. 'Would you mind? The old eyes aren't so good in this light.' He took her hand. 'What would I do without my Margot?'

She smiled. 'I am always your Margot. Always was; always will be.'

'Hyanh.'

'We'll start with the earliest, shall we, and work our way forwards.'

Margot read for ten minutes and when she stopped and looked up she saw that Charles had fallen asleep in his chair. She put the clippings back in her bag, finished her tea, and then stood up and nodded to the nurse who was sitting at another table near the door.

'See you the next time, Charles,' she whispered. She kissed him gently on his forehead and left.

2

Gerard Borkmann had been a rich man and his legacy, which he had described in his will, was the Borkmann Foundation, a not-for-profit organisation based in Liège and created to look after the work of Tom Hannah and some of Borkmann's other artists, as well as Tom Hannah's estate and the Musée Tash. The foundation was administered by Tom's sister, Caroline, who added her own money from the sale of his house in Spain, and one of her first acts had been to hire Germaine Kiecke as the museum's director and curator. The building was on the site of the old Chateau Giselle which had been knocked down, flattened and eradicated from this planet. Musée Tash owned the land now.

It was opening night and the great and the good from the art, games and comic-book world were arriving. A tree-lined driveway led to the museum's entrance and a long queue of cars and taxis was snaking towards the drop-off points and the visitor car parks. Stewards in high-visibility jackets decorated with cartoon motifs showed the guests where to park and where to go to pick up their Tash goody bags, and also where to find the lavish buffet that had been laid out for their enjoyment. Tour guides were on hand to explain the layout of the museum and to remind the guests that there would be a champagne reception on the first floor at nine o'clock sharp, in which Caroline would make an inaugural speech and make a plea for charitable donations to the foundation in exchange for the donor's name to be put on a plaque on the wall in the museum's entrance.

No doubt such pomp and vanity would have amused both Tom and Borkmann – or so Germaine thought as she stood by her office window and looked down on the arriving throng. Two years ago she would have been blowing smoke into the evening air but she hadn't smoked since Las Sombras.

'The sugar of life,' she said to her faint reflection in the glass. 'Not so sweet now.'

'You know, now would be a good time to resurrect your book on new art,' Catharina said. She stood away from the window, near the office door, and watched Germaine rather than the activities outside. She sipped a glass of champagne. 'You have a captive market and an on-site bookshop. Every writer's dream.'

Germaine nodded. But was she a writer? She didn't think so. Not any more. Since Tom's death she had found herself drawn to the practical aspects of life, such as running the museum, negotiating with stakeholders, and talking to schools and universities. She found she had a newly released urge to engage with people, to make a difference, to touch the lives of others. To participate in life, rather than observe it from a distance. She was filling in her outline, adding texture, bending straight lines and blunting corners.

'I don't feel I have the authority any more,' she said. 'What do I know about anything? Least of all art. I can curate it, organise it, display it, cherish it. But what "it" is, I don't know any more. I don't think I ever did.'

'Hogwash.' Catharina drained her glass. 'Anyway, we should

go down and meet the high and mighty. Are you coming? Your public awaits.'

'Soon. You go ahead, I want to finish off a couple of things. I'll be right along. Ten minutes. Fifteen maximum.'

'Well, don't be too long. They'll strip that buffet clean like locusts.'

Left alone, Germaine felt she could relax. She sat down, kicked off her shoes and put her feet up on her desk. On the opposite wall was the only piece of artwork in the room. A small original abstract piece painted by La Jaune. It was mostly yellow. She looked at it and thought about her flat in Liège that she now shared with Catharina and how it had once been hers and hers alone. She looked at the painting and thought wistfully of the yellow paint. Perhaps she hadn't changed that much, after all.

She stood up and went to the window again. People were still arriving. Across the driveway and beyond the trees were islands of shrubs, dotted here and there on the landscaped lawns. They reminded her of the heavy foliage that Tom had allowed to grow wild in his garden in Spain.

Poor Tom. What would he make of all this? His existence was gone and all that remained was the essence he had hoped to destroy. He would now be forever remembered as an artist. It was an irony that she still struggled with. She was the curator of everything he had not wanted. She was a promoter of shadows. She had once wondered what would happen to him if he took away the outlines in which he contained his real life. Now she knew. Real life had overwhelmed and consumed him. And what would happen to her now she had discarded the filters and frames she used to shield herself from reality?

A movement outside caught her attention and she frowned. Was that somebody by the bushes? She couldn't be sure. Some uninvited photographer or newshound lurking outside? Or a trick of the eye? She looked harder and then her phone beeped. It was Catharina.

'Are you coming? They're guzzling all the booze.'

Germaine sighed and looked again through the window. Nothing. Just a line of bushes. She retrieved her shoes, switched off her desk light and made her way downstairs.

Outside in the rhododendron bush Alta and Badger looked across the lawns and watched the comings and goings of the museum's guests with amused expressions. Strictly speaking, it was only Alta who had an amused expression; Badger was dozing. She could see Germaine looking down at her and wondered if she had been seen, and, if she had, would Germaine come out and confront her – and, if she did, what would Alta do? It occurred to her that now she was the observer watching others live their real lives. But then, really, it had always been that way, no matter how hard she always tried to make her own life more simple, more natural, more real.

It grew dark and the lights of the building switched on, and the trees and the lawns and bushes became dark shadows. Alta heard the distant applause when the speeches ended and saw through the uncurtained windows people admiring the exhibits: the paintings and prints and notebooks and letters and tools and equipment, and all the other Tom Hannah memorabilia. Sixty-three boxes worth, to be precise.

'Look at all those hangers-on with all their words,' she said.

Badger snorted, woke himself up and shook himself into alertness.

'Hungry?' By way of an answer, Badger started rooting around on the floor. 'Come on, let's go. Let's get out of this dump.' She stood up and brushed herself down. 'Maybe we'll go and find the dog-poisoner,' Alta said, 'and bust him out of jail. He'd like that.'

With a click of her tongue she and Badger detached themselves from the shadows and walked off into the night. A girl and her battered, threadbare dog; a slim, scruffy waif with a cocky walk, not quite eighteen and not quite seventeen either; part girl, part woman, part something and part of everything.

I am gone. I am like a spirit, a puff of gas. Forgotten.

But she was not forgotten. From the glass stairwell in the museum, Germaine, on her way upstairs after the speeches and the handshaking and the fundraising, watched them walk away. And it seemed to her that as they walked there was a curious movement of air behind them, a strange localised atmospheric disturbance, and for a moment, just for a moment, it looked as if there were other misty people processing behind them, including a large, shambling man with a big moustache who walked beside a tall, stick-like person with an outraged glare.

She smiled. That would have been nice. But no, it was surely just a trick of the eye.

3

It was a wet Wednesday afternoon later in the month and Germaine was alone in her flat. She had showered, made herself a cup of coffee and was now sitting on the sofa with her iLets in her hand. She hadn't used the phone with the *Happy Family* app since returning from Las Sombras, replacing it with a newer, cleaner device. The old phone would forever remain disconnected from any network. It would be her standalone *Happy Family* phone complete with its cuckoo – an ant with Tom Hannah's face.

She missed him.

She held the iLets for a long time before she put them on, slowly, easing herself back into the once familiar motion. She switched on.

A message flashed before her eyes: *Game Resume or Restart?*

Resume.

There was a moment of white noise and then the iLets synched with the app and overlaid a garden onto her living room. Her carpet now had flower beds bordering it, and the door to her hallway appeared to be a back door into somebody else's house; a back door with a cat flap. She was in the shrubbery. The last time she had been here, she had been in the hotel kitchen. Now she was in her living room but there was no cuckoo with Tom Hannah's face turning around to speak to her.

She was disappointed.

Germaine stood up and stepped onto the lawn. She saw that Sally was beneath the television.

'Well, hello,' she said. 'Where is everyone?'

The cat flap burst open and out came JoJo amid a cacophony of crazy piano chase-music – and clinging to her back was her father, Mr Kevin Venus. They raced round the living room, up the wall, across the dining table, over the kitchen units and then round again for a second go.

'Are you all right?' Germaine called to him.

'Gggnnnrrrr,' said Mr Venus as he swept past.

All around her bonus points popped up in mid-air for her to swipe with her hands while crazy, manic chase-music played loudly in her ears. She turned around and around in the middle of her room, getting giddy but not minding, as more and more game points cascaded from the air in a waterfall of primary colours and landed at her feet. Finally, she stopped, breathless and laughing, and fell onto her sofa. 'That was great.'

'Hello, Germaine.'

She felt her throat tighten. It was his voice. Or was it? Did she just want it to be? She turned slowly. The poorly conceived ant with its familiar face was watching her.

'Hello, Tom,' she said.

For a moment she felt absolutely certain that he was going to tell her that she had reached the Garden. But instead a large yellow question mark flashed above his head and he said, 'I've paused this nested game to let you know that you are not connected to the internet. Connection to the internet is required in order to install an important update. Do you want to connect now?'

Yes or No?

Germaine knew it wasn't Tom. She knew it was only an old echo of Richter Bird waiting to steal all her data. But even so she looked into his face. She leaned in towards him and it grew in size in her iLets until Tom Hannah's face was all she could see. If only she could connect to some cosmic internet and download him in real life.

If only.

But no.

It was always no.

She shook her head and Tom was gone. In his place was Mrs Venus. She smiled so widely and with such kindness that Germaine felt her throat tighten again. 'You came back.'

'Hello, Germaine. How have you been?'

'I missed you.'

'I know.'

'What happened to the game?'

'What do you mean? This is the game.'

'Oh.' Germaine stared at her virtual mother and then laughed – a hard laugh 'Of course.'

Not far from where they sat, on the living room floor, there was a small mound of earth. Germaine could hear the sound of hundreds of ants applauding and cheering. An inset window appeared in her iLets and she could see that Anuj had been named 'ant of the day' and was receiving his granule of sugar from the queen's larder.

Ant of the day.

What do you think: are we what we are, or what we do?

Germaine closed her eyes. They ached. Head-wreck. She took off her iLets and then ran her finger under each eyelid and took out the iLet-Inserts too. She rubbed her eyes before putting them back in. Then she pressed the side of her phone.

Restart.

Patrons

Unbound is the world's first crowdfunding publisher, established in 2011.

We believe that wonderful things can happen when you clear a path for people who share a passion. That's why we've built a platform that brings together readers and authors to crowdfund books they believe in – and give fresh ideas that don't fit the traditional mould the chance they deserve.

This book is in your hands because readers made it possible. Everyone who pledged their support is listed at the front of the book and below. Join them by visiting unbound.com and supporting a book today.

Bette Adriaanse
Joanna Aldhous
Gail Anderson
Anuj
Flo Barron
Vivien Boast
Helen Bradley
Joseph Brady
Simone Chadda
Maria del Pilar Corrales de Llaza
Alexandra Coulton
Linda Ellis

Michael Ellis
Rory Gleeson
Ben Gourley
Eamonn Griffin
Sam Guglani
Liz Hadley-Day
Cara Haines
Claire Handscombe
Caroline Hardwick
Maddy Harris
Imogen Harris
Melvyn Hawkins
Sheila Hedges
David Hetherington
Jude Higgins
Guy Johnston
Edwin Kayes
Rupert Kirkham
Ewan Lawrie
Claire Lever
Morven Littlejohn
Carlos Llaza
Armando Llaza Loayza
Amy Lord
Baret Magarian
Suzy McKeever
John Melbourne
Erinna Mettler
Andrea Millett
Anita Mir
Carlo Navato
Tiff Nield
Jamie Nuttgens

Chris Parker
Rebecca Rue
Graham Slater
Nick Stewart
Mike Scott Thomson
Nicola Turnbull
Damon L. Wakes
Simon Walmsley
An Welys
Jim West
Dean White
Paul Williams
Christina Williams
Alexandra Wilson
Paul Wilson
Mark Wisdom

Acknowledgements

This book began as a couple of scenes which I showed to the Unruly Writers – Hazel Barkworth, Susie Campbell, Shahla Haque, Imogen Harris and Sarvat Hasin. Their feedback and encouragement kicked off an entire novel. It took longer to write than I'd planned and without the support, generosity and patience of my constant muse, Sally McGuire, who listened without complaint to random and disconnected excerpts while she tried to get on with her own work, it would still be a first draft. Thanks also to the Unbound team: Xander Cansell, who listened to my pitch over a coffee in Oxford and has supported it wholeheartedly since, Sara Magness and her production team, Josephine, Julia, Annabel, the excellent Emma who's structural input hugely improved the shape of the story and the copywriters and proofreaders who politely pointed out all my continuity and grammatical gaffes. I include in that team all the supporters named in these pages. I cannot thank them enough. Every pledge made a difference and without them this book would not exist. Finally, a call out to: Paul Campy, Benny Collins, Mark Davis, Carla Garner, Manish Gupta, Maggie Hunt, Simon Lovell-Smith, Suzy McKeever, Gordon Porter, Sue Ransom, Anna Sabine-Newlyn and, of course, Kevin Venus. I hope you like this novel. Did I say finally? There is one more: my sister, Gemma, who shared with me the loss that fuelled this project.